To la

GENEFIRE

JAMES FLANAGAN

Print edition ISBN: 978-1-7394775-0-9

E-book edition ISBN: 978-1-7394775-1-6

A CIP catalogue record for this book is available from the British Library

Cover and Interior Design by: Natalia Junqueira

First edition published: 1st Sept 2023

To my wife,
who has always given me the most precious of commodities,
time.

And to my son,
who takes it all away.

Prologue

Anne sat beneath a tree in the arms of a man she shouldn't be with. The hill behind the meadow, so familiar to her from this view, was hiding the town of Bawnboy. She closed her left eye and then squinted her right to achieve the perfect illusion of seeing his strong muscled arm match the exact contour of the hill. The afternoon breeze swept through the field, where it rustled the long grass as if it were the soft blond hairs on his arm. Anne was content to sit with him, wrapped in his warm overcoat. She was eager to ask him to read to her again, as he had often done before.

The tall man stood, reached into the saddlebag on his tethered horse and removed a leather satchel. He pulled out a crisp book and opened it to a page that had been marked with a leaf. When he reminded her where they were up to in the story, Anne smiled, knowing what came next. She listened to his well-practiced timbre and dreamed of him being Will Scarlet as he told the tale of the wedding of Robin and Marian. She spent the afternoon wondering if there was a moment to interrupt and tell him her news. How would he react? She was certain it would be with the same love and affection he always showed when they were here, under this tree. Or would he act cold and distant, as he was when she saw him in the village? She listened and waited, but couldn't find the right moment, and didn't want to dispel the illusion of the narrative. As she watched the sun dip below the hill, she knew it was time to tear herself away from him again, if only for another week. Perhaps now she could reveal her news… but when she looked into his eyes, she hesitated.

A loud crack thundered above them. Startled, they both looked up to see embers of fire falling from the sky. The largest portion of a meteorite came frighteningly close and exploded into a field only half a mile away.

Anne squealed with delight, and before he could stop her, she lifted her skirts and climbed over the fence to enter the field, crunching through the last of the spring ice towards the hole that the meteorite had created. She ignored the calls from behind to leave it alone, and reached down with her hand to find the meteorite was not hot at all. It had cracked right down the middle to reveal a pea-sized metal capsule, like a seed embraced by two halves of a pumpkin. She looked up at the half-moon and wondered if the rock had come from there. The capsule was cold initially but warmed rapidly between her thumb and forefinger. Without warning, an explosive puff of dust from the capsule made her sneeze. Startled, she dropped it and turned to see her man arrive. She sneezed again and they both laughed as he drew her away. The proximity of the meteorite to the village was sure to attract attention; the place would be swarming with villagers within minutes. It was time to leave. They lingered for a kiss, then left in different directions, her on foot and he on his horse.

Anne meandered back down to the town. She touched her lips, remembering the warmth of that last kiss. She laughed in delight at a greenfinch that bounced along in front of her, hopping in step with her as she skipped along.

It was a long walk around the edge of the lake, through the meadow and across the churchyard that held her family's graves, and finally onto the main road toward the home of her friend Mary Ann Brady. Mary was a bouncy and excitable girl with a mass of fiery red hair, which was much nicer than Anne's dull black hair. Anne was aware that it was jealousy that made her think such things. On the other hand, Mary was the only friend Anne had. Perhaps it was time to start being nicer to her.

Anne was two steps away from the corner of the Keeper's Arms when she was pounced upon by Mary and swallowed up in a whirlpool of enthusiasm.

"I know where you been, Annie. You been with him, I can see it in your smile, girl. Why won't you tell me who he is, where you go with him, what you're getting up to? Tell me who he is. You can whisper in my ear, I know it's gotta be one of the Plunketts from the post office. It is, it is, it is, no?"

"Stop it, Mary," Anne whispered.

"The MacGuire boy, then. Listen, if you won't tell your little secret, I'll have to tell me Pa where you been, and he'll send you out to the workhouse. Oh, don't be that way, Annie. I won't tell. Don't walk away, it's just fun. It's— it's— it's a McGovern."

Anne blushed.

"Oh my, oh Lordy. Don't you deny it," Mary continued, "I can see you blushing, Ha – it's Michael, isn't it? I knew it, I knew it. No, no, not him. It's the cute one, what's-his-name, the son of the Miller, Bernie, I've seen you speaking to him at church. Oh, oh, there! I saw that smirk. No, it's not him, but you do speak to him at church."

Mary paused her monologue as she danced around the now seriously blushing Anne. "I'll just wait till Sunday, and see who it is then. A McGovern that goes to church and speaks with Annie, ain't gonna be too hard to work that out now. Annie, don't be that way, of course you have to go to church. The Lord won't wait for you. Of course, He's going to be mighty cross if you've been sinning out there with your mystery man, you'll have to confess this all to the Reverend. Oh, Annie, I saw that, it's not… not the Reverend? Terrence McGovern. Oh, my Lord, it's worse than I thought. It's the Reverend. Oh, Annie, how could you? That's naughty."

"Now you listen to me Mary Brady, you keep your fool mouth closed for just one minute. It's not him." Anne dragged the younger girl behind the Corner House and pushed her up against the wall, away from the eyes of the people streaming to the field where the meteorite had landed. Her muscles tensed as if they were being wrung dry.

"I know." Anne stopped to gulp down a large lump that had risen in her throat. "I know," she repeated, "what your father would do to me if he found out. But listen to me. It's worse than you think. I tried to tell him today, but I couldn't. Mary, I'm pregnant."

Anne watched the smile fade from her friend's face. As shame crept up within her, clawing at her insides, she turned away and spied the postman, Mr. Plunkett, down the street watching the sky where meteorite shards were still occasionally falling. He couldn't have heard her from that far, surely. Anne turned back to Mary and saw the change in the young girl's eyes. Her eyes were wide, mouth agape but closed into a smirk with a twinkle in her eye. The girl twisted out of her grip and bolted like a jackrabbit down the street towards their house.

"Don't tell," Anne called out in despair, running after her, hoping that she wouldn't tell, but knowing she probably would.

4

The kitchen door slammed as Anne rushed in to find Mary kneeling before her beloved father, Mr. Brady. This hulk of a man stood before her, brandishing his pipe like a rapier. He turned on Anne as soon as she arrived.

"You tell me who the bastard's father is," he exploded, swinging his pipe across Anne's head, and smashing a vase upon the table in his follow-through. Anne took the blow and stood up straight and stared back at him. Her lips tightened and she did not speak. "Right now! Or it's the workhouse for you. I'll not have this under my roof," he said. His eyes flicked to his daughter Mary, before returning to Anne. "You'll be seeing the Reverend about this first thing in the morning," he finished. He huffed and turned away as Mrs. Brady came into the kitchen having heard the commotion.

When Anne looked at the older woman, her resolve to face down Mr. Brady dissolved. She melted, wanting desperately to tell Mrs. Brady everything and accept the warmest of hugs. But she couldn't. She placed her hand on Mrs. Brady's shoulder, holding her at arm's length. Tears gushed from Anne's eyes, soaking her collar, and she could only say, "I can't tell you. I'm sorry."

"We'll speak about this in the morning, Annie dear." Mrs. Brady replied.

As Anne went to her room, she spared an evil glare for Mary, who had remained on her knees. Upstairs, her hands shook as she unfastened her skirt. Her chest heaved as she unbuttoned her blouse. She wiped her tears on her nightdress as she wrestled it over her head. She could hear Mr. and Mrs. Brady talking, whispering, and arguing about her.

Lying on her bed, Anne stared at the ceiling, watching the candlelight flicker over the wooden rafters. She imagined the flames reaching across the ceiling and down the walls of the next room, the flame hair of Mary Brady catching fire and burning her to cinders, the embers of her remains setting alight the house so that it too burned to the ground. Mr. Brady would be desperate, with everything he owned having burned. He deserved it. Her saviour would climb through the window and rescue her from the flames, and carry her in his firm arms to safety in the meadow. The meadow they shared, where he loved her. He would do that, she was sure.

The lights from the two candles flickered and dimmed. Anne replaced them with new ones. On either side of the wooden beam, she could now see love flickering in his eyes. His nose formed the beam with his nostrils flaring ever so slightly with each intake of breath, in time with the flicker of light. His smile gleamed as he mouthed the words, "I love you, Anne." She smiled back. She thought of the white dress she would wear if they were to get married, just like her Sunday dress but reaching to the ground, with a lace veil that would separate them until the moment he would kiss her. Her shoes would be white and tall, just like Mrs. Brady's Sunday shoes. Everyone would tell her how lovely she looked, and all the young girls would be jealous. She drowsed into sleep, dreaming of her happy future with her husband and child.

*   *   *

The next morning Anne found herself marched down to St Mogue's Church by Mrs. Brady and thrust into the confessional. The wooden kneeler bit into her shins as she rehearsed the words, "Forgive me, Father, for I have sinned, it has been six weeks since my last confession." The sound of heels clicking across the tiled floor announced the arrival of the Reverend. The musty air in the confessional was exchanged for fresh as the door opened and closed. The dividing screen slid open.

With the moment upon her, the ritual words of the confessional deserted her. Her mouth dried up, and she whispered, "Terry, I'm pregnant." Again, she wondered whether he would react with love and affection as he did at the hill, or cold and distant like in town. Her earlier confidence was draining away.

There was a long silence and then a sharp intake of breath, as if he had forgotten to breathe. "What will you do, Anne? You know you cannot tell anyone about me."

"Mr. Brady will send me to the workhouse."

There was another long silence.

"You will be safe there," he whispered. He paused, then said, louder, "I absolve you from your sins." The screen closed, and she heard his footsteps march across the tiled floor, faster than his approach.

Anne stepped out of the confessional with her legs shaking, and crumbled into the nearest pew. Her head sank to touch the pew in front, and she clasped her shaking hands together as though to pray, only she couldn't pray. *Why did he do that?*

Mrs. Brady kept her distance, perhaps having expected a long penance.

Although Anne had been born to a Catholic family, and the priests of the Catholic Church never married, it was different in the Protestant Church. The vicar at St. Peter's was allowed to marry. Why couldn't a Catholic priest do the same? He could leave the Church and marry – it had been done before – and why shouldn't he do that for her? He was a young man still, less than thirty. Why was he so distant toward her? Was piety so important? *He's ashamed of me.*

Doubts now flooded her mind. If others found out that Terrence was the father of the child, would he not be obliged to leave the Church and marry her? No – he had been clear. She couldn't tell anyone that he was the father. Another quiet sob.

She didn't understand why, but she would obey. She wiped her nose, stood up and straightened her hair. She would have to approach the workhouse on her own, with dignity.

The Bawnboy workhouse! Her father had been one of the workers that had rebuilt the stone houses. It was one of the few strong memories she had of him, holding his hand as he showed her the detailed craftsmanship in the stone that he had carved. It had appeared an impressive mansion, to a five-year-old. Designed to accommodate five hundred, in its first year it had opened its doors to fifty-two inmates: the poor, the destitute, the hopeless, and helpless. Ten years later, that was what Anne herself had become. The workhouse provided long, hard days of work for food and board. There was a laundry and nursery on the women's side and a bakehouse on the men's side. Anne had heard that the master, John Carson, was a harsh man, and the first matron, Jane Brownlow, was said to be equally hard on the women. Neither master nor matron tried hard to dissuade the community's prejudice towards the inmates during their only interaction at the Sunday Mass at the workhouse chapel. Anne had long feared ending up there after her parents passed and her cousins had emigrated – until Mr. Brady had taken her in. The frequent idle threats of the workhouse made being sent there seem so remote, until now. Now it seemed inevitable.

Chapter 1

I was with her when she was at the viewing deck, watching as each new flare advanced in every land, as the planet passed and twisted 'neath her and I. I can't define what it felt like, witnessing her planet annihilated. My planet.

She was as helpless as a medic watching the final death spasms in a patient she can't save. Her arms sank, drawing nearer her heart, knees melded with the metal girder near the glass. Staring silently. As I write this, tears darken my eyes and I keep replaying the events in my mind. Perhaps in time, I'll find the characteristics that defined her, like in all the tragic verses, as she was when I first saw her, still imprinted in my mind.

When I first entered the viewing deck it seemed deserted. The ISS was enhanced with a larger capacity when my parents met. They were the maintenance team at the time. Since then, it hasn't changed. It was tight when first designed, and the viewing deck was always small. Ten very dear friends standing in line can span the glass.

Halfway traversing the deck, I halted. I saw Gessica, delicate, gripping the fence near the glass pane, her face against the glass as if willing herself spaced and dead. Her ginger hair was tied in a twist, with a single ragged strand waving weightless past her chin. Her shape appeared petite in the standard ISS slim dress in genetics-team green, the same as the glass. She seemed like a tense spring, still and ready ta leap. Like me, she was there watching the planet. It was mesmerising.

The planet's air was thick, like caramel swirling in a milkshake. Flares fired here and there. With each new flare, we knew, many lives perished instantly. Everywhere, planet-wide – as I learnt later – all primates, apes, and men alike, were withering away in this miasma.

At that time, I had a strange feeling that I saw several spectres circling Gessica, criticising her as if it was her that killed the planet. They were spirits, hardly there, flickering like afterimages. I tilted my head and they persisted. They didn't strike me as scary, and I didn't fear them. I saw three, each wearing genetics green, yet they weren't crewmates that I knew. The male spectre was clearly in charge, aggressive and assertive. The lady with him had a face aged with sadness and the third was a girl with fair skin and a wide-eyed mien, and she had a partial name tag reading Sand that didn't match any name I knew. All three had fingers raised and they went after Gessica as if they hated her, like sharks circling, waiting ta strike.

Gessica didn't see them, and when they disappeared, I greeted her. "Hey ginger, ya perceive what is happening there as well," I said.

My first line wasn't the wisest, yet I will always recall her answer.

"Racism," she said, as she faced me, "ageism, spacism, even GM-ism I can take, never gingism. At a time like this."

I was entirely penitent. I didn't want ta start in a nasty way. If any man had the right ta defend racism, it wasn't me. Yes, I knew her, I knew all the ISS staff, yet I had never met her with names and all — we in maintenance never mingled with the genetics teams. It was red with red and green with green. I hadn't meant any levity. I started again and said my name was Tammy.

"Tammy isn't a man's name. What else did they call ya?" she asked. Her sapphire eyes glared at me.

I recited all my names: "Thames Impressive Henry. I had never learned why I was given my silly middle name," I added. "My dad was a Frenchman, and my mammy was English, and she called me Tammy and that was that."

"And a Gename patent?" she pressed.

I wasn't ashamed. I was a native at the ISS, I didn't fit the standard pattern. Yet, in hesitating and with her insisting like that, I realised I wasn't ready ta say it. I can't say why I felt that way. I changed tack.

"What genetic enhancements have ya had?" I asked her.

She sniffed as if I smelt rancid. I wasn't aware that this was a sensitive thing ta ask.

"It isn't a nice thing ta ask a girl," she said. She stared at the fire-riddled planet and added, "It hardly matters at this stage. I've had them all. My parents selected all the enhancements they had generated at the time. They were the geneticists that made them, here in the ISS. I've had strengthening ta increase skeletal density, lifespan enhancers which will add eighty years, gamma-ray-resistant skin, decreased dietary needs and," she hesitated, "intellect enhancers. They wanted me ta have all the advantages. What parents didn't want that in their child?"

She didn't add her Gename patent, yet I knew she had it. The Gename patent was the identifier every male and female alive had in their DNA, at least every legal male and female. I didn't have a Gename patent and didn't have any GM particles in my DNA. I hadn't any need ta hide my shame.

"Tell me, Tammy, did ya get a Gename patent?" she repeated. Her eyes penetrated like she was trying ta see my insides.

"I hadn't any enhancements," I replied finally, "and didn't get a Gename patent." My head sank after admitting this. Why did I keep telling myself that I wasn't ashamed? I think, seeing it written like this, I was.

She eased as if she had taken a large dram filled with chemical massage pills.

I stayed silent as I watched the flares dance an allemande.

"Never visited there, Tammy, have ya?" She knew I hadn't. Her eyes fastened the flaming Earth in sight and drew me in nearer ta her.

"Let me tell ya, then. They have aviaries and farms, saving all their animals." She sighed. "I feel certain that singing and classical tracks were invented ta replicate their avian calls, with the clarinet trills, the pipe whistles, harps and fiddles, and the heavy rhythms." She swayed and drifted nearer me weightlessly.

"It is magical there, Tammy. Sitting in the radiant warm light, eating a meal, a small finch will tweet his call, and its friend in the distance will pair with it and make an interlaced track with trills that fill the garden with happiness. In the evening, a geese gaggle can fly past and treat ya with their harsh, chatty speeches that will raise hackles." She giggled.

"Like a large family all talking at the same time. And the sights, Tammy. Will we recall the different shades in the parakeets' wings, and the daisies, the lilies, and lavenders when they germinate? There's a chance that these will remain, yet if there isn't any sentient man hearing them, seeing them, smelling them, will they stay the same?"

She halted. I heard her gasp as she watched the flares enlarge, and perhaps I heard a tempered cry. I sensed that she knew what was happening there. I asked her.

"Yes," she declared, "I'm aware what it is they released. I made it."

Chapter 2

The next thirty-five minutes would decide the rest of his life, leading either to a joyful existence of academic pursuit and an illustrious scientific career or to a life of mediocrity. Everything relied on this interview.

Larry Milton sat on an unstable stool outside a meeting room, his eyes focused on the curled corner of a poster. From his first school-boy science project to his most recent undergraduate research, Milton's entire education had been geared toward a career in the field of human genetics. Where better to apply for a PhD to further his training than the most prestigious university and the highest-profile genetics lab? Anything short of the best was unacceptable.

"No pressure," he whispered to himself. He took three deep breaths, causing the stool to wobble. His blond hair flopped into his eyeline, and he swept it back with a sweaty palm.

The poster showed a representation of the entire human genome in single bases, with genes of interest marked. It was a rather pointless poster as far as Milton could see, lacking any real details. It was historical, though, as it showed the first semi-complete human genome assembled, published in scientific journals long before he was born. The poster covered the glass window of the meeting room. He leant the stool to the right to peer through the gap where the poster curled at the corner.

Through the gap, he could see an attractive young woman sitting in the hot seat in front of the panel. She wore red lipstick and a tight business suit as though she was applying for a job as a stockbroker. The suit emphasised her figure, from what Milton could see of it. *Good-looking people get all the breaks*, he thought. The professor was bound to pick her.

The advice from his undergraduate tutor swirled in his head, like a ghostly visitation, repeating all his tutor's interview tricks. The venerable old institution of Cambridge had always been accused of instilling a sense of privilege in its students. In truth, this was not born out of snobbery or class, but out of confidence. Such confidence had been instilled in him from the day he walked through the door of Magdalene College, and he couldn't help but convey it in this interview. At least, that was what his tutor had told him. He tried to think confident thoughts.

In the five minutes that he watched her, the woman's face displayed a wide range of expressions. Her head tilted while she paused and thought. She scrunched her nose at what Milton could only imagine was a difficult question and nodded along with questions as though they were exactly what she was expecting. Towards the end, she was blinking longer than usual, and her lips drew thin. Her answers grew terse. Milton tried to imagine the questions that they asked her and pretended to answer them himself with confidence and poise. At last, the woman beamed, stood, and walked to the door, shaking hands on the way. When the door opened, Milton saw the welling tears that she had been holding back. As she passed him, the dam broke, and out poured the tears as she hurried away. *Excellent*, he thought, *perhaps I have a chance after all.*

The administrator called the next candidate. "Milton," he said. *Crunch time*, Milton thought. It was just like the Henley regatta finals with only five hundred meters to go, his muscles burning and the cox shouting obscenities, demanding one final effort. This time there were no teammates to rely on. It was time to shine, on his own.

Professor Anton Jerome was the head of the Westley Trust Applied Genetics laboratory, based at the University of London. His success had come on the back of his postdoctoral work with the Nobel laureate, Professor Mary Ambrose, who had discovered the genetic cause and treatment of male pattern baldness. It was rumoured that Jerome was bitter about not being considered for the award. His clean-shaven head was perhaps a statement to this effect.

Behind his silver-rimmed spectacles, Jerome's eyes were laser-like in their examination of the young man as he walked into the room. Milton's blood pressure rose as those beams fell upon him. He gripped the man's hand, egg-crushingly firm but not bone-crunching, and was introduced to the rest of the panel.

"Let me introduce Professor Anton Jerome," said the administrator. "This is Professor Dolores Ricard," pointing to the diminutive lady who looked like she wouldn't be out of place sitting behind a church fete stand selling shortbread. "This is Dr. Ann Hebren," he said, gesturing to the younger, serious woman who looked like she would rather be somewhere else, "and I am Ronny Allen, the Human Resources representative. Please take a seat, Mr. Milton."

Milton shook each of their hands and sat down. The seat was still warm from the previous occupant.

Jerome spoke with a deep voice, in a mild Jamaican accent. "As you are aware, I head the Applied Genetics lab, which has a broad remit of developing new therapies for genetic disorders. You will, of course, also be aware of my discovery of the genetic treatment for baldness that attracted quite a bit of attention."

Milton failed to stop his eyebrows from raising. His discovery?

Jerome continued, "Based on those methodologies, we are applying corrective genetic treatments to many diseases. Some of the projects include Down's syndrome, cystic fibrosis and Huntington's disease."

"This project will involve attempting to correct the genetic instability in the repetitive elements of the centromeres that is a classic symptom of the ICF syndrome. What does ICF stand for?" he asked Milton.

It was the first direct question, and Milton wasn't ready for it. He stuttered, "Immuno— Immunodeficiency— centromeric instability— facial aberration syndrome."

"Anomalies, not aberration," Jerome corrected. "Even my three-year-old would have got that right."

Milton couldn't stop his mouth from falling open, and he paused to give himself time to process the insult and try to set it aside. "So, my project will involve" – *that's right*, he thought, clicking his mind back into gear, interview trick number one, the oldest trick in the book: talking like it's already my job – "correcting the causal mutations in the DNMT3B gene that drive ICF."

"No," Jerome snapped. "We already have the constructs for that. The complex centromeric rearrangements are what we must fix and it will take a talented graduate student to accomplish." He wrinkled his nose when he said the word 'talented'.

Milton nodded.

Ricard picked up the questioning. "At this institute we are passionate about clarity in communication, about making science – and genetics in particular – accessible to everyone. Tell me…" She looked down at some papers as though searching for something. "Mr. Milton, how would you explain genetics to someone with no prior knowledge of the subject?"

Milton reeled at the question. What was she asking for? A lecture from GCSE level up, or the specific minutiae of the project as it had been provided to him, or a critique of the latest findings in their studies?

Milton glanced at the door, flirting with the idea of escaping. A whirlpool of ideas raced around his mind, eventually settling into place in a neat order. He launched into his pitch for the job.

"Where do I start? Obviously, with the basics. The human genome is made up of four rudimentary bases: adenosine, cytosine, thymine, and guanine, often written as A, C, T and G. That makes up your DNA. The genome encodes approximately twenty-three thousand genes that make up about two percent of the code."

Milton surveyed their faces as he spoke. Dr Hebren nodded along to his comments as though paying attention yet stared out the window. Professor Ricard retained her gentle smile and kept her eyes trained on him, while Professor Jerome shuffled papers as though he was already looking for the next candidate. He licked his lips to moisten them, but his rapidly drying tongue did not comply. The glass of water on the table tempted him, an oasis in which he could gather his thoughts. After a gulp, he continued, "Those genes are turned into messenger RNA that then gets converted into proteins, using the protein code. The protein code is represented by twenty letters of the alphabet for each of the twenty amino acids. Each amino acid is coded by a three-base-pair DNA sequence – for example, ATG represents methionine, the start of every protein. However, there are large portions of the genome that are non-functional, and were once referred to as 'junk DNA'. These parts are remnants from our ancestral ape days, or perhaps viral insertions that have accumulated over eons of history. The centromeres, the middle of chromosomes, are specialised regions of repetitive DNA that are there to allow proper division of the DNA when a cell divides."

Milton glanced at his interviewers again. Dr. Hebren was no longer nodding and just stared out the window. Professor Ricard was no longer smiling, and Professor Jerome was now just scowling with one raised eyebrow. He had studied for this interview by reading all the textbooks and all the latest reviews. He even read all of Jerome's recent papers. He wondered if he was faking enough confidence. He tilted his head and changed tack.

"But of course, you know all of this. If I was to discuss this project, I would start with the two limitations that I can see at this point. With the new DNA sequencing that is available now, reading the centromeres can be accomplished easily enough. However, trying to target a genetic change to a single part of this repetitive sequence might not be possible, unless you replaced the native centromere with an artificial centromere that retained the cellular function but not the repetitive sequence."

On saying this, Milton noticed Ricard's eyebrows raise with a wink to Jerome and the slightest acknowledgement from Jerome with the hint of a nod. They liked his idea. Milton sat a little taller and fought hard to hide the smile that wriggled onto his lips.

"The second problem is that you don't have ethical approval to administer the viral vectors to make these genetic changes *in utero* to babies when they are diagnosed in the womb, which would be the optimum time to do so."

"Not insurmountable problems," countered Ricard with a smile.

"That brings me to another problem with one of your most recent publications, Professor Jerome," Milton said, launching into another of his interview tricks, number seventeen: attack and see how they react. "The study you published on the correction of progeria, the aging disease. You didn't use the appropriate controls."

"And what would an *under*graduate know about such things?" Jerome retorted. "Four years of research, fourteen experienced scientists as authors on that paper, six expert reviewers, and an entire editorial board of the most respected genetics journal did not have a problem with the study, and yet you do, Mr. Milton."

Milton again warmed under the burning gaze and wondered if the sugar bonds in his DNA were melting under that intense heat.

"That is to say..." Perhaps his tactic had backfired. "I'm sure you will agree that every study, no matter what journal it is published in, can be criticised. Even you yourself have criticised the work of Professor Becken, who published in the same issue of that journal." He was on shaky ground, mentioning Jerome's competitor.

"Explain how sequencing works," said Ricard quickly, to change the topic, having also planted a hand on Jerome's arm.

Milton puffed a sigh of relief at the deviation from the potential disaster.

"If we start with the oldest technologies," he continued. "Last century, they used Sanger sequencing. That involved chopping the DNA into single bases, one at a time, like a salami slicer, reading each slice as you go. This was followed by the first-generation whole genome sequencing, which chopped the DNA into short fragments about 100 bases at a time and then made copies of that DNA, allowing you to take an image snapshot for each base as it gets copied. It then relied on mapping those short 100 base reads to a reference sequence, like taking a 100-letter phrase and trying to find matches within the works of Shakespeare, and then some. Any phrases that did not map to the reference were discarded."

Again, even as he spoke he sensed he was rambling and decided to wrap up.

"There were other methods, but these were all replaced about ten years ago by the technology that we still use today: native cell polymerase DNA replication, which uses live cell imaging of DNA replication as it happens *in vivo*."

"And how long does it take to sequence a whole genome?" asked Ricard.

"The same length of time it takes to copy the cell's DNA through the synthesis phase of the cell cycle – about twelve hours."

Jerome scoffed at his answer. "In the textbook it takes twelve hours. You do realise that textbooks are about two years out of date on the day they're printed? I can guarantee all the information you have just spouted came directly from *Molecular Cloning*, sixteenth edition. That book is four years old. I would know, because I wrote the dreadful thing."

Milton squirmed in his seat. That was exactly where he had found his information. He had somehow missed the fact that this man had written it. He breathed in sharply through his nose. *Who reads the name of the authors in a textbook?* he thought. *It was a textbook, for Christ's sake.* He pulled his collar away from his neck, releasing the heat that had been building up.

"With a host cell modified with an artificial rapid DNA polymerase, we can inject a nucleus of DNA from one cell into the husk of another cell," Ricard informed him, "that is, a cell with the nucleus removed, to synthesise and sequence the entire genome in about two hours."

Again, Milton shifted in his seat. That new sequencing technique was revolutionary. That must be impressive new technology developed in this lab. Milton was about to nerd out about the technology but was cut off.

"Okay, I'd like to steer this interview towards Dr. Hebren now," said Ronny Allen, "otherwise time will get the better of us."

Dr. Hebren had maintained a serious expression throughout the interview, but now she snapped a smile into place and started by inquiring about Milton's desire to undertake a PhD.

Milton responded with the usual drivel, but in a more euphemistic version.

"And what do you think is the most important characteristic for success?"

Persistence, obviously. "The ability to focus and think outside the box, and to work independently, and to operate as part of a team." *And all the other nonsense you're supposed to say in an interview.*

"Tell me, where would you like to see yourself in five years, or in ten years?"

Sitting where you are. "My hope would be to progress to postdoctoral work, aiming to develop my own areas of research and pursue my own ideas, ideally within a good department such as this one." *Or to put it plainly, to remain employed.*

Dr. Hebren seemed uninterested in his answers, and drew an end to her questioning. Ronny Allen then asked Milton to confirm his date of birth and information about his undergraduate degree, after which he too was finished, though he added, "Unless there are any other questions that you might have?"

Like the pull of the tide, the door tugged at him to escape as quickly as he could and leave this car-crash interview. *The damn textbook*, he chided himself. However, he had another trick up his sleeve. It was worth a shot. It couldn't get any worse.

"There is one thing I would like to ask Professor Jerome," he said. This was his next interview trick, number eleven: transversion. "You're sitting here questioning me about what kind of a student I might be. What I would like to know is what kind of a supervisor you might be. How many students have you supervised successfully? Are you the sort of mentor that would give me academic freedom to pursue a PhD, or will you treat me like a technician running a mundane project? I've heard stories..." Milton was about to say more, but he could almost hear Jerome's teeth gnashing.

Jerome stood and reached to shake Milton's hand. "That is irrelevant at this point, Mr. Milton, as we are looking for an intelligent, dynamic student who can drive this project forward. It will not be you. Thank you for coming in."

With that, Milton was dismissed, like a bothersome insect.

In the doorway of the meeting room, Milton paused, then turned. It was time to try one last interview trick, number forty-six: bargaining. "I hope you spend more time considering all the candidates than you have done just now," he said, "and if you do, you may realise that I am the best candidate that you will see today. Appoint me, and if I prove inadequate, I will leave the moment you tell me to do so. Thank you."

He walked out of the room knowing why the young woman had left in tears, presuming she had been treated the same. Instead of mist in his eyes, he made fists of his hands. He wondered if he could stand the mediocrity of failing, but would he even want to work for this man? Would he consider that a success?

He walked across the road and into the Jeremy Bentham pub, the old bastion of support for students throughout the centuries.

He slumped on the bench, gazing at the bubbles that ran up the inside of his glass. It was warm ale, so it didn't matter that it had sat there for more than an hour. The bubbles had diminished into a single stream emanating from the tiniest imperfection in the base of the glass. Much like the candidates in the interview, each bubble arrived, made its short journey, and departed. Occasionally, a bubble would cling to the side of the glass until the expanding gases, releasing enough hot air from inane answers, would inevitably depart. Despite clinging to the opportunity, like all the other bubbles, he had departed.

Milton wasn't aware of any laws that prohibited that type of behaviour when interviewing candidates, but Ronny Allen had failed in his duty to ensure a fair process. Sinking into an even lower slump, he rested his forehead on the table next to his glass.

He was two-thirds through his first pint when his phone rang. It was Ronny Allen on the line. "Mr. Milton, we would like to offer you the PhD position." There were other words about congratulations, impressing the panel, and receiving some paperwork, but Milton didn't hear them.

Chapter 3

I had lived in the ISS my entire life. I knew every ping and particle. An alert rang in my earpiece. It wasn't a typical ping. *Emergency in Maintenance.* Every vital system was managed there. Emergencies weren't rare and I was trained ta react. I left Gessica and yanked at the handgrips in the cylinder, flying the distance fast all the way ta the Maintenance wedge. Frank needed me.

The eight wedges in the ISS were designed with efficiency in mind. The Genetics wedge, Engineering and Maintenance wedge, Garden wedge and the Shared Activity wedge were at the "east" end. The Captain's, Physics, Kitchen, and Medical wedges were all at the "west" end. East and west didn't make sense in space. They were designated like that in the drawings and, as I knew, nicknames stick. In the middle were the first ISS parts and the new viewing deck. The cylinder passageway linked it all. All ISS spacers live and earn a living in their wedges.

As the gravity increased, I flipped and landed with my feet at the Maintenance hatch. Cranking it, I raced inside. My screwdrivers, wires and kit were scattered where I had left them, near my desk.

"Frank," I called. "What's the emergency?"

He was seated at his desk, tapping a screen, checking an air vent schematic. His eyesight was degenerating, and he held the screen an inch away, even wearing his glasses. He didn't even glance at me when I arrived.

"Clean it, Tammy. Always keep ya desk neat. Why d'ya race away like that?"

He was right, I had left a little hastily. I tidied my desk and stashed my gadgets. The device I was servicing didn't seem that pressing, given what was happening.

"Frank, have ya seen..."

"D'ya clean that air vent in the Garden wedge yet?"

"N'yet," I said. I clasped my hands.

"D'ya repair the seals in the Medical wedge yet? Dr. Chang needs that in the infirmary."

"I'll get it all finished, I will."

"Tardiness was never a character trait in ya parents. They'd have finished it already."

He always referred ta my parents when he was miffed with me. They were his staff in Maintenance. Then there was a freak accident.

Aged ten, I sat in the viewing deck, watching my parents fly. Masters at EVAs, they were like dancers in sync, flipping, twisting, repairing. Each task was handled with ease, each traverse like a leaf in the wind. Free. A panel needed replacing, and they were reattaching the wires when a leak vented my Dad's air. The air venting sent him careening at my Mamma. Mamma tried leashing with him, sharing her air.

At the time, I didn't realise what was happening. I simply saw that they were distressed. I smashed against the glass in the viewing deck, helpless. Frank raced ta retrieve them, dressing in his EVA, cycling the air and leaping. He didn't reach them in time.

Frank called them 'dark times'.

"They were the finest *Pan sapiens* I knew, Tammy. Never seen their like again."

He had a framed image near his desk: me, my parents and himself, taken a few weeks ere they died. He'd taken care a me ever since, all ten years. When Frank was in this frame a mind, we'd give the image a kiss and he'd reminisce.

There wasn't time ta reminisce, given what was happening. "Was there a real emergency, Frank?" I tapped my earpiece, reminding him.

"Nah – yanking ya chain. A few message alerts pipping in ya screen."

I had left the screen linked with my friend in Pasadena. He had sent many messages, then they ended sharply.

"Wanted ya ta clean the messy desk," Frank added. "Where were ya, anyway?"

"I was with Gessica in the viewing deck. Frank, listen —,"

"Gessica." He grinned at me and winked. "I knew ya'd find her."

He always ragged me when it came ta girls, even when there weren't any my age in the ISS. Since Gessica arrived, Frank knew that I'd tried meeting with her many times.

"Frank!" I yelled. "Ya have ta listen." I didn't need Frank's girl chat, and my meeting with Gessica didn't happen precisely as I'd planned anyway. My cheeks grew warm regardless.

Frank let his screen drift away as he glanced at me. His deep eyes had seen everything in the system, yet it was the first time he'd seen me this rattled. He gripped my shaking hands. "What is it?"

"Ya haven't seen it yet?" My speech faded away. Earth was typically greens and whites, tan-shaded deserts, and the pale teal sea. That was the way I had seen it my entire life. What I was trying ta tell him was that what I saw was red, dark and charred. "The Earth is painted in flames."

"What d'ya mean?"

"I mean the Earth is dying. Flares firing in every city. It's a disaster."

Instinctively, Frank swivelled his neck ta see the viewing hatch. It wasn't aimed at Earth while we were in the Maintenance wedge, and all he saw was space and stars. We always did it, reacting like whatever is happening we'll face it right where we can see it. If it's that dire, we'd see it, right?

"Why?" Frank said.

"Gessica said she knew."

"Well, get in there and ask her again. I'll alert the captain."

We parted, he ta the Captain's wedge and I ta the viewing deck. Gessica was still there, silent and still. *She made it.*

I stared at her and tried hard ta see the Hitler, the Stalin, the Stineman, the many criminals in the past with death ingrained in their minds. Yet I failed in seeing that in her. She hadn't made the flares, she hadn't pressed the keys and she wasn't even Earthed. She was here. Was I false and trivial in thinking she was pretty and sweet? She wasn't evil, as far as I saw.

And yet the fear in her eyes seemed married with her statement. *I made it.* Why? It was all I was thinking ta ask. I placed my hairy hands in hers, perfect and white, peering at her green eyes, wide and teary, reflecting the flames as if the devil hid within. I asked her again what it was that made her think that she was incriminated.

Chapter 4

No one had told him it would be like this. Before starting his PhD, Larry Milton had thought it would involve animated debates about the fundamentals of the universe, exciting discoveries around every corner, and that it would elevate him to a higher plain of knowledge. He had planned on saving the world, one disease at a time. He hadn't planned on having to play with kids.

He sat on a rug surrounded by three-year-olds in the middle of the waiting room. Joy, Andy and Zeke were all regulars at the ICF clinic, here for their monthly treatment. Milton was there to fulfil his patient engagement activities. He was supposed to be talking to the parents about his study.

He rummaged through the box of toys until he found the one he was looking for.

"Who's that?" Zeke asked.

"It's…" Milton paused for dramatic effect before launching the toy into the air, "Spider-Man." He caught it and pretended to swing across the room, jumping across the heads of the three children.

They all laughed.

"I can't believe you kids don't know who Spider-Man is."

"Joy Sinclair," the nurse called. Joy stood up with her mother and they were escorted into the treatment room.

Milton spotted a five-year-old boy, new to the clinic, sitting by himself. He walked over to sit next to him, and handed him the Spider-Man toy.

"What's your name?" he asked.

"Keith." The boy looked down at his feet. The toy toppled to the floor. Milton picked it up again. The boy displayed all the usual symptoms of ICF: slightly larger head, short for his age, detectable misshapen jawline, and lack of grip strength.

He's too old to start the treatment, Milton thought. Even without a medical degree, he'd spent enough time with these patients to be able to spot the signs easily enough. He couldn't quite understand how anyone else could miss it, but it was like that mole on your face: always there, but never noticed until someone else points it out to you.

Milton poked his tongue out at the boy. A smile crept slowly into place, as if Keith was trying to hold it back. Milton wiggled his tongue like a salamander. Keith chuckled.

"Are your parents here?"

The boy pointed to the bathroom. The door opened and a man came out, wearing a biker's leather jacket and boots that appeared to have the sole purpose of stomping.

"Hey. What are you doing with my kid?"

"Don't worry, sir, I'm just here to help with the clinic."

"He don't need no help."

"He looked worried to me. I thought I'd sit next to him until you were back. Keith, are you worried?"

The boy nodded.

"Well. That's my job, to tell you not to worry." Milton grinned so wide his teeth could see his ears. Milton glanced at the father, to check that it was still okay to sit next to his son, but he returned his attention to Keith. "My boss is a world-famous doctor, and he knows exactly what to do to make you better."

"What are they going to do in there?" The boy's father's voice had grown quiet, his hands resting on his child's shoulders.

"Standard genetic treatment. He'll do a few tests to work out the severity of the illness at the genetic level, and then will start Keith on a small dose of the medication that will correct the main genetic change in a gene called DNMT3B. Then over a series of months he'll gradually increase the dose until all the errors are patched up. It's delivered as an injection, and it's really very safe." Milton handed him a pamphlet.

"I just want my boy to get better."

"He will." *I hope. That's why I'm doing my PhD.* "Just out of interest," Milton was almost certain he knew what the answer would be, but it was why he was here, "would you be interested in consenting to have Keith take part in my study. I need a parent to consent on behalf of each child."

"Hell no. We ain't doing no study. I just want to see the doc and get out of here."

Typical. Milton hadn't signed a recruit in weeks and was falling behind his recruitment targets. He tried to hide his scowl.

The man picked up Keith, sat him on his lap and wrapped his arms around him. No matter what Milton thought of him, he was still a protective parent.

With impeccable timing, Cynthia, a post-doctoral fellow, arrived to drag Milton back to the lab. He had agreed to help her with DNA extractions.

"Let's go, Bruce Banner."

Milton sighed. Ever since he had pinned posters of his favourite old-school comic heroes above his desk, his colleagues had been relentless in their teasing.

The sun shone through the glass ceiling of the laboratory office as they entered. Milton's head turned in response to the smell of takeaway fish and chips, which came from the far end of the office where some of the students were eating lunch at their desks. The new version of fake fish, real chips, and really tempting.

Donning his lab coat, he followed Cynthia into the lab where the automated robotic DNA extractor was humming, waiting to be fed.

Urine samples. It didn't pay to be too squeamish in the lab, although the lab was all perfectly sterile. At least it wasn't Craig's faecal study. All samples were opened in the laminar flow hood, so that any nasty airborne droplets or contaminating DNA was prevented from entering the samples. The design of the hood said *these samples are more precious than you are*. Clean tubes, clean pipettes, an array of plasticware for the job, and Milton was ready. He set up a production line with Cynthia: her opening tubes, registering the sample IDs and handing them to Milton; he pipetting the correct amount of sample into each well of a 96-well plate. More than manual dexterity, this job involved stamina.

More and more, Milton found himself helping other lab members with their projects, rather than working on his own. With his project languishing due to failed experiments, technical problems and glacial recruitment, he was in a dark hole, unable to see a way out.

"How did you get through your PhD, Cynthia?" he asked.

"With great persistence and many tears," she replied.

"I've been working on this project for so long with no results that I think I'm just no good at it."

"If you were no good at it," she said with a smirk, "I wouldn't have asked to you help me. Look how quickly you're getting through these samples."

"I can do the manual stuff. I just feel like I shouldn't be here."

"It's classic imposter syndrome. I guarantee you, every PhD student has it at some stage."

Milton accepted this sage advice and continued to pipette. Twenty plates later, one thousand, nine hundred and twenty samples had been loaded into the automatic DNA-extracting machine.

"Thanks, Milton. I owe you one." Cynthia patted him on the back.

"Sure thing," Milton said, massaging the palm of his hand. "If I ever recruit enough subjects to do that many DNA extractions, I'll let you know."

With a few hours left in the day, he resumed his own experiments. The sequencing machine he had set up the day before was just about to finish, at which point it would automatically copy the results to the cloud server. This experiment was designed to identify non-heritable changes in centromeric DNA that formed the normal variation between individuals. He was sequencing mother-daughter pairs from GENERATE, a study designed to map human genetic variation. It was a longstanding practice in academia to come up with the most ridiculous acronyms for studies. This one was no different. GENERATE: GENeral sEquence vaRiATion in centromEres.

Milton had staked everything on getting his PhD, yet as he stared at his computer screen he wondered if any of his fruitless, confidence-sapping work over the last three years had been worth it. So far, he had found nothing. *A null result is still a result*, he imagined his supervisor saying. He sighed and rested his head in his hands. The trash bin icon on his screen seemed to be jumping up and down in anticipation. Although Milton was tempted to delete all the work he had done over the last three years, he resisted.

He loaded up the sequence of the daughter and ran it through the *de novo* scaffolding, piecing the sequences together like a jigsaw puzzle. Once complete, he mapped it back to the reference human genome and highlighted all the points of variation. He was scanning for differences in the centromeres, the middle of chromosomes that had previously been thought to contain only repetitive sequences.

Hey, that's unusual. His computer screen was filled with long lines of DNA code, the letters A followed by T, C and G representing each of the bases in a long line of combinations that stretched from the top of the screen to the bottom. To the untrained eye it was a jumbled mess, but to Milton it had become his domain. It was a genetic game of spot the difference.

A large chunk of repetitive sequence flashed with neon highlighting. The block of yellow text wasn't in the reference.

He copied the unusual sequence and ran it through the database. No matches in the human genome. No matches in *any* genome. That meant that it couldn't be contamination from some other organism. It only matched one other spot in this girl's DNA, six thousand bases away.

Milton tried to imagine the protein code that this sequence might make. It was unusual for repetitive sequences to form proteins, but this one looked as though it might. It had the classic start codon for methionine, M, in the sequence.

```
atg gaa att agc ggc gaa agc agc att tgc gcg
```

```
M   E   I   S   G   E   S   S   I   C   A
```

"Me is Gessica," Milton read. *What the hell?*

Milton turned and looked around the office. *Should I get someone to check this?* Cynthia was still in the lab looking after the DNA-extracting robot; others were at their desks. Craig, his unofficial lab advisor, was busy teaching other students in the lab.

They would all only laugh at Milton anyway, assuming it was a joke.

He looked more carefully and spotted a different start codon.

```
atg tat aac gcg atg gaa att agc ggc gaa agc agc att tgc gcg
```

```
M   Y   N   A   M   E   I   S   G   E   S   S   I   C   A
```

"My name is Gessica." *Oh my god. Someone has written in this girl's DNA.*

Milton's hands were shaking, but he copied the sequence six thousand base pairs away, and it translated into the same phrase. He leapt to his feet and pointed at the screen, shouting, "Hey!" No one paid attention to him. *It can't be real. Can it?* He sat down again.

"Nothing is real unless you validate it," he whispered. It was a mantra he had been told often by his supervisor. Milton wondered if he had time to sequence the DNA sample again. He looked it up on the record: rack five, box five, position E6.

"Wait," he said aloud. "I don't need to do that."

He loaded up the sequence of the mother's DNA, which was perfect for independent replication. If the message was an aberration or some sort of technical mistake, it would be absent from the mother's DNA. He aligned the mother's genetic sequence over the daughter's.

It was a match. The mother had the same repetitive sequence in her DNA too. Milton's heart started thumping.

It's heritable.

Chapter 5

"My name is Gessica Theresa Kelly, Gename patent 14806 Harry Alpha Whisky, and ya already knew my name," she stated as a plain fact.

Yes, I knew her name. She was the lead geneticist's child, and assistant head in the genetics department. It was said that she was enhanced far past the standard, having received intellect particles three times. Her parents always denied it. Regardless, the hearsay persisted. She didn't seem that different ta me.

"My calling is in genetics," she said, "and it is with genetics that we are eradicated. I made the genetic chemical that they released. All primates will perish. Ya can't even grasp the idea at all, can ya?" She snatched my arm and led me.

She directed me as if I was her leashed pet. We left the viewing deck and headed via the vast cylinder passageway, end ta end. We flew half the length, twisting and whirling in a weightless dance, and landed hand in hand at the Genetics wedge as the gravity increased.

"Ya said ya knew it was happening, Tammy. What gave it away?" she asked as we arrived at the wedge.

Her directness startled me, and I halted. I had ta think what ta tell her. Earlier, I had received a secret message via my friend in Pasadena. The message was a specific IP address registry. It had taken time ta crack the file, and man was I impressed when I did. It was an access address inside a satellite data farm, a replica internet, the entire light internet and many dark files as well. There were ministry archives that the States, Germany, Ireland and China kept in the self-managed data farm. Everything was there: classified papers and news, CCTV tapes and endless intimate vids. The farm held all past intelligence. My friend in Pasadena had sent this clandestine data cache in case any disaster happened. Seeing this emergency cache, I had ta think a disaster *was* happening. That was why I raced ta the viewing deck.

"I received a message, my friend in Pasadena, and it seemed like there was danger," I said. "I wanted ta see if my friend there was safe. He wasn't – Pasadena was the first flare I saw."

She twisted and held my face, like a hawk eyeing its dinner. She then eased as her hands released me; her strength melting. "I'm afraid," was all she said. All that needed saying.

Gessica lived in the Genetics wedge with her parents, Terrence and Gilly Kelly, and the twelve geneticists in their teams. When we entered the wedge, we were halted immediately – her stern-faced father.

"Papa," Gessica said. "What happened?"

"Child, the Illegals have released the chemical—" Terrence halted when he saw me.

Gessica gritted her teeth and hissed at the name "Child". She held my hand and led me inside her research den, passing her father's stares and her team, each craving her eyes.

Her skin was tender, yet her grip had tensed. I set aside the thrill that shivered inside me as we held hands. It wasn't a smiling time. She fastened the hatch and twirled the catch, and then we were inside her den.

Set neatly in the desk was a cell viewer, a sterile chest in which the cells were handled. There was a cell spinner, chip readers that read amplified DNA, and many research gadgets neatly attached ta the walls. I knew these machines, as I had serviced many myself. Gessica held a tray with three plastic dishes, and she placed them in the cell viewer. She directed me ta view the cells as she displayed them.

I saw lengthy stringy cells that she said were grey matter cells. The first were healthy, the latter were sick, and the third were all dead.

"These cells were treated with the chemical I made, increasing levels in each dish," she said.

She held an alternate tray, again with three dishes, and the cells in each were alive and well.

"The first cell type ya saw carried the Gename patent particle and died rapidly when they grew with the chemical. The latter cells had never seen the Gename patent particle and are resistant."

I still didn't get why the Earth was clapped in a red mist with flares dismantling cities, each acting like a cranky child, retaliating against each new city as they were drafted in ta the fight. I asked her ta tell me in simple terms.

"Alright, simple." She massaged her temple. "All males and females that have a Gename patent are at risk when they inhale this chemical. It kills grey cells, in a critical part." She tapped her head. "The first sign is fear, they then get deranged, and after that, they die. It is self-replicating, in a way. Cells that have the chemical catalyse DNA parts that then remakes the chemical again. It's like a viral particle spreading itself. The saving grace is if ya never had any Gename patent. There aren't many like that." She indicated me.

What was this chemical? Ta me it didn't make sense. Why make it?

She heaved a sigh. I think it was all the things I was asking that tired her.

"When the Gename patents were invented," she said, "the scientists tested all the native and synthetic chemicals. They tried identifying anything that might interact with the gene made with the Gename patents. They had all their clever minds imagining all the ways the genetic patent might fail, what might prevent it reaching the market. They didn't identify any way it might fail. The gene was silenced, and it wasn't even made in the cell. There wasn't any way it might harm –that they identified– and after that it was deemed safe. In the end, all Earth states were happy mandating it. They said that all legal children had ta patent their genetics ta stay safe. Fifty years later, nearly all, planet-wide, have Gename Patents. Any that missed it are Illegals, which means all in the space settlements Hisakatani and Marsstead and, it seems, a few Earth-side."

She then stared at me, thinking. She scanned my feet, my knees, then my chest and my eyes.

"And then there's my new friend."

I might have missed it since I wasn't fast, yet an idea in my mind held me. It was when we were in the viewing deck that she had said primates and apes were dying.

"Why the apes and primates?" I asked. "They didn't have Gename patents, as far as I knew."

"That's where I arrive in this tale," she said. "In the last three years, my research team have investigated a new idea. The Gename patent particle has mated with a native viral particle. It gives a mild fever, sniffles and headaches, the same as all similar viral strains. The Gename particle targets the viral DNA and hides in the central part in the cell's DNA. That viral strain has spread in all primates. At first it was harmless and there wasn't any alarm, yet in the last seven years it has spread far and wide. All primates have it. Ya might have seen that we haven't had any passenger ships arriving recently – since I arrived, in fact. The same in the settlements, Hisakatani and Marsstead. I realised that if any viral carrier landed here, we'd all get infected. When I identified this danger, I asked the Captain ta halt all traffic. He agreed.

"I didn't learn when and why it happened as it did," she reflected. "All that mattered was that any man thinking he hadn't a Gename Patent was clearly mistaken. Even the Illegals that released the chemical were infected with the new strain. They will die as fast as their intended targets. Sweet mercy! What a mistake."

She stared at the ceiling, shaking her head. And like I said earlier, she seemed helpless, like a medic with a dying patient.

Many ideas scratched inside my mind that needed answers. The largest was: why the flares? Why was the Earth a fiery hell?

"The fear and mental side effects made the leaders twitchy," she said. "Imagine a president with his finger wiggling near the trigger. Any slight sign that he was threatened, even imagined, might make him hit it. That's what happened, I'm certain. I saw in Africa even they had flares ta fire. Every land is a fiery mess."

She clenched her teeth, her eyes darkening like a shade had descended ta match her temperament. "In fairness, that is the preferred death," she added. "What happens when they get taken with the chemical at the end... it's sickening, Tammy. Then, if that wasn't the nadir, any that live will carry the chemical and spread it. Death will ride the wake like a water skier, spraying it everywhere."

There were many things I still had ta ask. Was there a chance the chemical was already released here in the ISS? What madness led them ta release it? Why did they even think it might end well? My friend in Pasadena – did he die painlessly? Was she really incriminated? Why did she make this chemical in the first place? I pestered her like a hyperactive child.

She faced away and didn't answer. I watched her trying ta think a ways ta answer, starting then halting, yet she stayed silent. In any case, there wasn't time ta answer me. We heard a rapping in the metal hatch that startled Gessica. Terrence Kelly, her father, called her name.

"Gess, a ship has left Earth heading here. They will arrive in a day. There's a leaders' meeting in the shared wedge in twenty mins."

Chapter 6

Larry Milton looked along the open plan office, the setting sun dimming now. The pale glow of screens lit the faces of graduate students, like little lampposts beaming weakly through the fog. He considered himself one of the hardest working, and with six months left of his funding, he had to be. He was the only one not immersed in social media.

The latest fad in social media was BuzzWorld, where virtual socialising was divided into alpha, beta, and gamma friends. With glazed eyes, you could stare into a different focal point and see the virtual world appear. Milton observed his colleagues and tried to guess where each of them were.

Cynthia was probably meeting her alpha friends in Singapore, sipping a cocktail in a rooftop bar, as she often did. It was an impressive location with a view over the city and the sun setting in the west over the edge of the swimming pool. She lifted her hands to her mouth regularly. Although Buzzworld commandeered the sounds made by her vocal cords, Milton could see her lips move and her face contort into laughter. Her embarrassing tumble off her chair was perhaps a sign that she had had too much psychological inebriation.

Craig was regularly pulling his hand to his mouth and pursing his lips, so was likely hanging out in one of his western movies again, smoking a cigar, gambling, and flirting with the working girls. Milton had joined him there once, but couldn't stand the smell of the stale beer and the clouds of tobacco smoke that stung his eyes. The working girls were nice on the eyes from afar, but when they drew nearer, he could see the realism in their haggard eyes and the stench of an unwashed body covered unsuccessfully by strong perfumes. Their clothes were ready to rip off and looked as if they often had been. It wasn't a fun place for Milton, experiencing all those senses.

As a beta friend you could watch an alpha conversation and contribute with text insertions that the alphas could read or ignore. Milton joined scientific conferences as a beta, so that he could ask questions with his interjections. The purpose of his interjections was not to ask pertinent questions, but rather to show off his knowledge of the topic, to grandstand in front of the important professors. It was a frequent ploy at scientific conferences. Like all others that tried this ploy, he was often ignored.

Tracey and Judith, two other PhD students, spent most of their time flitting in and out of celebrity events as gammas. They would watch casting calls and movie star interviews as a gamma fly, as close to the celebrities as if they were sitting on the couch next to them, buzzing around with other celeb-chasing flies, all pretending to be A-listers. They would go to meet-and-greets with celebrities, never sure if they were interacting with the real celebs as alphas, or whether the celebs were computer-generated. One never knew, as the AI celebs were as realistic as the live alphas, sometimes more so. And often more pleasant.

The lack of privacy in BuzzWorld had driven Milton away. That, and his lack of any real alpha friends to hang out with. His parents didn't count. As a result, he had made the decision to focus on his PhD rather than fritter away his time in social media. It was why Milton was still focusing on his computer this late on a Friday evening. That, and the genetic message he had just decoded.

For three years he had been staring at DNA codes, so that now he could see proteins and transcription factors, and the chromatin in a nucleus in a cell of the body. Milton had become a gene ninja. He could almost see the person behind the DNA code on his screen.

Excitement rumbled in his belly, as if he had missed both breakfast and lunch. He shook his head to try and dismiss what he saw in this DNA sequence. But it was still there. Milton sensed a presence behind him.

"Milton, time's up." Professor Jerome stood right behind him. "You're not going to get any more results by staring at that monitor. Come on, it is Friday evening – let's go and grab a pint, your shout." Tradition dictated that the supervisor bought the students drinks, so Milton's pained look in response to his well-remunerated supervisor's suggestion was only to be unexpected.

"I think you had better have a look at this before we go," Milton said. His certainty had evaporated like a puff of vapour. *Do I dare show it to him already? I'm not even sure of it myself.* He had just translated the full DNA code into the protein code, and now the letters fell across his screen.

"What is it?" Jerome asked. He was always curious about new results, like a bulldog with a chew toy. He leaned over Milton's shoulder to look at the screen.

"I think I've discovered something remarkable in the centromere sequencing project," Milton began. His voice now lacked any of his earlier confidence. Years of fruitless negative results, the unmovable impending submission deadline, and the impossibility of what he was about to show his supervisor all contributed to the shakiness of his voice. The excitement of a potentially ground-breaking result bubbled up inside him. "I've found a repetitive DNA sequence in this young girl's genome that's a little strange. See this 249 base pair sequence? It matched 100 percent to this sequence over here, six thousand bases away."

"That's not so strange, Larry," said the professor leading into his typical lecturing tone. "Forty percent of our whole genome is made up of repetitive DNA sequences. The centromeres are almost all repetitive. You know that."

"I know. If that was all it was, it wouldn't be so strange. The repeat doesn't match anywhere else in the genome apart from these two regions. I can't find it in any other reference sequence or in any other species. It's a foreign sequence. It shouldn't be there."

It was like finding an alien life form sitting next to you in a cinema. Even though it might be munching on popcorn like everyone else, it shouldn't exist. But there it was.

"Look," Milton continued, "there's a protein start codon here in the first repeat." He pointed to the methionine, the starting amino acid of all proteins. "And if you follow that frame, it goes for 2048 amino acids with no introns."

"That's huge for a single exon protein," Jerome agreed. He paused, performing the quick calculation in his head. "It would be 230 kilodaltons. There are no single exon proteins that big in the animal kingdom."

"And if you translate it, there are no conserved domains. It's not a normal protein," Milton added. "But look at this," he continued, his pulse increasing to keep pace with the adrenaline that was vibrating through his veins. "I thought this was the start codon here: methionine, glutamic acid, isoleucine, serine, et cetera, but if we go back in the same frame, there's another start codon methionine only four amino acids back. Now start reading."

Jerome leaned in to look closer at the DNA sequence on the computer screen translated into the 20-letter protein code.

```
atg tat aac gcg atg gaa att agc ggc gaa agc agc att tgc gcg

M   Y   N   A   M   E   I   S   G   E   S   S   I   C   A

acc cat gaa cgc gaa agc gcg aaa gaa ctg ctg tat ggc gaa aac

T   H   E   R   E   S   A   K   E   L   L   Y   G   E   N

gcg atg gaa ccg gcg acc gaa aac acc tgg gcg aac ttt gcg tgg

A   M   E   P   A   T   E   N   T   W   A   N   F   A   W

gcg acc gaa aac att ctg agc att aaa agc cat gcg cgc cgc tat

A   T   E   N   I   L   S   I   K   S   H   A   R   R   Y

gcg ctg ccg cat gcg tgg cat att agc aaa tat acc cat att agc

A   L   P   H   A   W   H   I   S   K   Y   T   H   I   S

att agc atg tat acc gcg ctg gaa

I   S   M   Y   T   A   L   E
```

"My name is Gessica Theresa Kelly gename patent one four eight nil six harry alpha whisky this is my tale," Milton read out. "I guess numbers are hard to write in the protein code."

"Holy smokes!" muttered Jerome. "My eyes hurt trying to read that. Read it for me."

"This is my tale," Milton continued. "In 2080, after ethics disintegrated in the seventies the Earth state finally legalised genetically altered man. First came GM plants, then GM pets. Finally, in 2088, GM man was accepted, with the Asians leading the way with their advanced designs. The space settlements Hisakatani and Marsstead and the NASA ISS demanded it, filling their large settlements with GM men. In time, the Earth permitted new tests in GM man designs that were fescennine even with their standards. They created GM men with green iridescent skin, and then with transparent skin and in the last series they reverse engineered a chimp-man, Pan sapiens they called it.

"The Earth state, realising its mistake, again illegalised GM man. IVF and all fertility treatments were halted as they were very easily altered with the illegal GM viral particles. This law wasn't implemented in the space settlements. They needed their GM men. As swiftly as the law was passed, as with any illegal activity, scientific advancement persisted in discreet places. In time, illegal GM men were everywhere.

"In their fight against the Illegals, the Earth state demanded all females attain legal child permits, a legal genetic patent, as it were. Three years later, they implemented the virally integrated genetic patents as a legal necessity. They called them gename patents. It stated name and a distinctive patent ID. The gene wasn't inherited since it was deleted in gamete genesis and was epigenetically inactivated.

"This was an appalling mistake. The Illegals created a chemical that wasn't identified in the early clinical trials. This chemical activated the patent gene specifically in the amygdala, giving severe psychiatric fear-related side effects. This chemical was released in the wind. With these fear-related side effects, the Earth leaders damaged the planet far past any help. The illegal GM men and the Pan sapiens lasted the chemical wave and saw the end arrive.

"We in the space settlements have created small viral gename particles that we have sent via a time-travel device. This particle will infect man with this message. This is a warning. There is still time. Please prevent this disaster. Keep in mind that the GM men weren't the mistake. We weren't a mistake. The patents were. My name is Gessica Theresa Kelly Gename patent one four eight nil six harry alpha whisky. This is my tale.

"That's it," Milton said, "2023 amino acids and a whole story. It's amazing! A patent in my genome." Milton whistled. "This could be an entire chapter in my thesis. I can finish my PhD!" His voice had risen an octave in his excitement. It wasn't every day that you discovered something truly amazing.

In contrast with the student, the supervisor's voice lowered by an octave. In his most serious tone, he said, "How did it get in this child?"

"And in her mother – I didn't show you that yet," Milton said.

Jerome's face turned from a scowl into a wide, white-toothed grin.

"Don't worry about it, Larry," he assured Milton. "It's probably just Craig pulling a fast one. Take the weekend off, and on Monday morning he'll be in here saying 'Gotcha!'"

"I don't get it," Milton threw his hands in the air and stood up. "This could be the most miraculous discovery in thirty years. I found it. You can't take that away from me."

Jerome growled, looking down at the student who stood a foot shorter. "Yes I can."

Milton shook his head, took a deep breath, and looked his supervisor in the eyes. The man's bald head shone in the glow of the screens and his forceful demeanour was irresistible. He saw he had no choice. Milton accepted the advice, switched off his screen and grabbed his coat.

As they walked out of the office together, he caught Jerome glancing back at the screen, his brow still furrowed.

Chapter 7

The shared wedge was the largest in the ISS, with gymnastics machines and games, a large eating space and an activity area. All crewmates spent time here staying active, and it was the wedge where we mingled. It was life in space. My chess set was still in its place in the central desk. The wedge's spin created a small gee that kept things in place a little heavier than when weightless.

Within the wedge were the eight department heads, their assistants, and me, hiding like a shy child. I wasn't a participant in this meeting since I wasn't a leader. I came in with Gessica and I was glad that the Captain didn't say anything. I stayed at the entrance where they mightn't see me.

Captain Yvegeny Petrykin led the ISS. He was a nice man, and he always kept the peace when things were heated. His assistant, Dr. Lee Chang, was standing at his side. Dr. Chang was the medic, and even if he was mean when he treated me, he was a decent medic. They were facing the remaining department heads and their assistant heads all standing in a semi-circle.

The genetics lead was Terrence Kelly, and his assistant was Gessica, standing near him. My Maintenance and Engineering department head, Frank, saw my red shirt and gave me a wink as I slinked away like a spider hiding in it's nest. Frank knew I wasn't meant ta attend this meeting. Since he liked me, he let it slide.

Petrykin was well respected, and when he held his hand high, he silenced the whispers. He repeated what Terrence Kelly had said earlier, that a ship had left Earth and was heading here. There were eight men, twelve ladies and a child in that ship, the remaining few that had escaped the flares that were spreading planet wide.

"The Earth is dead," he said.

Why the flares? It was the single thing that filled every mind.

Frank held his head in his hands. Andrew, the physics assistant lead, clasped his hands like he was praying. Marie, the Garden wedge head, was clinging ta her sides, like she was afraid she was falling apart.

They hadn't seen the red flares like Gessica and I had when we were in the viewing deck. They didn't appreciate the severity, and the captain didn't have all the answers. All he said was, "They will arrive, and I am determined that we will save them."

Still, there was a dilemma. The ISS was versatile and had physical space. The first challenge was feeding them and giving them air. Frank knew this.

"If they land and stay even three weeks, it might tip the stasis," he said. The levels we maintained in renewing air and water were critical. "We'd need a refill visit, and I daren't imagine we have a chance after this."

He was right. If we tipped the stasis past the renewing level, it was the end.

"Are they delivering refills?" Marie asked.

"Negative," the captain replied.

"If they stay a day past three weeks, we'll sign their death warrant," Frank added.

The captain regarded this statement with his typical calmness. "We'll limit the feeding cycles as well, half shares each, while they're here," he said. That was easy.

Frank was shaking his head.

Gessica stamped her feet and clenched her fists. Her eyes glistened with fire as if she was reflecting the flares we saw. She stepped away, setting aside her father Terrence Kelly, and said what I feared she might.

"We can't permit them ta land here."

The captain was startled, as if a child had slapped him. "What?" he demanded.

Terrence's eyes grew wide. "Gess, if they can't land here, they'll die," he chided her, as if she didn't grasp the stakes.

She clarified, "If they land, we will all die. Simple. They are affected with the chemical and if we release them in here, we release the chemical. We'll all die."

"We have ta risk it," the captain said.

"Risk implies it lacks certainty." Gessica glared at the captain. "I'm certain that if they land, we die." She stared at each crewmate, pleading with them ta see it the way she did.

"They need help," Dr. Chang said. "They're all that's left." Silence filled the shared wedge as all realised what that meant.

"Have ya even seen their genetic traces, Chang?" Gessica replied. "I checked their data. They're reverts." She gagged as if it made her sick saying *reverts*.

"Gessica!" Terrence chided his child with a stern eye. "I'll pretend I didn't hear that."

Reverts was a term I had heard rarely; it was a degrading term defining men that eschewed genetic enhancement. They were like the Amish regarding genetic advances. They had Gename patents and that was it.

"What if Gessica is right?" Andrew said. His eyes were red. "If they have this chemical..." He trailed away. He was trying hard ta agree with Gessica. With the captain glaring at him, it didn't last.

"They will need medical help when they get here," Chang added.

"Especially if they have the chemical," Marie snapped.

"Right." Andrew waggled his finger. With Marie agreeing with him, he grew in certainty. "And even if they're clean, in three weeks we'll regret it."

Ms. Anelka was department head in the Kitchen wedge, and general ship manager. She stayed silent, her mind already set. It was hard keeping the ISS fed as it was.

I watched the captain, and his typical calm face was challenged. New wrinkles appeared as he was thinking hard. His captaining style was generally *participative*. He craved their assent.

"What if we scan them with a chemical screen when they land here?" he asked. His eyes pleaded with Gessica. Did that satisfy her?

Her head was still shaking.

"If the chemical screen says they're affected, we'll deal with it then," he stated. "It's me that has ta decide this, Gessica."

Apparently, he had decided he didn't need her assent after all. He stared at Gessica like a hawk, daring her ta disagree.

He scanned his department heads seeking their assistance. "All agreed, raise hands."

Chang, Terrence and Frank raised their hands. Andrew, Marie and Ms. Anelka all declined.

"An even split," the captain stated.

"Gessica, child. Try imagining if I was in that ship," Terrence said. He was trying ta change her mind with empathy. She didn't have any with the passengers in the ship, at least that I saw. When he said "child" I saw Gessica tense.

"The deciding hand is mine, then." The captain sealed his eyes with a grimace. It was clear he was pained that it had ta happen like this. He raised his hand. "It's settled."

Gessica was deserted. She held her head high, stared at her father, and departed.

After she left, the meeting restarted with the department leads. With ample time ta decide the way we might receive the passengers, we decided it was right that we discreetly screen them and find a way ta keep the ISS clean, in case they were affected.

"Can we rig a segregated entry hatch where we can set the chemical screens?" the captain asked.

"Yes, easily," Frank replied. I knew Frank, and while his lips said yes, his eyes were wrinkled; he was trying ta think a ways ta make the segregated hatch ta satisfy the captain. His eyes danced till he had it. He snatched my arm and we left ta start right away. I always felt alive when there was a large maintenance task at hand.

Gessica visited while I was erecting the segregating walls, and watched as I set the master electric panel that managed the entry hatch. She set the chemical screen alerts in several places near the hatch and smiled at me when she had finished.

That day was tense, as if we were all sitting at an edge, waiting ta see if we might fall. The standard daily chatter in the airwaves grew silent and every man drifted, restless and ill at ease. Eyes were warier, and sinews tightened. I saw Andrew staring at a wall. I tried saying a few nice things and he didn't reply. He stayed silent, staring at that imperfect wall.

That day, we all learnt what had happened, and there was a chatter line linked with the passengers in the ship. They filled in the gaps in the tragic narrative. The chatter lines that linked with Earth were severed; the Earth had fallen silent.

Me aside, many crewmates had friends and family Earthed, and it didn't take an Einstein ta realise that they were all dead. I saw grief in many stages. Frank kept saying it was all fake, yet he kept making the sealed segregated hatch anyway, since the captain had asked him.

I saw raging fists directed at the Earth, and crying as the crew threw every negative feeling at the planet itself. The viewing deck was filled with the crewmates in savage fits, fighting ta witness the flames. I saw yelling at Gessica and even if I hesitated in defending her, I had ta wipe away a tear. Three times she received a shellacking served with spite when a crewmate saw her setting the chemical readers. I didn't get why they kept asking her ta repair the damage – she didn't have any way ta retract the chemical. She had made it, yet she didn't release it. She wasn't the villain, yet they said it and she accepted it. She didn't cry a single time, even if I wanted ta cry in her stead.

Dr. Chang kept asking her if we had a way ta reverse it, engineer an antithetical chemical, a medicine, a way ta make it right, yet there wasn't any medicine she knew.

"When the chemical is inside, there isn't a treatment," she stated.

It's interesting that I didn't see any acceptance, the grieving end stage. Perhaps Earth's death happened far faster than the mind can handle.

We talked with the ship's passengers as it came nearer, and they clarified a few things. The chemical was released instantly, in fifteen attacks in capital cities, an integrated attack. It was planned and devastating. The latency meant that it was a day after the release that any strangeness was seen. In a single day, the carriers had travelled everywhere with it. Panic, severe mental states and anarchy spread in all large cities and left a devastating trail, matchless. Within a week, every male and female, every child and grandparent with a Gename patent was affected with this chemical.

What little research had happened in that week had determined that any Earthers affected with the chemical were inhaling it, resynthesising it in their DNA and spreading it when they respired. They died after a day, the heavy chemical strangling their airways. It emerged that all primates were infected with this erstwhile harmless variant Gename particle, like Gessica had said. They were then devastated as greatly as man. Did we lament the primates, as we did man? I did, at least.

It was simply the greatest devastating chemical warfare ever seen. The Illegals, the men that eschewed the gename patent, had initially claimed they released it when the first victims appeared. Then, when they saw the real devastating effects, when apes and Illegals themselves were affected, they realised their tragic mistake. They then denied any claims, a little late.

Madness manifested indiscriminately, in state leaders and in vagrants alike. Allies damned allies and keys were pressed, setting it all alight like a daisy chain sparking at each link. Flares spread in what seemed an instant. Even the Illegals had perished in the carnage they created. A single ship was ready in the Cape Canaveral gantries, and NASA filled it fast with their families and sent it flying.

And here it was, drifting ever nearer, twisting like a dance partner, with a shimmy this way and a wiggle that way. Gas drivers fired left and right, aligning it with the hatch.

With a clang, it met the ISS.

We waited as the air in the ship integrated with the ISS system within my hastily made hatch. At least, even if they had the chemical, we were safe. While the air was integrating, the captain again asked the passengers if they were affected with the chemical. We had asked this every time we chatted with them.

"Negative, Captain. We are clean." It was the same reply each time. We had all heard it. Even if we weren't certain, the captain accepted it.

We released them in the segregated area where the air was sealed. The first passenger that left the ship was a man, his hair a mess, his eyes dark. His hands were shaking as he gripped the wall. The few that left the ship were the same, haggard and sick; they hadn't travelled in space, and it was clear they didn't have the training. Dr. Chang tried entering right away ta administer his medical checks.

He keyed the panel, yet it didn't release the hatch. I scratched my head. It was my hatch; I had made it. I tried the panel release mechanism myself. It failed. I feared that Gessica might have tampered with it when she set the chemical screens. I recalled that smile she gave me. Was it a sneaky smile?

"Release the hatch," the captain said, addressing Frank and me. He wanted Dr. Chang in there. I tried again, and all that happened was the electric panel release failed and sparked like it was angry. The wires fried. It was permanently sealed.

I leapt away, afraid the sparks might get me. I scratched my head and stared at the fried panel, then at Frank, then at the panel again.

Frank didn't have any answers, even with the captain glaring at him. Glaring didn't seem ta make anything right. Then my fear was realised. I heard Gessica in the speakers.

"Captain, they are affected," she said. "My chemical readers have detected it. I have retracted the release system. The hatch will remain sealed."

"Terrence, can ya verify that she is right." The captain slammed his hand against the wall.

Terrence replied, "Captain, Gessica has sealed herself in her research den with the chemical readers. She has sent me the analysis and it seems she's right; the chemical is present, and the passengers are affected. I can't say anything else since I can't see the raw data."

I recall that statement clearly; *I can't see the raw data*. It's still lingering in my mind. Did she fake the data?

I was distressed that the passengers were sealed like that, and I remained watching via the glass that separated the segregated area like a fish tank, with my hands pressed against it. The area had air ta last a few hrs. We had ta either release the air vents ta replenish it, else let them strangle in the thinning air.

I pressed my face against the glass and prayed they'd live. In their eyes I saw scared caged animals, pleading ta release the hatch. The largest man tried inflicting damage and instead damaged his hands. My hatch was tight and withheld against this attack. They were indeed caged animals.

I remarked that there were thirteen in the segregated area and asked them where the remaining eight passengers were. Their reply was weird, ta say the least.

The first man said, "They're sleeping."

A different man said, "They're ill with space sickness and remained in the medical ward in the ship."

A third man tried ta speak, then was grappled, the large man and his mate pinning him. They wrestled him till he was still and then yanked at his neck.

Whether they intended it this way, I didn't see. The third man's eyes stared directly at me. He was dead.

A lady snatched at the first assailant's hair, and he repelled her like she was an empty vessel and she hit the glass panel. The wrestling and fighting grew and three passengers were harmed in the mêlée. They screamed in pain, with arms and legs snapped and heads lacerated.

The captain yelled at them, "Cease this fighting. Please!"

I repeated, "Please!"

Dr. Chang grew frantic and slapped the hatch. "Gessica, let me in there. They're dying," he said, crashing his fist at the panel that activated the speaker.

"Negative," Gessica denied him.

Chang steamed away. At the time I was thinking he was headed ta the Genetics wedge ta attack Gessica. I wasn't thinking like a medic.

Fifteen mins later, Chang was inside the segregated area.

"What the hell! Chang!" Petrykin raged at him.

Chang had taken his EVA in space, ta the peripheral hatch in the Earth ship, and traversed their ship ta the segregated passengers. He remained helmeted as he administered medicine ta the distressed and eased their pain.

"They aren't affected with this damn chemical," he said. "My readers in here verify it. Gessica is lying. End the farce and let them in." He detached his helmet.

"Chang!" the captain yelled. He wasn't impressed.

This was what he had ta decide: did he agree with Chang's insistence; did he marry with Gessica's resistance? Were the passengers affected? Were they safe? It was a killer thing ta have ta decide. I was glad I wasn't captain.

In any case, their air was ending. It was time ta release them; if we didn't, we had ta let them die. The captain's face was calm and his eyes twitched, like he was weighing it all in his head. Standing there with him, I felt he had already decided. He faced me and asked me ta affirm his plan.

"Why did we let them land if we'll them die like this?" he asked.

A child held hands with her parents. I faced away, disregarding their pleading eyes. I wanted ta have faith in Gessica, yet I didn't get it. Why might she have faked it? Was it a grievance with a passenger? Why hadn't she released the raw data? That was in my mind when I replied ta the captain.

"Yes," I said. "Release them. I agree."

I had ta dismantle the entire segregating hatch ta let them in. The final panel drifted away, and I saw the passengers' faces. Relief.

I smiled at their happiness. They leapt and high-fived me. The little girl wept. Even in tenth gee a tear can fall. I placed my large hand in hers and she kissed my finger. The captain clapped my neck and thanked me. Chang carried his patients and the passengers dispersed in the ISS.

In less than a day we saw that Gessica was right.

Chapter 8

Milton did as his supervisor advised and travelled to his parents' country house for the weekend. Sitting at the breakfast table, he squirmed. His father, Richard was his usual unkempt self: unshaved, hair a mess and still in his robe. His mother, Bethany, was prim and proper and ready for the day; she had probably woken before dawn to do her hair. Before coffee, no one in this house talked, and afterwards it was rare, and woe unto anyone who disturbed the peace. A muttered hello and a nod of acknowledgement was all that normally passed for communication. But the unexpected weekend visit required explanation. The silence hung above them like a teetering chandelier.

"Laurence," Richard prodded.

"Dad, I need..."

"Here it comes. How much?"

"What? No, I don't need money." Milton telegraphed a pained expression. "Well, I do, but right now I need advice."

"You know that doesn't come free."

"I'll pay the booze toll later. Let's just say, for argument's sake, I made a discovery in my PhD. Like, world-changing, Nobel-prize-winning discovery. Really important."

Milton's mother clasped her hands together and beamed.

Milton shook his head. "No, Mum. Just hear me out. I thought it was important, but my supervisor just threw cold water over it, like it was nothing. He told me to drop it."

Bethany's shoulders sagged, but Richard nodded his head, like a wizened therapist.

"He knows best," Richard said. "You should always do what he says. He's your boss."

That was what Milton had been afraid to hear. Richard had always been the loyal company man, working for the same company for forty years.

"I don't think I can," he said. "I thought you raised me to have integrity. To stick up for what I believed in."

"Just don't believe in nonsense. Too much of that these days." Richard motioned to the news site open on his rolled-out screen. "If he says drop it, then do it."

Milton held his head in his hands and gazed at his Marmite toast. Humans were hardwired to look for patterns in everything: faces on Mars, butterflies in paint splats, an assortment of creatures in the stars. As he stared at his toast, a pattern started to emerge: the letters N and O.

"No," he said quietly. Then, louder, "No, I don't think I can."

Bethany stood up, scraping her chair across the tiles. She collected Richard's empty plate and, when she passed Milton, placed a hand on his shoulder.

"Love, why don't you come for a walk with us in Buzz-World to clear your head," she said. "We're going to meet up with your cousins and Aunty Wilma in the Cotswolds. Wilma has made a lovely autumn trek for us to enjoy."

"You know I hate going in there. Can't we just go for a walk in the woods here?"

"Your father's knees can't cope." Nor could his waistline. Public health officials had always warned about the dangers, but with BuzzWorld overtaking all other social media, the obesity epidemic had inflated at an alarming rate.

Milton left them zoning out into their screens and walked down the garden path into the nearby woods. The wind was chilly and blew through the empty branches. The path passed through a gully that had once been a riverbed, now overgrown. Pheasants blustered out of his way, and he could only think of the shot he would hear from his father's gun, during their walks in his youth.

In the afternoon, he rode a horse around the yard with his mother, trying to remember what it was like when the most important thing on his mind was to decide which social media platform to share photos of his horse on. More than once, he tried to broach the topic of his PhD and the genetic message, but the topic never escaped his lips.

He tried to forget all about the DNA sequence, but the message ate away at him, like an earworm. Staring at the fireplace on Saturday evening, mesmerised by the dancing flames, he pondered what the message meant. He pictured the flames dancing across buildings, across cities – flames of destruction wiping the Earth clean of the human disease.

That night he lay awake, trying to imagine ways the message could have been faked. Any DNA sequence could be generated and inserted into a tube of DNA, spiked into his sample so that he would sequence it. Milton couldn't think of any reason that someone would do that. But there was every possibility it was fake.

After another quiet breakfast on Sunday morning, he packed his bag and said, "Mum, Dad, I need to get back to the lab early tomorrow. I need to check those results again."

*   *   *

He returned to London, and early on Monday morning, he arrived at the Institute to inspect the genetic message again. It was a mistake. He knew it the moment he stepped into the lift. *When will you learn?* He asked himself. *When has life ever rewarded diligence?* The lift creaked as it stopped between the second and third floors.

Milton sat on the floor of the lift, growing ever more morose. The air could be thinning or filling with a noxious gas, and not just the ones he produced. At least he was alone. It would be worse if he was stuck in there with someone else driving him crazy with small talk. His watch strap was wearing a red mark into his wrist as he twisted it around and around. *What are they doing up there?* Every small noise bounced and echoed around the lift. He could hear his own panting breath, as if he was a hyperventilating madman.

He looked at his phone. No signal. He could only wait for help to arrive. *I need to check that sequence. It must be real.* With an hour gone, Milton started to wonder how long he might be stuck. With enough body fat in reserve, he could survive a few days if needed, but water might be a problem. *I don't want to die in here.* Drinking his own urine would only happen at a time of greatest need, he decided. He wondered whether security could see him on the CCTV, sprawled on the floor of the lift, desperate due to boredom more than anything else. *Come on, can't you see I'm here?*

Indeed, they did. Milton finally heard the voice of a security man outside the lift saying, "Okay, time to get out of there."

Milton breathed a heavy sigh. He was saved.

The doors of the lift were manually separated and the security man, like Samson between the columns of the temple of Dagon, held the door open. Milton stepped up the six inches from the lift to the third floor. As meek as a penitent nun, he thanked the guard, recognising the simplicity with which he'd been rescued. Fortunately, only two other senior postdoctoral lab members had been present to see him extricated from the lift. His student peers would be relentless in their banter.

The day had started badly, but maybe it would improve if he got a chance to investigate the source of the genetic message in the DNA. A few ideas had crossed his mind while he reclined on the floor of the lift for an hour. For example, he should check the parent's DNA again, plus the father's this time, to confirm whether the message was maternally derived. He also planned to ask Craig if he had anything to do with it.

He sat at his desk and opened the minimised window of the remote desktop to he shared server from which he had read to his supervisor on the previous Friday evening. The DNA sequence filled the screen from top to bottom. He scrolled to the segment of chromosome four, where he knew the message to be.

Milton screwed his face and squinted at the screen, then looked away and back at the screen again. He blinked a few times, as if his eyes needed cleaning. It didn't help. The message was gone. The strings of A, C, G and T were replaced with a long string of Ns.

With his blood pressure rising and sweat escaping from new and interesting places, he surveyed the office. Milton craved a suspect. Craig had been near Milton's desk when Milton had arrived but was now with Cynthia at the other end of the office, engrossed in their own screens. Milton dismissed them as potential villains – too obvious.

He typed in the genomic location again and pressed the enter key, hoping he'd simply made a mistake. Again, the screen scrolled to the segment with all the Ns. He checked the desktop folders in which he had saved the analysis from last week. Empty. The saved files from the last month, the last year. Empty. Empty. The only sequence that remained was the one loaded in the program. Sweat dribbled into his eyes, forcing him to blink it away. He closed the program and opened it again. Turn it off and on: the classic IT solution to all problems. The sequence didn't load up again, presenting only a blank screen. Milton realised with horror that the file stored in cache had been overwritten by a blank sequence. The only thing left to do was yell.

His porcine squeal echoed down the open plan office. He cursed all the cartoon characters he could, from Porky Pig to Batman, the pictures pinned to the board behind his screen. They had nothing to do with the lost data, of course, but it felt cathartic, nonetheless.

Craig and Cynthia, who had been happily ignoring him up until that point, could no longer do so. Craig stood up and regarded Milton with a sneer. "Pipe down. It's too early for that, Milton."

"What have you done with my sequences? You've tampered with them," Milton shouted, throwing books from the desk to the floor like a petulant three-year-old.

"Now hold on there, Ninja Turtle," said Craig.

"Don't call me that," Milton wailed. "My files are all gone. Someone's deleted all the work I've done over the last year."

Craig leaned over Milton's shoulder and scanned the screen.

"It must have been Jerome, then," Milton wailed. "He's had it in for me from the start."

"Impossible," Craig said.

"Unthinkable," Cynthia added, joining them. "You know, deep down, he really does care about everyone. You can't see that yet."

"And what about the cloud storage backup?" Craig said. He was always full of good calm advice. "The university backs everything up to the cloud."

"And everything is synced automatically, so don't worry," said Cynthia.

As though a ray of sunlight from God himself had lit Milton's face, his heart lightened. Of course, it would all be backed up in the cloud. He clicked the link to the cloud and the ray of sunlight blinked out again. His link gave nothing but an error message and he lost access. He typed his password into a new link, which only opened an empty folder in the cloud. There was no other way into his account.

"Bollocking bull carp!" he yelled again.

In life there are often challenging times when one should take stock of assets and liabilities and, with a rational mind, come to a decision and meet one's challenges. And having made a rational decision one should feel comfortable, for the rest of one's natural life, with a clear conscience that the right decision was made. Unfortunately for Milton, he did not see things that way at that moment. The decision he made set in motion wheels that would not stop turning no matter how desperately he may have wanted them to, later.

Milton walked into his supervisor's office and exploded.

Jerome listened to him intently at first but then, having lost his patience, he put a halt to Milton's rant. "Larry, stop. Enough. I understand you've lost files. These can be recovered. The sequence you showed me on Friday was a joke. Right now, I'm hoping that it wasn't you who started this. I'd like to think that you were brighter than that. I would be willing to forget about this and let you get back to work. I can turn a blind eye once. If you can forget about it, you still have six months of lab work to add to your thesis."

It dawned on Milton what Jerome was insinuating. That he, Milton, had faked it and should forget about it. But that would be impossible now. He couldn't forget about it. That would be like discovering you had won the lottery and decided not to cash in the winning ticket. It had kept him up to all hours over the weekend. He had dreamt about it. It had to be real. There was no other explanation. If he didn't act on this discovery, the world was doomed. It was also the first exciting result in his PhD in over three years. He had even spent time drafting a report on it over the weekend.

"No." Milton was shaking. His entire body was revolting against the assertion that the message was a hoax. The very fact that it had been deleted, that someone had gone to the trouble to hide the evidence, proved it had to be real. "Unless you can prove otherwise, I will continue to believe it. Why else would anyone delete it? I didn't make it up. Craig didn't plant this. He as much as admitted that, just now."

"You will do as I say, or you're out!" his supervisor exploded. "Do you remember what you said during your interview? If the time ever came that I thought you have proven yourself inadequate, you would leave of your own accord. That time may have come, but it is your choice."

Milton sat with his mouth agape, like a man witnessing his own execution. The blasted man remembered what he had said in the interview all those years ago. Milton was stunned that it had come to this. He slumped out of the office and sat on a couch on the stair landing. How could he forget this result? What possible work could he do now to get his PhD back on track? Everything would be dull grey in comparison.

He needed to think, but his nerves were still vibrating from the negative energy emanating from the office, like a strong electrical field making his hairs stand on end. He needed space. He walked down the stairs, not yet trusting the lift, and found himself walking along the street like a homing missile, not knowing where he wanted to go but getting where he needed to be.

Milton marched with a scowl across his face and his lips pinched tight. He jerked his head left and right, staring at the people passing by. He almost wanted to shove the slow walkers out of his way as he barged through, not caring if they had more important places to get to than him. He was, in theory, walking aimlessly, not thinking where he was going. Nevertheless, within a short distance he found himself in a familiar setting.

He walked up the stairs of a big white building with columns like a temple, into the foyer and to the first exhibit on the left. The British Museum, to Milton as much a temple as any church or cathedral, was where he did his contemplating. One of the best places to do so was from behind the Perspex cabinet that held the Rosetta Stone. On one side of this granodiorite block was writing in Greek, Egyptian and Demotic script, from which Champollion, among others, had deciphered the Egyptian hieroglyphics in the early 19th century. It was one of the few real treasures of the ancient world. Yet, ever since the invention of flash photography, a strange thing always happened around this particular treasure. Despite its magnificence and importance, a constant flowing river of tourists, never less than twenty, arrived, took flash photos of the stone, and moved on within seconds. These people never realised that the flash would reflect in the Perspex. They would never understand the beauty of looking at the stone itself. There were books and 3D virtual reality videos that you could buy about the stone, with high quality images of exquisite detail.

Unlike the tourists, Milton preferred the reverse side of the stone. That side featured no writing, but there were veins and discolourations in the granite, chips and chisel marks that told an even more interesting story than the written side. The script described the decree of the ancient king Ptolemy V, celebrating his coronation and describing his gifts to the farmers and priests. A more important story, Milton thought, was the one about the man who carved this granite stone from a quarry 2245 years ago. Milton decided that the man must have been left-handed, judging by the direction of the score marks on the back. Incredible conclusions could be made about the past by looking at the stone as it was in present. Archaeology was one of Milton's great loves, second only to genetics.

If the genetic story was true, and if the disaster was going to happen in the future, and someone from the future had reached out to him, shouldn't he at least try to help them? Might they be reading the score marks he had left, in their own present? What would those marks be? What could they interpret about him? Could they even have planned for him to be the one to receive the message?

After staring at the stone for a long time, Milton decided that he would follow through and do something about the message, and that those that sent it must have known he would.

He walked back along the street, one of the many pedestrianised streets in London. There were people walking in the bike lane, biking in the walking lane, and riding any number of devices in both. Milton avoided anything with wheels and plodded along slowly, occasionally shoved aside by people passing him. He found himself outside the stone building that held the office of the Westley Trust, the agency which funded his PhD and most of the work in Jerome's laboratory. In the lobby he asked the man behind the desk if he could speak to the junior grants administrator, a woman called Judy Spencer, the postgraduate advocate, who provided pastoral care to the students funded by the charity.

There were two items that he needed to discuss. Firstly, he wanted to talk about extending his PhD funding due to extenuating circumstances, *vis a vis* the data tampering and deletion of the majority of his work. That would take a bit of convincing, he was sure, but with three years of data having been deleted, he thought he would have a strong case.

Secondly, he started to suspect that his supervisor had himself performed the tampering, which amounted to scientific misconduct, and gross mistreatment of a student. These were serious accusations that must be handled diplomatically. How often had a student wanted to accuse their supervisor of some malfeasance, mistrust, harassment, or just plain meanness? And yet, in this bondage, a student had no choice but to accept the abuse, or else forfeit their chance of gaining a PhD. Milton knew he was not the first to have experienced this situation, but Judy could be trusted to act discreetly.

He was ushered into an empty office to sit behind a large desk, and was told to wait for Ms. Spencer to arrive. Milton sat patiently for at least five minutes before he started wondering what was taking her so long. He didn't care if she had other important work to do. His complaints ought to take precedence over any mundane tasks. He glanced at his watch to find that a whole two minutes more had passed. To occupy his racing mind, he looked about the office. There were no discernible features that might indicate its occupant. There were no degrees framed and on display, as if that was all that was needed to convince any visitor that you were important. The terminal on the desk was logged off, and Milton didn't dare risk trying to log in. The books on the single shelf contained the gamut of medicine from genetics, behavioural psychology, obstetrics and gynaecology, mental health disorders to dentistry. Milton considered scribbling a letter of complaint onto the blank pieces of paper he found in the desk drawer, but decided discretion was still warranted at this stage. He watched the minute hand of the wall clock make a three-quarter turn before someone arrived.

It was not Judy Spencer.

Professor Sir Angelo Williams, the director of the Westley Trust himself, entered the room. A man in a very smart suit followed him inside. They were both so serious, that Milton wondered if someone had died.

"Mr. Milton, I'm glad you chose to come in for an informal chat. It will make things much easier," the professor said. "Let me introduce Mr. Lawson, the head of our legal department. He will be joining us for this chat."

Milton sank into his chair, wary of the need for lawyers at an 'informal chat'. The lawyer nodded at Milton and sat beside him while the professor circled the desk like a ravenous reef shark and chose a seat on its far side. Much like other professors, he had laser-like vision that could see through bullshit and turn flesh to jelly. The lawyer rasped his pen along the edge of a sheet of paper like a butcher sharpening a knife on a whetstone.

"It has come to our attention that you have generated a DNA sequence with a message in it, which is absurd," the professor said. "Moreover, you have tried to pass this off as real, even going so far as to say this could inform a chapter in your thesis."

Milton stammered. "I'm, ahh…"

"If you cannot come up with a satisfactory explanation," the professor continued, "you will be charged with scientific misconduct and dismissed from the graduate programme. This is an extremely serious matter that can have implications for the reputation of the university and for the Westley Trust. You need only say that you made it up, forget about it, and the matter will be dismissed. But if you insist on your story, then..." The end of the sentence hung over the edge of a cliff.

"No, not me," Milton found the words to say. "It was Jerome what has done the misconduct." He had somehow forgotten simple grammar. "He deleted all my PhD work. I've got nothing left. Why would I have made this up? It's real! If I don't do anything about this, the future won't find my score marks and the Earth will explode. You must help me get the data back. The whole world depends on it."

"Mr. Milton, your attitude is disappointing. I have no choice but to invite you back for a formal public hearing. I had hoped we could settle this informally. You will receive a message later today telling you when the hearing will be held." The professor and the lawyer left as though they had somewhere more important they would rather be.

The room became a ghost town. Milton found no fun in poking around the desk drawers and found nothing of interest in the filing cabinet. He did find an amusing breast-shaped stress ball advertising a cancer charity, which he slipped into his pocket. It seemed a small reward for his sufferings. Before anyone asked, he hurried out of the office and down the stairs to the exit.

Chapter 9

I played chess with the little girl in the shared wedge. I hadn't seen a child in the ISS in many years. It was a nice change. Her hair was straight, like fine spaghetti, and her eyes were shining like emeralds. Like a fairy, she danced weightless and with ease. She was still wearing the same dress she'd arrived in, as we didn't have any new ISS dresses that small. She didn't mind that we didn't have a clean dress when I asked if she wanted it.

"It's my special flying dress, Mammy said," she said.

She was very attentive when I displayed the chess pieces and said what each did. I think she had already learnt chess, since she played fast and nearly had me in the third game. She giggled when my large fingers tipped my king when I was reaching ta play my pawn.

"I win, I win!" she said. "That means I win."

I was dismayed. I didn't mean it, and in space these things happened all the time especially with weak magnets.

Andrew always said that chess was a gentleman's game, and it was meant as a civilised pastime. I never resigned, even when checkmate was in sight. It was a gentleman that let the winner have their winning play. I tried telling the girl this.

"Please let me replace it," I said. I felt silly asking this little girl ta permit me ta keep playing. It was my chess set, after all.

Her mammy was watching and came ta my aid, "Dear, that was an accident. A kind and nice player might let him replace it."

The little girl wrinkled her face as she was thinking, then tipped her head as ideas wriggled in her mind. She set my king in its place and grinned at me.

I smiled at the lady, and she dry retched.

Lightning panic flashed in her eyes, like a lie had escaped. She placed her hands at her face. "Stay here," she said. "I think I need ta see the medic." She patted away the startled child, insisting she stay with me and left the wedge.

"She'll rest fine," I said ta the little girl, ta keep her calm. "I've seen space sickness many times when new crew arrive here. Dr. Chang will have her medicated and right as rain."

There are times when I say a phrase I've heard in a film, and it seems strange that I never realised what it meant. Right as rain? I'd never seen rain and didn't think it was right at all. Perhaps a farmer might say this and mean it. In any case, the girl knew what I meant, at least, and was happy ta keep playing the chess game.

After a time, the game stagnated as the girl started fearing her mammy wasn't well. She didn't make a play in ten mins, as if she was elsewhere, dreaming. I neighed like a mare, indicating that she might play the knight. She didn't take my hint. After a while she started wiping her eyes as tears filled them. I realised what she needed.

"Listen, let's visit Dr. Chang," I said, "We'll see that she's right as rain." I was still certain it was space sickness.

The little girl agreed, and we left the shared wedge. I held her hand as we danced a weightless spiral, traversing the cylinder passageway. I twisted her faster and she seemed ta like it. Like whirling dervishes, we arrived at the medical wedge. Her giggling was like a fragrance splashed in the air.

I twisted the hatch and levered it wide. We were greeted with a harsh, panicked scream in Dr. Chang's accent. "Tammy! Get her away. Seal the hatch!"

The scene I saw was a disaster area, like in all the war films I'd seen. There were three new passengers as well as the lady, all retching and gagging as if their insides were escaping. They were strapped in ta their stretchers and shaking like the devil was inside them. Dr. Chang was racing like a firefighter, treating their fevers as fast as he dared. He repeated his demand ta seal the hatch and I reacted fast, slamming it.

The last speech I heard as the hatch clanged firm was Dr. Chang's. I wasn't clear if it was directed at me, at his predicament, at his mistake.

"Damn it!" he yelled.

The little girl reacted.

"Mamma, Mamma," she screamed, and tried hard ta evade my grip. She twisted like a slippery eel, trying ta reach the hatch, yet I held her away. She relented and went slack in my arms. She started whimpering.

It was then that I started fearing it was Gessica's chemical that had made them ill. Was the chemical spreading in the Medical wedge? Did I trap it in there with them when I sealed the hatch? Was I already affected? My insides were twisting like my intestines were vacating. I started hyperventilating.

The girl sensed my panic and started replicating it. I tried hard ta grind my teeth and think. I didn't want ta spread fear.

The sweat in my skin tickled my face as it dripped. Deep in my mind I knew I was safe, even if I didn't have it clear in my head at that time. The answer was there when I recalled what Gessica said. Since I didn't have a Gename patent, I wasn't affected. The chemical reacted with the genetic particle in the Gename patents, and I didn't have it.

The little girl wasn't. I realised this fast and with great pain, like a needle in my eye, when I saw the change in her face. Her cheeks grew paler and sweat lathered her face. Her health faded within ten mins like she was preparing ta depart this life. I held her arms and legs and tilted her head sideways as she retched. She needed medical help. I engaged the speaker in the hatch ta speak with Chang again.

"Dr. Chang, please let me in. The girl is sick and needs help."

"Tammy, I can't," he replied. "I've sealed the hatch. It isn't safe in here."

"Dr. Chang! Please." I hammered at the panel and tried engaging the speaker again.

The speaker was silent.

I slapped the hatch till my hand ached. If Gessica was right, this girl hadn't a chance and was dying right there and then, yet Dr. Chang wasn't willing ta help her. I peered left and right trying ta see anything that might help. I didn't have any skills ta save her and there wasn't any crew in the cylinder that might help either. I was all she had, and I was helpless. I felt less than a man. A clever man might have saved her, with first aid – at least he'd try. It saddens me ta think that I gave in as easily as I did. What else might I have tried? I didn't have any answers.

The girl gagged and retched as her mammy had.

"Red alert, red alert," I heard the captain say in the ISS-wide speakers. "There is an emergency in the Medical wedge. All wedges are sealed till the emergency is rescinded."

I heard the clang as each hatch sealed and fastened. The little girl and I were sealed in the cylinder. The red alert alarm, which we hadn't heard in years, rang like a steady headache, drilling in my mind, digging deeper and seeking the rawest pain. The red lights that lit the passageway flashed in time with the alarm and made it seem like the ISS was aflame in hell.

The red lights palpitated like the veins in my temple. I realised the captain had made a vital mistake. The emergency wasn't in the Medical wedge. It was everywhere. It was right there with me.

The chemical death was fast and messy. The heavy gas filled the little girl's airways and thinned her air, as she spewed and gagged. Her dry retching released the chemical in the air, and I imagined I saw the devilish gas swirling. I held her hand and tried ta let her see that I was with her. Her eyes wide, she started inhaling in tiny gasps. With her last gasp, she stared at me, then departed. She died in a dignified way; she didn't have time ta cry and didn't have time ta live the years I think she deserved.

I held her till her skin chilled and then I let her drift away in the passageway, like a Viking pyre in a calm sea, sending her ta Valhalla. I wished her well in her travels – sweet child.

The captain realised his mistake when every wedge called in with new sick crewmates. He cancelled the red alert and released all the hatches. His last statement in the speakers was a sickening thing ta hear. He was defeated.

"My crew, my family. This mistake was mine; I accept that. We are all affected with this damned chemical and there isn't anything we can change. Feel free ta die in any way ya see fit."

It was the first time I'd heard him as desperate as that, like he had already given in ta despair.

The silence killed me, like I was a singer and my scream-ing fans had disappeared the instant I started ta sing. What else can define my feelings as that day ended? The last escapees vacated the Earth, came here, and killed my ISS with this damned chemical. I hadn't any direct family after my parents departed, yet these crew were my family, the captain my father and Frank the grandfather that always gave me treats. Gessica was the distant relative that I fancied.

Like a child watching his parents and sisters marched away in Hitler's Germany, I'll never release that pain.

It seemed very little time till the crew were all affected as the chemical spread via the air vents. Their frantic attempts ta hide themselves and evade it were ineffective. Like sprayed insects fleeing the nest, they spread it farther afield. Fifty crew and thirteen escapees scattered and died, each in their different ways. I realised then that the eight missing passengers had already died, and the rest had lied.

I tried ta ease their pain. I fetched medicine when asked. I held hands with any that feared death, like a priest giving them their last rites. Several panicked and attacked crewmates. I was larger than them and they were easily sedated when they tried attacking me. They resented the fact that I wasn't affected. I get that. I hated it as well. Can ya imagine? I was ashamed that I wasn't dying.

I watched the lads that wanted ta leave a message and I taped their final vids. My eyes misted as I registered in my mind the very few that might see these tapes replayed. I saw several crewmates space themselves, escaping the pain. Like wreckage drifting in the night, they slid away in the darkness. They didn't scream, they didn't flail, they drifted. When Frank did this, I sank ta my knees in the viewing deck, watching him till he was a small speck, like a distant star that dissipated in a final twinkle.

The ISS grew silent, like a graveyard. I rewatched the last vid messages, and I passed time in the ISS viewing deck, weightless, watching my tears dance in the air and glint in the green and red lights that lit the wall panels.

I wrapped myself in my arms and my chest started heaving like an asthmatic. I hadn't given it time and grief clenched me immediately. My eyes were pained, and my head ached as if I was gnashing my teeth. I rammed my naval with my fists again and again. I kicked my legs and smashed my knees and ripped the hairs in my arms. I sagged and whimpered. I asked myself: Why hadn't it taken me as well? I wished that I had a Gename patent and died with my friends. I wished that I wasn't a *Pan sapiens*, the last alive. I felt the need ta space myself like Frank did and leave the ISS empty. I didn't want ta live here like this and didn't think I deserved it.

Near the viewing deck there's a hatch. I sat in that hatch. I was ready ta seal it. I was ready ta hit the keys. I was ready ta end it all. My eyes were filmy. My heart was tearing apart. I stared at the keys, and repeatedly reached my fingers nearer, nearer. I didn't hit them. Then a new sense was alerted.

I placed my fingertips in the wall grips ta steady myself. A smell permeated the air in the vents and awakened me. As a maintenance man, a new smell is always a signal that a thing needed repairing.

It smelt like fennel. The entire ISS stank with rancid fennel. I decided it was death that I smelt. Did death even have a smell? If it did, I didn't think it was a veggie. I'd never seen death as viscerally as this and my senses may have wearied and started faking smells, imagining things like it needed a facade. The cadavers were in pain, twisted and inverted. I realised it was the chemical that made the smell.

It fell ta me, this grim task: sending their remains inta space. All spacers receive their rites in the same dignified way. I recalled my parents when they died; the captain delivered a nice speech and we said a prayer and vented the hatch. I sat at the viewing deck and watched them disappear in the darkness.

Each crewmate and the new passengers alike I carried ta the hatch and I repeated the rites. Many I hadn't made friends with, yet I had ta say nice things anyway. Marie tended the Garden wedge and made tasty veggies. I prayed and vented the hatch. Lenard was in Physics and he had a friendly face and was always pleasant with me. I prayed and vented the hatch. Andrew was in Physics as well and I played chess with him. He never let me win; I'd miss that challenge. I prayed and vented the hatch.

The little girl that had held my hand and died in my arms, I didn't even ask her name. I called her the last Earth child and prayed as I vented the hatch. Her remains drifted like she was a little bird in the sea, carried away in the tide till she was a little pinprick and then she disappeared.

Each drifted in the path the vented air sent them, in a spiral like a small-scale Milky Way with each representing an arm in the system. Depending which way the ISS spin sent them, a few made a flaming spear in the Earth sky and the rest drifted in space, many with the farthest reaches as their destiny. If the paths aligned, they might get a chance ta draw near the gas giants. If I aimed well, they might track the crafts we sent in earlier years ta the darkest reaches.

Dr. Chang was in his Medical wedge and had died at his desk, helping the passengers. I hesitated when I saw him dead. I wanted ta hit his face, as it was his insistence that made me say ta the captain that we release them. It was him that made it all happen. It was him that let the little girl die in my arms. As little regard as I had, I tried ta find a nice thing ta say. I was thinking what my mammy might have said ta me. She always had a nice thing ta say, even if she was mad. All I arrived at was: he was a medical man that cared. It was right try, even as I hated him. I didn't pray and waited till the ISS spin vented him sharply ta flame in the Earth's sky.

Captain Petrykin was nearly the last, and I said a speech that he deserved. He was always kind with me and was a great captain. He always listened. I said he was like a father ta me since my parents departed. I appreciated that. I said many things that lasted several spins in the ISS. The captain made me cry as I vented him ta the far reaches. He deserved a distant view, travelling past all the planets that he knew as if they were his children.

At last, there was Gessica. I had kept this pain till the end. My heart catches every time I recall the instant that I reached the hatch ta her research den. Like a man cremating his canine friend, an ancient man interring his wife, my heart was heavy. I didn't have the right ta feel as if I'd married her fifty years, yet I did. I twisted the hatch and heard a terrific scream.

"Wait! Tammy, leave it."

My ears didn't deceive me.

Gessica was alive.

Chapter 10

Milton had nowhere to go. He couldn't return to the lab and risk facing his colleagues. By now, they would all know what had happened in Jerome's office. The fire safety doors were no barrier to gossip, which spread like wildfire through the lab, and there was no way such a secret would be kept. His only remaining refuge was his one-bedroom shoebox apartment in student accommodation.

A small Perspex table and two chairs filled his kitchen. A few pizza boxes remained on the table. He used a worn-out second-hand futon as a couch, pointed at the only screen on his walls. He rarely used the screen as a television, as the power to run it was too expensive on his stipend. The fridge and a lightbulb to read by were the only essential electrical devices he could afford. Fortunately, his work screen was paid for by the lab. Resorting to non-electrical entertainment, he had his books and comics and a backgammon board. Above a small bookshelf was his only prized possession, a framed seventy-year-old Spider-Man comic book, number 181 from 1978, which he had inherited from his grandfather.

As was his habit upon entering his apartment, he opened the fridge. It was stocked with ready meals, grab food and a single bottle of champagne. The champagne was a keepsake from the party he had attended after his induction to the lab. The remaining unopened bottles at the end of the party had just been left there as the students cleaned up. Of course, the students took them home. Milton planned to open it after his graduation. It had been long forgotten at the back of the fridge. With his imminent expulsion on his mind, he noticed it, pulled it out of the fridge and inspected it.

So easy to give up, he thought. He turned the bottle around and looked at the label. The 2043 vintage had already aged a few years. *Admit that you were wrong.* He only had to drink the bottle, get drunk and forget his PhD. He held the bottle at arm's length, as though it was the skull of Yorick. "Only, I'm not wrong. Am I?" *Why am I talking to a champagne bottle?* He placed it back in the fridge, grabbed an apple and closed the door.

Wracked by indecision, Milton barely slept that night. On one hand, he had seen the evidence with his own eyes, but on the other, as time passed, it was harder and harder to remember every detail. For all scientists, experiments are like your own children: you conceive them, you grow them and nurture them until they blossom and provide the thrill of the seeing them achieve their aims. But then a doubt is raised and niggles at your mind. Did you forget to add that reagent? Did you mix this sample up with that one? And once that doubt is nailed in, the whole experiment is ruined, and you can't even trust your own results. That was what occupied Milton's mind as he tried to sleep. But each time he recounted the experimental procedures, he discounted every doubt he raised. He was certain there were no mistakes. He was certain no one could have tampered with his samples. As the dawn light crept through his bedroom curtains, he realised that in truth there was no indecision. There was no mistake. By the morning, he had reached a decision.

He needed to publish his story and get it out there before it was muddled by false accusations. He called his friend Roger Campion, a reporter who wrote science articles for the Metro newspaper.

"Meet me at the usual spot," Roger said. On the numerous occasions Roger had come to Milton to fish for university gossip or explanations of complex genetic research, they had always met in the same coffee shop that was equidistant between the research institute and the newspaper head office.

Rain pelted the window as Milton sat in the small coffee shop just outside Goodge Street station. He gripped his coffee as though it was lifebouy, ignoring the searing heat, burning an imprint of the famous logo into his hand. Above him was an oversized painting of coffee beans that he knew well. His eyes gravitated to the single green bean that was the artistic focal point of the painting. He wondered if the green bean represented him, bucking the trend, inexperienced, unaware of the pain encroaching on him as he becomes roasted like the rest of the brown beans. Would he toe the line as the head of the Westley Trust had instructed, or would he tell Roger his story? And would Roger publish it? Would the newspaper publish factual science that was stranger than fiction? He would let Roger decide if it was real or not.

Milton stared at the back of the head of a woman occupying the table in front of him. Two chopsticks were crossed over to hold up her smooth blonde hair that fanned out in a spiral. She sat alone, wearing a tan trench coat, reading something on a rolled-out screen. Her hand twirled the remnants of her coffee in the tall, empty glass. Chopsticks, as Milton decided to call her, tilted her head upwards at an angle that would have made reading her screen difficult. Perhaps she had seen something through the window or was pondering.

Milton was swirling the dregs of his own coffee when Roger burst through the door, at the precise time he had said he would. Some people have an ability to avoid attention no matter what they do, like a fog at the edge of peripheral vision that vanishes when you look directly at it. Others are quite the opposite, setting off firecrackers everywhere they go, glowing brightest in the night. Roger couldn't help but captivate the eyes of everyone who fell into his orbit. He wasn't attractive in the usual sense, but he enchanted men and women alike. As he walked toward Milton's table he smiled at Chopsticks, winked at the Italian barista behind the counter, and turned the heads of several tables.

"Hey little man, do you have a juicy story for me?" he asked as he sat down. He flicked his long black hair from side to side, like a whinnying horse, until it all fell neatly behind his ears.

"How much time do you have?" Milton asked.

"Depends on how juicy the story is. For front-page news, I have all day."

Over the next half an hour, Milton gave an account of the events of the past few days. Roger wrote occasional notes in his old-school notebook, which he preferred to use for security reasons. Milton watched Chopsticks as he spoke, and noticed that she stopped swirling her coffee cup but still peered out the window. He wondered what she might be thinking.

"Okay," said Roger, "let me summarise. You've been conducting your PhD in the lab of the world-famous Anton Jerome for the last three years. Last Friday you found a hidden message in a young girl's DNA. The message was from the future, purporting to be from a Gessica (with a G) Theresa Kelly who has a Gename patent. In a few years from now, ethical science will break down and it will be like the Wild West, with genetically modified humans who will populate the International Space Station, bases on the moon, Mars and, of course, the Earth. The government will implement a new law that means everyone has to have a patent in their genome, which sounds like a good idea. But some illegal rebels will then release a chemical that will make everyone who has a Gename patent go crazy, at which point the Earth will explode. Gessica is on the space station, watching this happen, and decided to send this message back through time into the girl's DNA so that you could find it and stop this disaster from happening."

"That's about it," said Milton. "I know it sounds crazy."

"But it doesn't end there, because you've taken this to your boss, who rejected it as a hoax, and then you went over his head to the funders of his research, who also rejected it, and are now bringing charges of scientific misconduct against you. Where did you go wrong?"

"I don't know," whimpered Milton. He looked down at the dregs in his coffee cup, like the worst of society floating to the bottom of the gene pool. This might be his fate: failure and mediocrity, to become the dregs of society. He showed Roger the message inviting him to a formal hearing next week.

The public hearing was due to take place in the university's BuzzWorld Pro, in a room decked out like a courtroom. The Westley Trust suit that he had met at their office, Mr. Lawson, would conduct the hearing. *What an appropriate name for a lawyer*, Milton thought. The panel would also consist of Milton's supervisor, Jerome, the new head of faculty, Professor

Thomas, a Westley Trust representative, Mr. Underwood, who Milton hadn't met, and the university HR representative, Mr. Ronny Allen, of whom Milton held such fond memories related to his PhD interview. He would have Judy from the Westley Trust postgraduate office to defend him in the hearing against this panel of heavyweights intended to intimidate.

"I'll tell you where you went wrong," continued Roger. "Time travel doesn't exist. Haven't you ever heard of the Fermi paradox? Where are all the time travellers?"

"That's aliens. Where are all the aliens? That is what Fermi was on about. But I can see why it works for time travellers too." Milton paused, searching for the right words to explain. "It seems they could only send a small particle. It might not work with anything human-sized. If you could send a one-gram message, what would you send? Electronic, no – imagine you sent a USB key back to 1980. They couldn't read it. DNA is the answer, but it's risky."

"After all the sequencing we've done, how come no one found this before?"

"Firstly, for so long we relied on mapping the fragmented sequences back to the genome. Anything that didn't match was thrown out. It was only with our new method of reading rapid DNA replication that sequencing the centromeres this thoroughly became possible. Secondly, how do you know they didn't, and were hushed up? What if the people in the future have been sending hundreds of desperate messages, and I'm the single recipient of this message that refuses to be hushed up? I must speak out."

"Is there any way to prove this isn't a hoax or a prank?"

"The response from the higher-ups wouldn't make sense if the message were a hoax. I was uncertain about it myself, until they deleted it. Why would they try to hush this up? If these

Gename patents are going to be implemented in a few years, I'd bet there are already secret projects developing them. We need to find evidence of that."

"They've accused you of scientific misconduct, of having made this up."

"I know. My PhD could be over because of this. Why would I do that to myself?" Milton hesitated, looking at his friend. "Why would I do that to myself?" he repeated. "So, are you going to post a news article on this? It could really help me out, a pre-emptive strike against this stupid misconduct charge."

"To post a news article I'll need hard evidence, corroboration. It might take weeks – or months, even."

"I need it this week, before the hearing."

"At the very least, I'd need to speak with Professor Jerome."

"No, you can't do that. He'll kick me out of my PhD for sure."

Roger considered this, looking out of the window in the direction of the Institute. Then he faced his friend again. "How about a gossip piece? Anonymous whistle-blower reveals scientific misconduct in high-profile lab."

"Yes, that might work – but you have to write it like it's true, not some conspiracy-theory."

"Listen, Larry, it does sound far-fetched to me." Roger put a hand on Milton's shoulder. "But I have one more question. Do you believe it?"

"Yes, I do."

"Then I'll try to fly the gossip piece past my editor. Meet me here again tomorrow, same time, and we can see what the buzz is and if there's any follow-up story."

With that, Roger stood up and walked out of the coffee shop, clicking his heels along the floorboards, like a stallion stomping its horseshoes. He waved to the barista as he stepped out into the rain.

Milton returned to the thought that he needed to find evidence of the Gename project. In order to be implemented soon, the project must have already started. The idea must have hatched in someone's brain. Someone must be developing the technology. He recalled Jerome's facial expression when Milton read the genetic message on the screen to him. Had the professor flinched when he mentioned the Gename patent? He recalled Jerome's backward glance at the computer screen as they had left. Was he involved? Milton's memory seemed to force him towards that conclusion.

A private company developing Gename patents would consult with eminent genetics experts. Jerome would be one of them, Milton was sure. Did Jerome receive money as a consultant? If he did, he would have to declare it in publications, to acknowledge a conflict of interest. He pulled out his screen and flicked through Jerome's papers, but found no conflicts declared. What about undeclared? On the university website there was a section of Jerome's CV that declared additional incomes. A few companies were listed: GlaxoSmithKline, Pfizer-EliZeneca, Sanofi, Westley Trust. All these companies had genetics departments and could be working on Gename patents. There were no obvious answers.

Milton yawned, despite the caffeine and the early hour of the day. He realised he was exhausted. It was time to go home and get some real sleep. The story was now with Roger, and he would wait for the next morning to see what the news would bring.

When he returned to his empty flat, he didn't even make it to the bedroom. He crashed on the futon couch with a news station playing on his screen.

Milton slept fitfully all afternoon and into the night, dreaming of impending disasters on a constant loop. Exploding chunks of rock flew through space on elliptical trajectories towards the Earth, nestling like well-placed Tetris pieces, one after another. Large, nebulous mushrooms formed from the dissipated grey clouds and absorbed into the ground. The bricks that lay all over the ground, all over the cities, threw themselves into the air and landed neatly to form buildings. Glass formed on all the windows, and in an instant reflected the bright sun. People leapt from the ground high into the air, like seeds bursting from flowers, to land on the windowsills of the 74th floor. People hurried around faster and faster, and just like that old Ginger Rogers quote, women were doing all this backwards and in high heels. Cars drove the streets in reverse gear in a mad ballet, seeming destined to crash on every corner, and yet they didn't. A man leapt out from in front of a reversing train and ran backwards along the platform, hurdling barriers and running onto the street. Milton followed this familiar young man backwards along the street, losing him in a crowd and picking him up again as the man paced backwards into a coffee shop, sat down, and in slow motion, banged his fist on the table. The fist stopped and raised from the table again as the man leapt to his feet, kissed a girl at the open door, then burst through the door and weaved into the crowd. The dream played like a film reel playing forwards and in rewind as Milton tossed and turned throughout the night.

The next morning, Milton sat at the same table in the coffee shop as he had sat yesterday, a fresh coffee in his hand and the Metro newspaper spread over the entire table. There were fewer people in the coffee shop than the previous day. By the door were two men in matching suits, drinking from espresso cups. The same Italian barista stood behind the counter, serving a couple who ordered a skinny flat zero dark latte and a crunchi-caramel frothed oat milk cappuccino. Chopsticks once again sat at the next table, also with a copy of the Metro spread out, instead of the screen folded into the side pocket of her backpack.

Milton flicked through the entire newspaper a second time. He found no mention of his story. It was clearly not the front-page news it seemed to be in his own mind. The front page instead covered the arrest of a Scottish comedian for driving under the influence and crashing his Mercedes into a children's park. It wasn't hidden in the political section, although to Milton it had become political. Milton's story wasn't sports news, yet he flicked through the back pages anyway. Milton even read the entirety of the readers' comments section.

There was no story.

Perhaps the senior editors had rejected it, or maybe Roger had grown cold on the idea with no hard evidence, and had decided not to publish it. His regular science column was filled with an old story Milton remembered from weeks ago. Did the Westley Trust pull rank and block the publication? Could they even do that? Then something occurred to him that worried him more than the missing story.

Roger was late.

Roger was *never* late. He pranced about and flirted with everything that moved, male or female, rock stars or rocking horses, but he was never late. Milton looked out of the window, up and down the street, but saw no sign of his friend approaching. He scanned the interior of the coffee shop: the barista and the seated couple sipping their skinny dark light carefree crunchi-cappuccinos. The two suits were still sitting by the door. Chopsticks pulled the straps of her backpack over her shoulder, slowly, discreetly. Had she eavesdropped on their conversation yesterday? It seemed possible. A sliver of doubt passed through Milton's brain and, in that instant, everyone became an enemy.

The girl in the trench coat became a Stasi commandant. The two CIA operatives with earpieces and dark glasses – despite the darkness outside – still sat at the door. *Who orders such stupid coffees, anyway?* The couple could be undercover spies for MI5, about to take him down; the man seemed to be speaking to his lapel. Milton decided it was better to leave than wait any longer for his friend.

He left his half-drunk coffee and the Metro on the table. He folded his screen into his pocket and drifted towards the door. The two suits stood in unison to block the doorway.

"Excuse me, Mr. Milton. I believe we should talk," said the one with short stubble over his entire head and face. He looked like a hairy cue ball.

Milton didn't know who these men were and wasn't inclined to find out. He tried to push past one of them to leave but was unable to move the mountain of a man.

"Please, Mr. Milton, we insist," said the other man, who was mouse-like, with a twitchy moustache. The two men remained unmoved and Milton was too small to compete with them. He resigned himself to doing as they said.

Before he sat down, Chopsticks walked towards the door and asked the two men to allow her to leave. Hairy cue ball moved out of her way and Chopsticks opened the door. Before she stepped over the threshold, she reached out, grabbed Milton's arm, then yanked him through the door, and pushed him down the street with the forceful command, "Run!"

Milton ran, and the girl ran ahead of him, her trench coat flying behind her.

Milton didn't look back to see if the men were pursuing them, but his imagination insisted that they were. Milton wasn't athletic; he ran crouched over like a hobbled rabbit, dashing through the crowd of people, stopping, then straightening up, looking this way and that, then crouching to run some more. Each time he stopped, he heard a repeated command from the girl to keep running, so he did. Eventually, he ran into a side alley and ducked into the sheltered eaves of a building, followed by the girl.

"Who were they?" he asked.

"Witless," the girl replied.

"Witless – what is that?"

"It's what we call them: Westley Trust Legal Enforcement Security Service, WTLESS. They're the hired hands of the Westley Trust, to enforce scientific security and investigate misconduct."

"I've never heard of them."

"They could hardly be a secret service if you knew about them. I recognised them because I've tangled with those two before. Have you ever been at a conference when a study is withdrawn? That's the work of WTLESS. When competitors are getting too close to Westley-funded research, WTLESS are there to sabotage the rival research. When papers at the third stage of review are looking like they'll be accepted for publication and are inexplicably rejected? Again, the work of WTLESS leaning on peer reviewers and journal editors. It's a dirty business."

"Why would they be after me?" Milton exclaimed. He knew exactly why, as soon as he said it, but was reluctant to divulge this to the woman. The misconduct investigation. "I'm just a PhD student, I work on genetic sequencing. I'm a bit of a gene ninja, actually." *Man, that was a stupid thing to say*, he admonished himself. It wouldn't impress her. "But I haven't published anything yet," he added, hoping to gloss over the 'ninja' comment.

"Well, they want you for something, Gene Ninja, and that makes you interesting to me. The enemy of my enemy is my friend." She handed him a card with a London address on it. "Come and visit me, friend."

Milton heard someone walking down the alley towards them. Before he could react, the woman's warm, moist lips against his as she curled herself and her trench coat around him, like an angel wrapping him with her wings. After a long and lingering kiss, the footsteps receded, as did the wings and the lips.

Milton reached out for more, but the opportunity was gone. His heart beat faster hoping for more.

"I've discovered a message written in a girl's DNA," he blurted. "It's rather disturbing, and the Westley Trust and the University of London are accusing me of making it up and have levelled a charge of scientific misconduct against me."

"I suggest you get that DNA sample and bring it when you visit me. Maybe I can help."

She turned, and Milton watched the chopsticks bouncing up and down as she ran down the alley and into the crowded street.

Chapter 11

I was thrilled ta hear her scream. My heart leaps every time I recall that. Like seeing a dead friend spring ta life again, a shiny new dawn after the darkest eclipse. Yet, it wasn't clear why she still lived, and the rest died. I asked her.

"I have capped the air vents in here," Gessica said. "The chemical can't get in, and I can't leave here. I sealed it when the ship landed. My air will stretch a day farther like this. Then, well…" She waited.

"Every crewmate and passenger has died." I said it as if I was telling her that her dinner was ready. I think at that time my energy and sadness were finished and I was an empty vessel. I was ecstatic ta hear her alive, even if it didn't seem that way.

She still didn't reply. I sat and waited. I said again I was happy she was alive.

"Tammy, I had a chance ta save them all and I didn't take it," she said.

I knew why she felt like this, as if the weight was all hers. It wasn't fair that she take it all. She tried preventing the ship's landing, she tried ta prevent the affected passengers' release, and we dismissed her advice. Her father even discredited her, like she was a child, and it was clear as day that it didn't sit well with her.

Me? I deserted her as well and neglected her warnings. I agreed with the captain. The weight was mine ta take and I wanted ta take it. I said the same. She denied my charity.

"Tammy, there isn't time ta fight. The chemical. Ya have ta clean the ISS. If even a small part remains dirty with the chemical, I'll die. Start here in the Genetics wedge. If that's cleaned, I'll have a larger air space. If ya can't clean it, I'm finished."

All the taint in my mind was cleared, like a scene change in a film. There was a maintenance task ta save her. Eager ta start, I fidgeted like a child with a new gadget, yet I needed ta sit and listen ta all her training. First, she said I needed ta make the same lids capping the air vents, placing all free dirty items in the cylinder passageway. Then I had ta wipe every panel with methyl spirits, which made the chemical inert. And at each stage I had ta screen with the gas meter ta see if it had decreased. At last, she released me and I ran.

I started the gas meter. It read twenty ppm. It had ta read less than detected if Gessica was ta remain alive and safe in there.

The inlet air vent lids were easy ta make with hard plastic sheets and D-tape. The away vents I left, as I wanted them ta take the affected air. I analysed the Genetics wedge, determined the air aggregate, and checked my maths. With a clean tank filling the air, it'd last a few days with her and I inhaling the air. I spent time finding and discarding all the free items. Dresses, sleeping sacks, research machines and materials I placed all in the passageway. They made a weightless trash wasteland, like plastic in the sea, that I had ta pass in each transit.

With the vents capped and the trash replaced, the gas meter read thirteen ppm. It was decreasing already. I started wiping all the panels in the first research den with methyl spirits. Having never treated panels with methyl, I'd never realised its strength. After a time, my head ached and was spinning like a whirligig. I dismissed these effects as necessary pain, a penance I had ta make, and kept cleaning. I needed ta finish in time, since Gessica's life was in my hands. With each swipe I felt like I was saving her. The catch was that, with all that swiping, I was tiring fast. In little time I was asleep.

I dreamed a paradise where I was a family man living in an estate in a grassy field. I sat in a deck chair drinking my tea, watching my wife, Gessica, tanning in the shining light, my angel. Finches were trilling in the garden, and I read a newspaper like it was a typical thing. We had three children. I recall their likeness: ginger hair like their ma, and tall like their pa, as they ran in the garden playing games. The smallest child threw a plane in the air, and as it hit the grass it clanged like a metal pan crashing.

A fracas in Gessica's den stirred me awake. She was desperate.

"Tammy! Tammy! I can't hear anything," she cried. "Are ya there?"

I staggered near her hatch, like my legs were missing a few ligaments.

"I fell asleep," I said. "I think I'm really tired."

I hadn't slept in three days since the ship landed. Even if I was tired, I felt silly admitting I'd anaesthetised myself.

I saw the time and realised I had slept three hrs and still had a cracking headache.

"Gee, Tammy, there isn't time ta sleep," Gessica said with a sigh. She seemed relieved, as was I, incidentally, since I might have died. I didn't tell her that.

She was right that I needed ta get cleaning again. I was energised. I learnt that ventilating the space with clean air was needed, which I did with a fresh air tank, as I wiped. I had finished half the panels in the first small den and my first methyl spirits canister was empty. The gas meter read ten ppm.

Methyl spirits are made with the gases when respired air is tied with H-three, an efficient way ta recycle the spent air in the ISS and make water and heat at the same time. Marie, the Garden wedge department head, had left a half vat ready in the methyl distiller, which was handy. I knew the distiller very well since I did its maintenance. Starting it again was easy and I left it distilling a new vat, while I carried the first half with me ta Genetics.

I renewed my attempts ta immerse all panels in the newly distilled spirits, in a well-ventilated manner. I waited till I had finished cleaning the three empty research dens and I checked the chemical levels again. The device displayed fifteen ppm.

I flapped my arms like a chicken and yelled at the gas meter. I checked the time again. I had cleaned five hrs and slept three, and the chemical was increasing. Gessica's air was a third finished and I hadn't made a dent.

I sped myself ta the Garden wedge and grasped the new vat. It was a little less than a tenth filled with fresh methyl spirits. A heavy weight filled my insides and I deflated. I was failing at everything. Why was it empty? I scratched my head as I didn't get it. The distiller was meant ta distil the respired air.

I cast my eyes past the walls and dens in the Garden wedge and the emptiness hit me like a smack in the teeth. My eyes filled again, and I watched my tears escape me, drifting like little lakes sailing in the air. There weren't any spent gases since there wasn't any crew left ta spend it.

Gessica had sealed her den. It was me, myself, and I that was spending all the air, and that was it. I didn't satisfy the distillers' needs. It was vital I find a fast way ta spend the air and make the gases I needed.

In the end I did find a way, and I didn't like it.

What is the last thing ya want in space? I can tell ya: it's fire. And what is the single thing that can spend the air as fast as I needed? Fire. If I had any way ta make a safe fire and vent it in the distiller, it was the answer.

I didn't dare. After all, as a maintenance man, everything I did was ta prevent fire. *Never light a fire in space.* Frank had said that many times. Yet needs eclipse wants. With Gessica in my mind, I risked it.

The venting was easy with a cylinder attachment; the spark was easy, and we had the shielding. It was finding an incendiary material, the kindling, that was hard. Methyl spirits can make flames, yet that defeated the intent, spending what we needed. What I was seeking was a lethargic fire. I spent a time thinking my way everywhere in the ISS; in Physics, Medical, and in Maintenance. I didn't see what I needed. In the end, the answer was right there in the Garden wedge. I spied the sacks filled with dehydrated sweet yams. They were a delicacy at dinner, and they'd make a nice lethargic flame. I felt sick wasting the yams, and the scent made my insides ache, like they did whenever we had a captain's feast. I saved a single yam and ate it as a reward, then waited till I saw it distilling new methyl spirits. I left the flame alight.

With the remaining methyl spirits, I cleaned a few dirty panels and in less than fifty mins was again in the Garden wedge. It had distilled a greater weight, which delighted me. I always liked when my ideas achieved their aim. With a few yams added in the fire I was again in Genetics wiping away. I glanced at the gas meter and my spirits sank again. I wasn't satisfied that it still read ten ppm.

Again, I flapped my arms like a chicken. I say this, even if it is silly. When I was a child I always reacted like this when things rankled me. In fact, this time it did a splendid thing. I sniffed my armpits. It made me realise that my red maintenance attire smelt like the same rancid fennel as the chemical. I was plastered in it and carried it everywhere. It wasn't that startling, since I had carried all the affected cadavers everywhere in the ISS.

I had ta strip and wash myself in the spirit and then re-enter the Genetics wedge naked. I capped my privates with my hand as I was a little ashamed entering naked, even if it was deserted. I wasn't the type ta parade myself like that, as if I was a marketeer displaying my wares. At least Gessica was trapped in her research den and didn't see me.

I analysed the wedge again and the gas meter read five ppm. Reading the meter naked made a difference. My chest swelled with faith that I might still save Gessica in time. I glanced at each panel that needed cleaning again and at last reached the hatch that held Gessica. With her in my mind, I started wiping every panel in each den, and then the entrance. Keeping my air ventilated, I cleaned like a machine. I even revelled in it after a time, and danced a little as I wiped each panel. I was nearly finished when I wiped the last panel near the entrance hatch, which had a small dark glass circle in it. I hadn't any idea it was there till I wiped it. It was a CCTV camera.

My cheeks warmed with a red flash. Hell, I was ashamed. I capped the camera with my hand, and I prayed Gessica hadn't seen me parading naked. I heard a giggle in her den and knew she had watched the entire time. My shame and chagrin allied, yet I permitted myself a cheeky grin as I raised my hand and smiled at the camera. At least I hadn't had a hard... well...

"Tammy, Tammy." She giggled again. "It was the right thing, and clever."

She said it ta lift my spirit. The endless giggling said it all and left me red in the cheeks. I lifted the gas meter in the camera's view and presented her with the reading *less than detected*. At least the cleaning was finished.

I checked the meter in all the dens and the entrance again, then arrived at Gessica's hatch. Her air was less than a tenth left. After all the death and pain since that ship landed, we had a win. I was eager ta see her alive in the flesh, despite her having seen all mine. I twisted the hatch and then held my hands in place.

Her eyes gleamed as if there was a light within. Her ginger hair fell free and framed her face like a swaying red sea. It was like seeing an angel set free. Yet she appeared tired and weak. Her eyes were weary. She hadn't eaten in days. Despite this, her smile was wide with white teeth.

She presented me with a fresh green ISS dress.

Chapter 12

Time is cyclic. Milton realised this in a momentary flash of drunken brilliance. Over three years ago, he had sat in the Jeremy Bentham pub in this precise seat, with a glass of this same brand of beer in his right hand, waiting for the phone call that would signal his acceptance to his PhD position. Ever since he had exploded in his supervisor's office when he first discovered his sequences had been deleted, he had felt the wheels of time inexorably turning. He was on this path now and there was no way of turning back.

The cycle was repeating only this time he was waiting for a phone call from a colleague who would let him into the lab late at night, not to start his PhD, but perhaps to end it for good. The sinking feeling in his stomach signalled that he was about to commit a crime against himself. The university would never let him back in to complete his PhD if they discovered what he was about to do.

Milton swirled the beer around the glass and disrupted all the bubbles, thousands of them chasing each other around the whirlpool and accumulating at the head of the beer. Like before, he considered himself a solitary bubble floating through life, and he had no doubts that he would follow the course set out for him. How could he fight against that current?

Milton cast his mind into the future. He looked towards the space station where he imagined Gessica sat, beyond consolation, staring at the desolate Earth. He wondered if London was one of the early targets for destruction. What must she be thinking, seeing that destruction? What was her personality like and what did she look like? Looking around the pub, he wondered if any of the men he saw might be her great-great-grandfather. Kelly was an Irish name, after all.

He spotted one of the young men behind the bar, cleaning glasses and placing them on the shelf. His name tag read *Evan Kelly*. It could be him.

The grandfather paradox crossed his mind; if he were to kill this young man, then the Kellys of the future would not exist, the message would not be sent, and Milton would not be wondering about whether to kill an innocent young Irishman just because his name was Kelly.

It wouldn't make sense though, Milton concluded. What motivation could he possibly have to kill the man? Gessica wasn't the enemy. It was a rubbish paradox anyway, when you considered that time is not linear but a complex spider web, a network with links backwards and forwards to all other points in the network. End products could all be reached from many different points. Besides, the time difference was one hundred years, a mere two thousandths of the time modern humans had been occupying the Earth, so they were very close together in the network. Yes, time was a spider web, he decided, and Spider-Man was its master.

He took a long sip of his beer and swallowed a large amount of froth.

It was so easy to believe that Gessica's story was true. It seemed inevitable that events would lead to the disintegration of ethical science. As far as Milton was concerned, it had already started, with his being dumped out of his PhD program. With egotistical professors like Jerome in charge of the research budgets, it was not hard to see this grim future realised. The future was in trouble, and that was where his mind was focused.

Milton's phone buzzed. Cynthia was ready to open the door to the loading dock. He tipped the last drops of Dutch courage into his mouth and headed towards the institute. He crept around the block, careful to avoid the one CCTV camera on the street that he knew about, and crept through the open door, as inconspicuously as a purple kangaroo.

"Make it quick – it's 11 p.m. now and security will come by in about one hour. I'll wait for you in the Bentham," Cynthia told him as she handed over her pass. The security guard on the graveyard shift was usually Aaron Weeks. He was an old man, with a goatee, a terrifying turn of speed and a slight air of madness.

"Thanks," replied Milton. "I owe you one."

He reviewed his plan. Sneak in, find the DNA samples, then sneak out. There were four tubes of the DNA samples that he knew about, two from the daughter and two from the mother, in his own freezer and in the stock samples in the backup freezer. It would take no longer than ten minutes.

Recalling his misadventure in the lift, and hoping to avoid CCTV cameras, he decided to take the stairs. He bounded up the first flight. By the third flight he had slowed down, holding the handrail, and dragging himself up the last couple of steps. He paused at the landing before passing into the corridor that led to the lab. After a few calming breaths, he walked down the corridor, automatic lights firing and darkening as he passed them. He arrived at the freezer room. He opened the door to his freezer space and found the entire drawer empty.

"What!" he cried out, forgetting the need for stealth. His voice echoed around the room and down the deserted corridor. Not only had they cleaned out his computer files, but all the DNA samples as well. Many of those samples had come from experiments that he had created, worked on, slaved over. All his boxes were gone, his samples were gone, like he had never existed. As if he was never going to get his PhD. As if he'd never started it.

It was outrageous! It was a mistake, it was misconduct! *The miserable miscreants!* he screamed in his head. He slammed the freezer door shut, unsatisfied at the slow automatic seal that prevented it from making a good, healthy bang. As the door sealed, so too did Milton's rage, and he allowed himself a moment to think.

The stock samples, then. They would never have thrown those out.

Milton crept along the hall again, more ninja-like, to another freezer room. He opened freezer number three, where the cohort samples were stored. He remembered where the DNA samples were held: rack five, box five. Easy. He found the box and opened it to find it full of tubes – apart from two empty slots. Of course, they were the two he sought. It was a dead end. Milton closed his eyes and ground his teeth together so hard they hurt.

He clutched the box and raised it high above his head. Chopsticks had asked him to bring the DNA samples, but they were no longer here. He couldn't bring her anything. There was no more hard evidence of the message in the DNA at all.

They had beaten him to it. If there had ever been any truth to the message, if there had ever been anything he could have done about it to save the planet, then without the evidence there was no story, and the planet was doomed.

As the temperature rose in his blood, he raised the box above his head. Steaming like a bull he boiled over and threw the box down to smash on the linoleum, scattering the tubes across the floor. He pulled from the freezer the entire rack of boxes representing the entire cohort of thousands of samples and smashed it on the floor for good measure.

Tubes scattered across the ground as though they were little humans fleeing a giant. The deafening crash produced by the metal rack reverberated throughout the silent building. Milton stomped over the DNA tubes, cracking them like little beetles under his feet.

Through the glass panel in the door, Milton spied movement in an adjacent lab. He snapped out of his Godzilla-like rampage. The security guard must have heard the noise. Milton closed the freezer, scraped a tube off the bottom of his shoe, and stood still, reasoning that the motion-sensor lights would eventually blink out. As he counted to ten, he glanced around at the mess he had left on the floor. At least he had remembered to close the freezer door; its alarm could wake a three-block radius.

He stood motionless in the middle of the room, counting to twenty now, and realised he would be too easily caught. As soon as the guard investigated the room, he would be done for. He cursed himself. He would have to move to a better hiding place. Spotting one, he squeezed his belly into the gap between two freezers. His movement reactivated the lights, resetting the minute timer.

Sweat dribbled down his back, also down his forehead, into his ears. The tickling sweat in his ears was the devil trying to make him twitch. He resisted with all his Christian valour and, with a sweet blessing, the lights went off, leaving a faint green tinge in the air from the freezer dials. Milton breathed as much of a sigh of relief as was permitted, with his lungs and belly squished between the freezers.

From his hiding place he could see through the glass door, and noticed the corridor lights turn on as the security guard walked towards the freezer room. Milton inhaled through his nose and wheezed out through his mouth. He heard the footsteps echoing down the corridor, ever so slowly, pausing, then starting again. A bright light shone into the room through the glass door, its beam passing from one freezer to the next. Milton closed his eyes, afraid that they would shine like the glow of cat's eyes in the dark. Fortunately, the torch light neither fell on him nor passed over the floor to reveal the incriminating evidence of his actions. Milton was safe enough where he was. He peeked out to see which security guard it was, expecting to see old Aaron Weeks.

It wasn't Weeks at all. It was the hairy cue ball. WTLESS!

If Milton's belly wasn't so jammed against freezer four, his legs would have crumpled underneath him. Their trembling was so bad that he felt like he was tap dancing. He bit his lip and tensed his muscles to stop them from setting off the motion sensors.

The torchlight passed as the man moved further down the corridor. Milton exhaled, but still didn't dare move until he guessed the man was on another floor of the building. *Just a moment longer*, he told himself. His legs kept tapping and his mind kept spinning, slowing down, like a centrifuge encountering friction.

He waited, and when his mind calmed, it floated down like an autumn leaf and settled on a single question. What was hairy cue ball doing here? The simple answer was that he was up to no good. Much like Milton was. The idea of following him to find out what he was up to was unthinkable. If Milton were a smart lad, he would get out of the building as fast as he could. Yet his mind started to think the unthinkable. What would Batman do? If he did follow the man, at least he wouldn't set off any new motion sensor lights – they were already on.

He sucked in his belly and climbed out from between the freezers, reactivating the motion detector to turn the lights on. This revealed the mess of tubes on the floor, a bit like dead cockroaches on the kitchen floor of a student shared house. The shame of his actions in destroying the cohort samples was clawing up inside him, but he tensed his diaphragm and shoved it back down. He couldn't afford weakness or guilt. He tiptoed to the double doors at the end of the corridor and ex-ited to the landing above the stairwell, just outside the boss's office. He caught a glimpse of the back of the man's head as he descended the stairs.

The boss's office door was still closing. Had the hairy cue ball been in there? Milton decided that this was the perfect chance for him to look for evidence of the Gename project. He psyched himself up for a potential run at the office door. Batman would investigate. It was the obvious thing to do.

Jerome's glass-walled office was dark, and the door was never locked. Jerome had disconnected the lights from the motion sensor long ago, due to his habit of staring trance-like at his screen. As a result, the lights did not flash on as Milton slunk through. The glow of the moon though the skylight pro-vided enough ambient light to see.

Jerome's office was a zen minimalist's dream. In the cen-tre of the room was a glass desk devoid of any clutter, a com-puter screen rolled across it. A single shelf on one wall held a teapot and three books. One – Milton could just make out the dust jacket – was *Molecular Cloning*, volume sixteen, written and edited by Jerome himself. The other two books were also written by Jerome and were easily ignored.

The office proved quite uninteresting. Milton reached down to log into the computer screen, but then recoiled. It didn't seem like such a smart idea, now that he thought about it, given the fingerprint activation code.

He looked around the moonlit office and was about to leave when he noticed a small vial on the seat behind the glass desk. It was a strange place to have left it, unless it had fallen out of Jerome's pocket. It was unlikely, though, to have landed upright. It was as if someone had left it there deliberately for Jerome to find in the morning. That could have been only one person: hairy cue ball.

Milton took a closer look at the vial. It was clear plastic with a screwed-on cap, about the size of his thumb, and inside it was a small metal capsule. On the side of the tube was written *GP*.

"Right, I'm having that," said Milton aloud.

He slipped it into his pocket in an unplanned theft. GP could be an abbreviation of Gename patent, he reasoned. It could also be a prescription from Jerome's GP for some unknown ailment. The fact was that Milton didn't know what it was, and if Jerome hadn't seen it yet, he could hardly miss it. With one last look around the office and no detectable evidence of the Gename patent project, he left.

He returned through the still lit corridor and down the back stairs. It was much easier going down than coming up. His heart was pounding again. He had never had so much exercise and panic at the same time. He was out into the cold evening, and the sweat that had drenched his shirt, unnoticed before now, became cold and uncomfortable. Exhilarated by the daring adventure, and despite leaving without the DNA he had been seeking, he walked taller as he crossed the street. Like an alley cat slinking in the shadows, he avoided brightly lit areas, trying hard to avoid any further encounter with the hairy cue ball if he happened to have hung around. He hurried through the back door of the Bentham pub to find Cynthia waiting for him. As though they were in a spy movie, he palmed her swipe card as he brushed past her, and slipped it into her hand, whispering, "Sorry if I caused you any trouble."

"What trouble?" she called after him as he strode out into the crisp night.

Chapter 13

My legs and arms were strange in green attire. I had never seen the Genetics green with large, hairy arms like mine in it. I wriggled my arms and stretched my legs and held myself a little taller. I thanked her as the warmth in my cheeks diminished.

When I was dressed, Gessica drew near and wrapped me with her small arms. She held my chest with her last strength, her head fell in and rested.

"Save me," she said.

It was as if the princess had asked the shining knight ta clasp her in his arms and carry her away. I had already saved her.

Her fingers caressed my sides, feeling my shape like artist preparing ta draw me. At first, she sighed and sniffled and afterwards she started shaking like as if she had an epileptic fit. All the criticisms, all the pain and the weight seemed ta reach her in that instant, like death calling when the time is right. She maintained her steady shaking as my arms encircled her. I held her as if she was a cracked egg. I didn't mind at all staying as we did, while time remained still.

When time started again, I saw that she'd fallen asleep, and I attached her sleeping sack ta the wall grips and let her rest.

I had time ta rest myself, and my mind set itself ta thinking what else needed cleaning. The ISS at that end had the Garden, Kitchen, and Medical wedges. Ta save Gessica, I needed ta clean that entire end ta give her the space and safe air she needed. The cylinder passageway was still filled with all the parts I had left and that needed cleaning as well.

Cleaning aside, there were five vital tasks ta deal with ta stay alive in the ISS. The Captain's wedge held the ISS steering, rarely needed, yet pretty vital when it was. In the Maintenance wedge, the air and water were managed, which was my task anyway. Since we had many dried packets already, and Gessica had the genetic enhancement that meant she ate every three days, the Garden wedge wasn't vital. The Shared Activity wedge was needed every day, else we'd wither in space. My activity was already high, with the cleaning, yet Gessica needed it. In the Physics wedge was the star tracking, which was the least vital task at that stage. It didn't matter where the stars were at when we were fighting ta stay alive.

I watched Gessica sleep. My heart still sank with the emptiness in the ISS. I missed Frank. Yet there she was, a light that filled my darkness. Her small frame drifted like she was dangling attached ta strings. I didn't think she was the type that was yanked with strings in any way. She was her master, that was clear.

Her eyes seemed alive, twitching left and right in a captivating dream. I tried thinking what dreams she might have had, and I saw endless nightmares. The Earth stayed silent, the ISS crew were decimated, and a chemical gas spread death wherever it lay. I didn't need a dream ta see that. Her ginger hair was dishevelled and framed her in weightless, rippling waves, like the seaside at dawn. In time, she slept deeper, with a gentle rise and fall in her chest. I decided it was right ta clean this end, saving Gessica first. The remaining tasks had ta wait.

My cleaning system needed a plan, as I'd have ta clean myself every time I entered Genetics. I may as well leave the clean dress in genetics; naked was the cleanest way. I started with the entrance that held the different wedge hatches, cleaned it till the chemical wasn't detected. I fetched a treadmill, cleaned it and set it in the Genetics wedge. That way Gessica had it when she awakened, and I didn't need ta clean the Shared Activity wedge. I left her sleeping and visited the Garden wedge.

As I twisted the entrance hatch, a dark grey gas swirled in the air and escaped the wedge.

Never light a fire in space. I heard Frank's statement in his plain matter-a-fact way. Why didn't I listen?

I knew that leaving the fire alight wasn't safe. I scanned the damage and assessed the site. The fire with the yams tipped in the small gee, and flaming yams drifted near the methyl spirits canister. The canister that held the new methyl spirits was aflame, and tendrils licked the panels and the distiller near it. The increase in flaming gases kept feeding the distiller in an ever-increasing cycle: as it made increased methyl spirits, the flames grew higher. It was igniting all the methyl spirits I needed. The wedge was a flaming mess. And I was naked.

The fresh air I'd added when I entered made the fire dance and flash higher, yet it gave me an idea. There was a fire mat hidden near the entrance hatch. I leapt at the mat and cast it at the flaming canister. My casting was dire, and it served ta flip the canister, sending the flaming methyl spirits in small vesicles that spread everywhere in the wedge in a weightless flaming dance, like fairies permeating their light and winking as they spent their spirit. The wedge was an even larger flaming mess. And I was still naked.

Ya never saw a naked firefighter. Ever think why?

I retreated; it was the sanest act. As always, the simplest idea is the right idea, even if I wasn't clever in thinking it fast.

Less air was less fire. That was it.

With the electric panel in the hatch, I had the capacity ta vent all the air in the Garden wedge. I did it and it cleared the fire in a flash. All I needed then was time ta fill the air in the wedge again. When I was ready, I released the hatch again and inspected the damage.

I calmed when I saw the damage was very light. The flames were dissipated, and all my new methyl spirits canisters were empty. The largest damage was that all the living plants were vented ta space. I had a large wedge filled with desiccated pre-flamed yams.

The smell that greeted me was a treat. I ate a few crispy grilled yams ta ease my sadness.

With my newly dried yams and increased enlightenment, I relit the fire and held the distiller in place with D-tape. I started cleaning wedges, starting with the Garden wedge. I cleaned the ISS with a steady plan: sleep, eat, clean, rest and repeat. I cleaned all the free-drifting items in the passageway and placed them in the wedge when they were clean. I discarded anything I didn't clean.

I was satisfied in this task, as it was the largest maintenance task I had set myself in ages, and the rhythm gave me the sense that I was always making headway.

When I spent time with Gessica, while eating and resting, I asked her many things. Why hadn't we cleaned the passengers with methyl spirits when they arrived? Why hadn't we tried it with the crew?

"They were affected, Tammy," she said. "It didn't matter if we cleaned them. If any spewed the chemical again, we were finished. We can't clean insides with methyl spirits."

Her answer satisfied me at the time, yet I still think we might have tried. I wished that we had tried.

I wanted ta ask her why the Illegals had the chemical anyway. If she had made it, why did they have it? Did they steal it? When did she learn that they had it? Yet I was afraid ta ask. If we ever neared that matter, she shied away and didn't answer. I think she was afraid that I mightn't like what I heard.

Instead, I asked her why we hadn't heard anything sent via the Marsstead and Hisakatani settlements.

"The transmitting links are all in the Captain's wedge," she replied. "The messages decreased steadily in the last weeks since we halted the traffic. They haven't any interest in the ISS. Their messages will arrive in the Captain's wedge. It isn't clean yet," she said. "Check the messages when ya get there."

I cleaned that wedge right after, and I saw there weren't any messages; neither settlement had sent anything. I sent a few messages asking if they were still there and advising Marstead and Hisakatani that we still lived – despite the devastating events. I didn't receive any answers.

This led me ta think that they were devastated with the chemical as well. If they weren't and they were evading – neglecting their replies – it meant we were deserted. Gessica didn't have an answer when I asked her what she inferred.

After many days cleaning and many chats with Gessica, she remained rigid and terse when I asked things regarding her family, the crew and the chemical deaths. It was the reverse when we addressed the stars and planets and the ISS mechanics; she was animated.

"What if we pass time in Physics, staring at the stars?" I asked her.

She delighted at this idea, and we spent a pleasant time staring at the gas giants, watching their satellites. We tried inspecting the Mars settlements and saw evidence that they were still active. That was heartening ta see, at least.

After a time, I asked Gessica if she was alright. It wasn't healthy ta keep everything inside. If she needed ta talk, I was there. She declined.

Yet, I still needed ta talk. There were many things in my mind that weren't settled. Grief hit me at different times in the day. When I cleaned the Maintenance wedge and I saw the things Frank left. When I saw the images I kept in my den: my parents. I kissed the image as always. If they were alive, they'd have stayed safe as well. Like me, they didn't have Gename patents.

While I rested, I watched several vids, repeating them again and again. My parents had made many training vids, and there was a vid that detailed air cleaner maintenance. In it, my dad made a mistake and said that we needed ta vent all the air in the ISS. He meant all the air in the cleanser. My ma, with the camera, giggled and made the camera wiggle. My dad cracked and grinned a wide smile till he settled himself and repeated the line right. The year after they died, I watched that vid nearly every day. And while I was cleaning, it kept me inspired ta keep at it.

I cleaned the ISS in thirteen days. The last cleaning day I spent traversing the entire ISS with the gas meter, seeking the chemical. My fingers were raw, my skin dry like parchment. I emptied many clean air tanks, finished all my dried yams, and the remaining methyl spirits. Replenishing the spare air tanks was vital, and the yams needed time ta germinate again. The methyl spirits I didn't want ta see ever again.

It was a giant task finished. I snickered at my childish idea, signing the maintenance register: *Thames Impressive Henry - Cleaned ISS with methyl spirits while naked,* tick. Afterwards, my arms, legs and fingers all ached, I staggered inta my sleeping sack as intense malaise gripped me. I slept dreamless and deep.

A day later, Gessica did a magic thing, like that princess with her shining knight that saved her.

I met her in the Kitchen wedge while she was eating her cereals and drinking tea. When she saw me, she wriggled free escaping her seat and came nearer. She leaned in, came nearer still, and held my face with her tiny fingers. Her lips tickled mine and I shivered. It wasn't an air kiss, cheek-ta-cheek, it was the real thing. My heart leapt a mile. I wrapped her in my arms and kissed her again. Her lips yanking at mine as if trying ta decide which she preferred. She was tasty, like a fresh mint tea.

She stared at me with intense interest, like pride, and she said, "Impressive."

"Well, it's my name," I said with a wink.

She giggled. I can't say if I did kiss well, having never really kissed a girl like that. I imagined myself as characters in the films I watched, which was practice in a way. I have a little pride and can say at least it impressed her. It was the first hint that she liked me.

"Tammy, I can see why ya did it." Her fingers traced my arm in my green dress. "Why ya spent the last weeks cleaning, naked and stressed till ya fingers were raw, keeping the ISS alive, keeping me alive." She kissed my fingers. "I see why ya did it."

She shivered as she held me tight. "Tammy, I see shades drifting past me. They're sitting there eating. They scare me. Can ya see them?"

She indicated where she saw them. I admitted that I had seen them in the past, while cleaning. I never knew them. They were always strangers and since they didn't harm me, I left them in peace. While I didn't see the spectres that Gessica saw, I said that I did, ta make her feel alright. I said they weren't scary at all since they didn't affect anything. They were figments.

She didn't accept that, and steered clear when a spectre came near her.

An alarm rang. Gessica leapt like a startled feline, yet she didn't appreciate what the alarm meant. I knew. It was the alert that rang when a satellite was nearing the ISS.

"I wished I'd learnt ta fly the ISS," I said.

Gessica's eyes widened and she raced away heading ta the Captain's wedge, screaming a phrase I daren't repeat.

Chapter 14

Milton hesitated at the warehouse's corrugated iron door, half-way along the alleyway in the middle of Hackney. Hackney had always been the London borough that oscillated the most, from poor to posh and back again like a sinusoidal wave. Currently, it was trending downward, and the trendy crowd had left.

Milton checked the address again and, having confirmed that it was correct, tried the door. It was unlatched. He slid the door along its metal rail, causing it to screech, vibrating his teeth like a dentist drill. Milton grimaced at having announced his arrival to the residents of Hackney and nearby boroughs. He snuck inside, peeking back into the street to check that nobody was watching.

Looking into the expansive interior was like wearing dark sunglasses. Low-grade bulbs hung from a high ceiling. Milton felt certain that any demons present were tracking his movements through that darkness. Yet there were pockets of bright illumination in sealed-off regions around the periphery. In the centre of the warehouse was a kitchen area containing several dusty couches. A bearded man was coaxing coffee from a percolator jug as if he were squeezing the last drops out of a sponge. He looked up as Milton stepped into the light.

"I'm looking for a woman," Milton stated.

"Aren't we all, laddie," the man replied. He was large and reminded Milton of a Viking, without the helmet.

"Short, blonde, has chopsticks in her hair," Milton said. "She said I could find her here."

"That would be Noah. Trust her to lead a stray dog in here. Third lab on the right." The Viking put a hand on Milton's shoulder, pointed him in the right direction, then gave him a slap on the bum.

Milton jumped and hurried in the direction of the sealed-off lab. He tapped on the soft plastic before realising that it made no noise, then parted the leaves to enter the lab. Unlike the warehouse, the lab was pristine, wrapped in plastic, and it contained benches, fridges and freezers and what looked like a cobbled-together DNA sequencing machine, the old bench-top MiSeq. Sitting at the computer screen was the woman, as intriguing as she had been when Milton first saw her. She wore a bright white lab coat and her hair was pinned up and covered with a disposable paper hat.

"I'm sorry, we never got a chance to introduce ourselves," Milton began. "I'm Larry Milton."

She spun around in her chair and smiled at him. "True, it wasn't exactly a first date," she said. "They call me Noah. Welcome to my lab. I'm guessing you haven't heard of the biohackers movement."

Milton shook his head.

"Rarely do we show our heads above the parapet," Noah added. "Nothing too illegal, mind you, but the 'real scientists' get nervous around us."

Noah explained. The cooperative was known as Bio-Hackspace, a community of like-minded, do-it-yourself biologists and garage scientists. This was the London chapter.

"Why?" Milton couldn't understand why people would do 'pretend' science like that.

"Some join the cooperative for nostalgic reasons, trying to emulate the scientists of the eighteenth or nineteenth centuries. Some are just curious, others disaffected by society or shunned by the regular academic scientific community. There are even some who were expelled from universities for scientific misconduct or other misdemeanours."

Milton wondered which description might apply to her.

"We have twelve labs here. No one uses their real name in here, FYI. The others doing genetics are Wellzy and Jackknife. We sometimes work together on projects. People like Grube and Ralph do the computer stuff. Don't even ask what magic they can perform. Most people share their labs, but I keep mine clean and tend not to invite unnecessary DNA contaminants in here." Noah looked Milton up and down, as though wondering if she would have to do another deep clean. "For me, it started as a hobby, sequencing all the organisms that had missed out on the gold rush of sequencing in the first decades of this century. You'd be surprised how many organisms were sequenced just because they tasted good or looked cute, from truffles, to fugu, to pandas, lobsters and minke whales. I sequence the untasty, the ugly and forgotten animals, two by two."

"How do you fund it? Sequencing is expensive," Milton said, remembering countless arguments with his supervisor about whether his experiments were cost-effective.

"We rely on donations, crowd-sourcing and other less reputable benefactors. I have an anonymous donor who keeps sending me money. Don't ask, don't tell." She shrugged. "You'd be surprised, though. It's cheaper than you think." She indicated the machines dotted around the lab.

"This bench-top sequencing machine, from the now defunct Illumina company, is forty years old. I spotted it at an auction at the Sanger Institute – it had pretty much fallen off the back of a truck, so to speak – and we set it up in here. It's my trusty old war horse."

The main sequencing machine was a large box with tubes poking in and wires and other peripherals attached around it. It was hooked up to the large computer screen at which Noah was sitting. The shelves around the lab were filled with familiar reagents and kits. Centrifuges, freezers and a small DNA amplification machine covered the remaining bench space. He could see it was well provisioned.

"How do you pay for the electricity? This kit must burn through a lot of kilowatts." Milton could count on one hand the electrical appliances in his own home that he could afford to keep powered.

"Don't ask. That's one of the fringe benefits of working with Grube. He tapped into the grid for us."

"You steal it?"

"Trade is a better word."

Milton didn't dare ask what it was that Grube traded.

Noah continued, "Once people stopped buying these sequencing machines, the company tried to survive by selling reagents, but most of the reagents can be reverse-engineered and made on the cheap. It cost me about two hundred pounds to sequence a male and female marmot last week. The hard part was catching the little blighters. Damn things nearly bit my fingers off."

Milton didn't know what a marmot was, but was too shy to ask. Noah stopped talking for a moment and looked at him. Then she said, "Do you mind telling me now why they were following you?"

Milton sat on the only other seat and recounted his story. He started calmly, but as he continued, his voice grew weaker, whining like a child whose toys have been taken away.

He told her about the first discovery of the message in the girl's DNA, being maliciously trapped in the lift, to the bust up with his supervisor, his missing reporter friend, Roger, and then being chased down the street by WTLESS, which Noah too had participated in. He ended with his clandestine visit to the lab, which he had found devoid of any evidence of his PhD work. Milton had been excised from the lab like an unsightly growth.

"Do you have any of the DNA samples?" Noah asked him.

"No, they took everything," Milton wailed. His despair from the previous evening washed over him once more. "My whole PhD is gone."

"You didn't back any of it up? Surely you can't be that stupid."

Milton sat with his chest heaving, trying to take calm breaths. He *was* that stupid.

"Think, Larry – there must be a backup somewhere they haven't looked."

His data folders on the university servers had been wiped clean, his laboratory samples were gone, and his desktop links to the cloud data were scrambled. Shaking his head, he felt his brain was becoming equally scrambled.

"Hold on. Your cloud links are scrambled," said Noah, "but the data is still floating in the cloud. You just can't access them."

Noah had an answer. In this case it was Ralph. Ralph, she explained, was a bearded *silico* hacker working in an adjacent lab. He knew all the old-school computer hacker tricks. Milton recognised the description of the man he had met in the kitchen.

Noah tapped her phone to link up with Ralph and explained the problem. Within minutes, a weblink popped up on her screen that circumvented the security to access Milton's account.

Ignoring the ease with which his secure folders had been opened, Milton pointed out the correct folders, and soon found the right file. He opened the genome sequence and zoomed into the centromere of chromosome four, right where he had found the message before. The message was gone, replaced by a long string of Ns. It must have synced with his desktop version. Milton's stomach couldn't escape that sinking feeling.

Syncing, bloody syncing, he thought.

For a moment, Milton doubted himself. Had the message ever been there? What mental health disorder could lead to delusions of such detail? No – he couldn't entertain the possibility that it had been faked. It had to be real. It was real. Jerome saw it and had argued with him about forgetting it. Jerome had authorised its deletion. Why would he have done that if he knew it to be fake?

"It looks like it was never there," Noah said doubtfully. "Why would the sequence be a string of Ns, though? If you were going to hide it, you'd paste in a real sequence."

Milton hadn't thought of that before. It was evidence of tampering.

"But if it was ever there and now it isn't," Noah continued, "then at least we know that WTLESS are thorough. You know, I hate those guys, and if you can get one up on them, then I'm going to help you as far as I can."

"Why do you hate them so much?" Milton asked.

"Ask me another time," she said, deflecting the question expertly. "We'll just have to find the girl and sequence her again. That's the only evidence I'd believe. They can't wipe her clean."

Milton wondered whether that was true.

"How are we going to find her? She was anonymised," Milton said.

"You *are* rattled, aren't you? I thought you said you were a gene ninja."

God, Milton thought, *I wish I hadn't said that.*

"Prove it," Noah said. "What can we tell about this girl from her genome sequence?"

She loaded the DNA sequence into a computer program and initiated analyses faster than Milton could follow, so he started off with the simple things that first occurred to him.

"We need to start with the variation in the genome," he said. "With principal components analysis of population-based studies, we can estimate the main components of variation in her genome and estimate her geographical origins based on her unique variation."

Within seconds, the plot showed on the screen. It was a world-wide map with a heatmap showing the probabilities of the individual's origin. There was a striking increase in the intensity over Cardiff. "This graph is pointing to somewhere in Wales," Noah said.

"Genetic association with various traits can give you a probability of hair colour, eye colour, height and build," said Milton.

Again, Noah clicked buttons on the keyboard. "From this, we have an 83 percent chance of her being blond, blue-eyed, tall and slender."

"We could estimate her chance of developing cancer," he added.

"Milton, you said she was a young girl. That won't help us find her."

That was all Milton had.

"What about other traits?" Noah urged. "From the epigenetic signature for gene regulation that you conveniently linked to the genetic data, we can tell whether she smokes, what she likes to eat, whether she drinks alcohol, but, more importantly for us, we can also tell her age to within three years. This says that at the time of DNA extraction she was between six and nine. When was the sample taken?"

"I'm not sure," Milton responded, scratching his head. "The study recruited over three years in 2043 to 2045. That was four years ago, so if she was between six and nine then, she would be between ten and fifteen now."

"Now comes the interesting part," said Noah. She was animated, enjoying the detective work. "In 2007, some scientists from Canada showed you could calculate the surnames of 80 percent of anonymous donors to genetic studies based on the variation inherent in the genes. This collapsed any pretence of anonymity in genetic research studies, but there has been an unwritten ethos in the scientific community that we would refuse to do such research. Well, when I say we, I mean they." She twirled her hair around a finger.

"Biohackers are not so constrained, and I've developed these methods further. Trained on all the data the was publicly available from ancestry sites where names and genetics are linked. We use the genetic variation in the chromosomes to estimate the probability of any given surname assuming normal conventions of naming after the father; and, using the mitochondrial DNA, which is passed through the mother's line, you can estimate the maternal surname."

"Wow," Milton said. "How accurate is that?" Although he was studying for a PhD, Milton hadn't really bothered with the literature unless it was published in the last ten years. Anything beyond that was considered old and archaic. Clearly, he had been wrong to dismiss old ideas.

"Accurate enough. Using this, we can see we have a high probability of the father's name being Evans – not surprising, given the Welsh genetico-geo-positioning – but for the mother's name we get three candidates: Walsh at 73 percent probability, Bishop at 84 percent and Kennedy at 86 percent. Those probabilities are too statistically close to one another to say for sure."

"So, we're looking for a teenage girl called Evans," Milton summarised. "Blue eyes, blond hair and tall. How tall is tall for a teenage girl?"

Noah raised an eyebrow and put her hand on her head, indicating that she expected the girl to be about her height.

"If they follow normal naming conventions, yes, she'd be an Evans," she added. "Remember, like all statistics, this is based on big assumptions."

Milton acknowledged this, even though he had always blindly accepted statistics without bothering to test the assumptions they were based on. It was typical of most PhD students.

"Not all assumptions are safe, though. It's our family tradition that the women in my family keep their maiden name, usually because the men in our family are deadbeats that either leave or deserve to be left. We might have to do more digging to be sure." Noah opened a couple of browsers and typed in web addresses refering to onions that appeared unusual to Milton.

"The next step is to look at marriage records from, let's say, 2030 to 2040, again assuming normal marriage conventions. These marriage records are all online, but it will take a while to collate it all."

While Noah worked, Milton looked at newspaper website on one of the desk screens. It reminded him again that he still hadn't heard from Roger. Was it worth letting him know he and Noah had made progress? He tapped a screen to access Buzzworld and popped into some of Roger's private habitats. His virtual mansion, where he held parties that Milton rarely joined, was empty, with not a soul floating around. Milton ghosted into the AI newsroom that Roger used to meet with sources, but it too was deserted. A ping from Noah's computer rattled him out of the virtual world and it took a moment to refocus his eyes on her screen.

She had narrowed the search down using some filters.

"Here we have eight different men in Wales called Evans, who've married any of those three maternal surnames. Birth records from each of these pairs shows that three of them have had children and only one of them is a girl, born in 2038. Alice Marie Evans, born 5th August 2038 to parents Gerard and Margaret. She's 14 now, probably still living at home."

Milton's mouth opened as he stared at the final analysis, featuring just one name and with extensive details, all taken from the genetic sequence.

"Let's pay her a visit," Noah said.

Milton was veering between embarrassment about how little he knew and being impressed at the speed at which Noah had performed this analysis. For the first time he admitted to himself that he was looking at her, really looking.

When he first noticed her, she was an unknown woman drinking a coffee with an unusual hairstyle. The second impression had been of a commandant in a long trench coat directing him away from the gas chamber as she rescued him from WTLESS. Looking at her now, his third impression was that she was young and beautiful. The chopsticks crisscrossed at the back of her head clasping a spiral of hair like a galaxy. Looking at her profile, he saw her long eyelashes against the backdrop of the computer screen. He turned away when he realised she was looking at him with raised eyebrows.

"Impressive…" he stammered, now aware of his blushing cheeks. "Analysis," he added.

He was dealing with, he realised, a grand master gene ninja. Her skills far exceeded his own.

"How did you get all of these records?" he asked.

"Biohackers talk to *silico* hackers. I have friends in dark places. What can I say – a girl must keep her secrets," Noah said with a twinkle in her eye.

"How did you get so good at genetic analysis? You're a genius, Noah," said Milton.

"For someone trying to get his PhD, you sure don't know much. Reading is what makes you smart, not degrees. You should have learnt that by now. Listen, I don't know whether your story is true or not. I have my doubts, but it would be spectacular if it were. I'd like to find out. Besides, if WTLESS are out to stop you, then I can't help myself. Come on; let's go to Wales. Where was that address?"

Chapter 15

The magnified image hit me like a steam train. It wasn't a satellite at all – it was a stiff cadaver, a dead crewmate that I had vented. It had vented in an elliptical circle and was headed right here, a missile with revenge in its heart.

All I was thinking when it appeared was *Heaven help me if it's Frank*. I tried magnifying the image. It was shaking as if agitated. I mapped its flight and estimated its arrival time. My fingers grew white gripping the panel when I saw it was hitting in twelve mins.

Gessica was already at the panels, scanning reference chapters that detailed flying the ISS. I watched as her fingers danced, wiggling levers and swiping at panels as she familiarised herself with the system. I tried ta help, and she waved me away like a pesky insect.

The challenge in shifting the ISS wasn't in getting the small drivers firing – that was easy. It was in navigating past all the remaining satellites, as well as the litter and wreckage. Imagine a man screaming as he traverses an eight-lane highway filled with speeding vehicles. It was like that. That was why we had several trained crewmates and the captain all taking shifts.

Gessica picked it apart in five mins. Her intellect enhancements made all the difference. If I held my heart it'd swell with pride. She really was first-class. The drivers kicked in and my legs grew heavy. I saw the height relative ta Earth changing in the altimeter. My heart leapt at the idea we might miss it. It was seven mins till impact, and we were shifting at a few metres per min.

The ISS was never meant ta weave like a high-speed racer. With rapid mathematical skills, Gessica estimated the new paths the cadaver and the ISS were taking, and their lines still met.

"Tammy, help me. Lift that lever, change that driver, flip it left."

I leapt and yanked at levers and hit keys as directed. I ran in circles, wayward and distracted, trying ta hit the right keys.

"Gah!" she yelled. "Tammy!" Her face wrinkled and she wrenched me away. She flipped the levers the way she meant me ta hit them.

I stepped away and let her finish. Despite my hindrance, we increased the gap where the lines met. Yet they still met.

"It's likely it will hit, yet it isn't certain. It's maths after all," Gessica said, spitting at all the mathematicians in the past.

There weren't any drivers left ta add. I clenched the handgrips and spent the last three mins praying.

When I magnified the image again, I saw it wasn't Frank. I can't say why it mattered. I didn't want ta think I might die at his hand. Frank was gentle. I accepted that it was my venting this man, that had sent him in this elliptical circle. I hadn't even imagined that it might happen. My eyes welled with tears. My end was nearing and wasn't ready.

I prayed like I had never prayed since my mammy died. "Have mercy, have mercy," I repeated.

The sweat dripped in my eyes, and I wiped it away with my green sleeve. I said ta Gessica that even if it did hit, I was impressed with the speed she learnt the levers and drivers. She gave a wry smile.

The mathematics was right. We were late and he was early.

He hit as if it were a giant icicle ripping a gash in the ship's side. The entire ISS rattled as the dead man met with the large wings generating electricity. He had vented in a freak alignment, higher than the ISS and then flying in an elliptical arc, fired directly at the ISS with great speed. I was heaved inta the wall with the energy it imparted as the ISS twisted in a spin, catching the speed that the dead man carried.

Several alarms rang at the same time. The first indicated that the electricity grid had taken a hit and needed repair. Many panels went dark as the grid minimised its activity. There were alarms that said the new spin had messed the ISS alignment with satellite links. All the messages, links with the space settlements, and the planets went dark.

We had the drivers ta reset the alignment, yet with the weaker electricity we didn't dare fire them ta right the spin.

I searched all the satellite tracking fields. They were spitting images, the ISS's spin killing the image stream. I feared I might find new dead crewmates that I had vented. The scanners didn't differentiate these and satellites. I saw a few that might intercept.

"Even if they aren't hitting, they're an immediate danger," I said ta Gessica.

She clenched her teeth and stared at the panels, thinking. She replied simply, "We fly high, then, higher than she's ever seen."

I liked the plan. Ta make that happen, we needed the electricity grid repaired, and that meant a maintenance task, and an EVA in space. When I realised that, my heart skipped, and I wavered, snatching a hand grip ta steady myself.

I tried ta hide my eyes, as I didn't want Gessica ta see my fear. I spied the EVA hatch in the Captain's wedge, ready as always.

My EVA training was still fresh. Since space had many repair tasks that needed EVA, I had ta learn. I recalled my first training day like it was stamped in my mind. Frank had dressed me; we had revised all the dials in my arm panel and tested the air. The vent had cycled, and I drifted away. I'd kept drifting, flailing my arms, and Frank had leapt after me.

"Always leash in." He chided me with a *tsk*.

As calm as he was then, I was terrified. I had disregarded my training in the very first instant. And had nearly died.

With his arm linked with mine, I had finished the EVA training tasks, like I had training wheels strapped ta me the entire time. After my tests, Frank said that if ever there was a maintenance task that needed finishing, and I was the last man alive, he'd let me at it. In the meantime, he'd take all the space tasks.

Well, here I was, the last man alive.

With Gessica watching me, I feigned a calm face. With her help, I dressed and screwed in the helmet. I knew I was the man with the training and Gessica wasn't. It was my task. With the dark helmet glass shielding me, she didn't see my eyes. I was certain they were giving it all away, like a frightened deer telegraphing its fear as the circling tiger stalks it.

What kinda man was I if I didn't save her? I knew she heard my panting. Even with a fresh air tank, my hyperventilating was making it empty fast. I heard her talking in my helmet speakers.

"Calm, Tammy. This is like any repair. I'll keep talking and keep watching the camera. I'll tell ya what's needed. Inhale calmly. Wait, wait."

She held me and prevented my entering the hatch. She inspected the panels in my chest and arms and held my hand tight. I kept that image with her hand in mine and saved it in my mind like it was the last sight I'd have.

"The dead men ain't waiting," I said. They flew fast and I had little time. She dismissed my haste.

"Calmly, Tammy, always calmly," she said.

As was the standard practice in space, I kept talking, telling Gessica everything that happened. The first thing I said was that the air in the helmet seemed dry and smelt dirty.

"Want ta change it, Tammy?" she asked.

I replied that we didn't have time. I hit the panel that cycled the air in the hatch ta vent myself. It wasn't like the rapid vent I had fired the dead crewmates and passengers with. It was a five-min cycle. I had time ta check my air, my arm panels, and repeat the readings ta Gessica. I had time ta let the dread in and fester. The air seemed alright in the readings despite the smell. I linked my leash with the inside grips, ready ta vent and let the hatch swing wide. As I departed the ISS, the lights inside diminished and left me in darkness.

The ISS was in the Earth's shade at that time and the darkness in space was stifling, as if dark glasses had hampered my view. The stars didn't shine, as if they were hiding.

The darkness was enhanced, with my eyelids firmly clenched.

Chapter 16

The small town of Narberth appeared to be an idyllic little village in the heart of Pembrokeshire in Wales. Its single high road was populated with antique shops, local restaurants and three pubs. Despite the economic boom in Wales over the preceding decade, Narberth retained its village feel, with ancient oak trees surrounding the community car park and expansive fields encompassing the cluster of remaining houses. It was obvious there was significant wealth in the area, as the village was as pristine as a postcard, with hedges trimmed inch perfect as if they were as solid as the stonework of the house. The streets were clean, and the shopfronts were all freshly painted. The clean village made Milton feel uneasy, being so used to the dirty, graffiti-covered streets of London. He wiped his hands on his jacket in case he needed to touch something.

After checking into their bed and breakfast, he and Noah walked out to the edge of the village in the direction of the Evans' house. Milton walked close to Noah, almost near enough to hold hands, but he didn't dare.

Like most of the town, the street they found themselves on was picket fence perfect, with small cottages set back from the road. At the head of a short driveway, they found the house they were looking for. Milton knocked several times but there was no answer.

"Maybe they're not home?" Noah suggested. "Let's try the neighbours."

They had moved five houses along the street before they found someone at home. An elderly man opened the door, holding back a large Rhodesian Ridgeback who was eager to greet the visitors.

"Back, Dante. He's ever so eager to meet people," he said, addressing his visitors.

Noah prodded Milton forward to speak.

"Hello, my name is Larry Milton. We're looking for a family a few doors down. Evans. Do you know them?"

"Lots of Evans, around here. Margaret is number fifty-two, and Jennifer and Michael are bit further down, seventy-three, and I think there's another one on the corner."

"Margaret. She's the one." Milton said clicking his fingers. "Do you know if she has a daughter, about fourteen years old?"

"Yes, I think so. I don't know them too well."

"Have you seen them lately? We need to speak with her. It's urgent."

"No, sorry, I haven't. I've been away for a few weeks. Listen, I'd better take this boy for a walk. He's very eager now that I've opened the door."

"Well, thanks for helping."

"Alright, no worries. Come on, Dante." He leashed the dog and closed the door behind him.

They tried a few more doors, asking the same questions, and found the occupants of most households either unhelpful, unoccupied, or decidedly rude.

It was late in the afternoon when Milton and Noah approached the main road again. Milton's pace slowed. Ahead of them, a crowd of about two dozen people walked along the street.

"I've got a bad feeling about this," Noah muttered, vocalising the same sentiment that Milton felt.

It looked as though the crowd was trudging along the main road in a slow procession. They were dressed in sombre colours, like a river of dark molasses. They were following a black hearse.

Milton and Noah joined this river of people and followed them to the quaint Catholic Church of the Immaculate Conception, located at the end of Church Road, as if the church had simply known where it should be.

The churchyard appeared weary, with withered granite stones askew in the ground, like old man's bad teeth. The smell of fresh earth came from a hole in the ground, a cavity that needed filling. The procession surrounded the hole to watch it be filled.

Milton cast his eyes about the crowd, hoping to see a tall, blonde fourteen-year-old girl.

"I don't see her," he whispered to Noah. A handful of children were amongst the mourners, but all were too young. "With my luck, I bet she's the one in the coffin."

"I don't think so," replied Noah. "The coffin looks too big, too heavy. Let's wait and see."

Milton agreed. The box appeared to be of similar proportions to the priest who stood behind it.

The priest intoned the standard Catholic funeral rites, ashes to ashes and dust to dust. "May her soul and the souls of all the faithful departed, through the mercy of God, rest in peace."

The priest had said "her". Milton convinced himself that it must be his girl. He wanted to interrupt and ask someone who it was, but Noah kept a strong hold on his arm.

"Almighty and ever-living God, in you we place our trust and hope, in you the dead whose bodies were temples of the spirit find everlasting peace. As we take leave of our sister, give our hearts peace in the firm hope that Margaret Marie Evans née Walsh will live in the mansion you have prepared for her in Heaven. We ask this through Christ our Lord. Amen."

"The mother," Noah hissed.

Milton nodded. It wasn't the girl. That was a relief, but the mother also had the message written in her DNA and had been his backup plan.

"We need to find out how she died," Milton whispered. "I don't believe in coincidences."

The small service concluded with dirt being tossed on the casket by each of the mourners. After the line of people finished their duty, the priest gestured to Milton and Noah, the only remaining mourners yet to take their moment with the deceased. Milton stepped forward and scooped up a fistful of soil, paused, and thought of everything he knew about this woman, a numbered test tube in a box, used for his sequencing experiment. That test tube had become a person in a box ready to be buried.

He tossed the sod of dirt and said goodbye to her. The dirt was wet and stuck to his hands, and it landed with a thud on the casket. He brushed his hands, trying to remove the stain it had left, but before too long he had to move on.

At the end of the service, the crowd dispersed, and Milton approached the priest.

"You're not from around here. How did you know Margaret?" the priest asked him. He was a tall man in dark robes, and his ever-cheerful Welsh accent made it difficult for Milton to follow.

"In a way, I knew so much about her. Do you mind me asking how she died?" Milton replied.

"It was rather sudden, last Sunday evening. The doctor diagnosed a heart attack."

"And her family, are they here?"

"Her husband is," he said, pointing to the grave next to Margaret's. "But their daughter hasn't been seen since Sunday service. She wasn't here today. We're quite worried about her – but if I know Alice, I'm sure she's safe."

"Why would she miss her mother's funeral?"

"I hear they were having a bit of trouble. She's at that age."

"I'd like to speak with her. If you see her, can you send her to the Plas farmhouse across the road? That's where I'm staying. My name is Larry Milton."

"Yes, I will, Mr. Milton. Bless you for coming today. I'm sure Margaret would have appreciated it."

Yes, she would, Milton thought. If Milton could save the world, then her death would not have been in vain. *She must have been killed.* It was the single explanation he could entertain.

Noah spoke to several women gathered around an elderly lady in a wheelchair, while Milton stood by the fresh grave, wondering what to do next.

They returned to their bed and breakfast and sat in the common room, each with a warm cup of tea. Milton recounted what he had learnt from the priest.

"Well, that *is* interesting," said Noah. "I spoke with several of the ladies. One, Margaret's neighbour, Mrs. Winthrop, seemed to suggest the family hadn't been having as much trouble as the priest suggested. Both Alice and her mother were at home on Sunday afternoon when two men visited for afternoon tea. Mrs. Winthrop was invited over but declined. It turns out those men were the ones who reported Margaret's death and accompanied her in the ambulance to the hospital."

"Let me guess," said Milton, "one had a mousy twitch and a moustache, and the other looked like a hairy cue ball."

"She didn't describe them, but I agree… it does seem suspicious." Noah whistled. "This must be big, then, if WTLESS are willing to kill for it. The little girl is missing. Either kidnapped by WTLESS, or still hiding from them."

"She could be anywhere by now. That was five days ago. It's a catastrophe!" Milton slammed his fist into the sofa cushion. His tidy plan was unravelling leaving no loose threads to pluck at.

"Logic, logic, logic," he admonished himself. With enough information, he could work out what he needed to do. All he needed was a source of their DNA. "How much DNA do you need to sequence on your MiSeq?"

"Not much. Two hundred nanograms is enough for a whole genome read. What are you thinking?"

"Two hundred nanograms is about the amount you'd get from a few hair follicles. We could sneak into their house and steal a toothbrush, a hairbrush, or sweep for DNA in clothes. There must be loads of DNA in there."

"Yeah, I've got all the tools for that – but there are two problems I can see. You'd want to make sure the DNA is all from the same person, otherwise the sequencing gets messy. What if they share the same hairbrush? The other problem is if they've cleaned the house. If WTLESS cleaned it, it will be clean. Trust me."

"Sure, but that is the best plan I can come up with," Milton said with his eyes downcast.

"No good – we need another plan. I have a feeling if we wait here long enough, the girl will show up." Noah closed her eyes and took a deep breath, exhaling with a sigh.

Milton leaned back into the couch and stared into the fire burning in the hearth. The flames licked at the fresh log of yew tree that Noah had placed onto the embers. The smell of burning wood filled the room with a relaxing aroma. The white, fleshy wood soon browned and blackened as the yellow flame spread its tendrils across the hard outer bark of the log. A small shard of wood lit and was soon reduced to ash as it was consumed. Sparks exploded from a moist part of the log and filled the chimney with little fireflies that danced up into the night air. Milton stared long and hard at the mesmerising flames as the log transformed into ash.

Noah moved to place another log on the fire, but Milton stopped her.

"Wait," he said. "Ash. Humans reduce to ash when they're cremated. Why didn't they cremate her? If they were so worried about her DNA, if WTLESS could arrange to kill her and then forensically clean her house, it would have been a simple matter to arrange for cremation. You can't extract DNA from ash."

Milton leapt to his feet. "Dammit!" He dropped his teacup on the table and stomped outside. Milton ran back to the fresh graveyard and stood over it, panting. Eventually, Noah caught up to him and handed Milton his coat.

"You don't think…" Milton looked at Noah, then back at the grave. "Could we dig her up?"

"What? Larry, we can't do that."

"We can get some of her DNA for retesting."

"It's illegal. It's disrespectful to the dead. It's not right. We have to find the girl."

"The mother's DNA is sitting down there in that hole. Six feet away. We don't need the girl if we can get the DNA from the mother. She can't have decomposed that much. Post-mortem DNA is degraded, but I'm sure you can use restorative methods to at least read it on the sequencing machine."

"That's true – but Larry, it's wrong."

"I need to verify the results for my PhD."

"Would you forget about your PhD for a second? A woman has died. This is more important than your stupid PhD. I'm not going to dig her up." Noah stepped between Milton and the grave, like a barrier holding back the tide.

"You don't have to. I'll do it." Milton looked towards a shed. A large-handled shovel was leaning against it.

"Do what?" a voice called from the darkness, behind him.

He turned to see a young girl carrying a large bouquet of flowers. She was tall, with blond hair, and probably blue eyes too, if only he could see them in the dark.

Chapter 17

There were many things in space I didn't like. The first was the emptiness. My feet always kicked like a diver swimming in the sea. It was the first thing that Frank criticised in my training. *Ya kick like a wet and wriggling child*, he said.

While I hadn't meant it, my kicks had drifted me away a few meters. I waved my arms trying ta find the leash.

"Calmly, Tammy," Gessica said. "Take the leash with the left hand. It's there. Gee, Tammy, ya might have said ya didn't EVA well."

"At least I had the training," I panted.

With Gessica directing, I gripped the leash in my left hand and reversed my drift and reached the handgrips. I linked my spare leash with the grips and released the first. It was like scaling a cliff, always attached. With my feet linked with the ISS steel shell I calmed and remained still. I drifted via the main ISS cylinder till I reached the area that was hit.

"Right, Tammy, keep that head camera there. I can enhance the image and see the damage. Let me analyse it."

I held still, inhaling, trying ta stay calm, tasting the dirty air in my helmet. The spin, imparted when the dead man hit, was very distracting. In all my training, the Earth had stayed in the same place relative ta the ISS. It was a steadfast friend. With the new spin, the Earth was circling the ISS like a giant hammer as an athlete prepared ta heave it. My palms grew cramped as I held the leash with all my strength. I changed hands several times while Gessica analysed the damage. The Earth was spinning three times per min, and I imagined the athlete letting it free ta fly away in the darkness.

The day dawned as the ISS flew in the light, and I saw the damage myself. I saw the cadaver. It had a face, and a name. Andrew, my physics friend. Chess games played in my mind, pawns and kings. He was tangled in the electric panel wings and the free, dangling wires that were meant ta keep the wings in place. The panels were delivering thirty percent less electricity ta the ISS, and with the crack in the grid the entire thing was incapacitated.

"Alright, Tammy. I see three things we need," Gessica said. "First, we have ta release the dead man and send him Earthwards."

"It's Andrew," I sighed.

"It's a cadaver, Tammy. Keep at it. The panels that are cracked we'll leave, as we haven't any replacements. Then we have ta rewire the grid ta pass these cracked panels. And last, the electric transfer in that panel has fried, and we have ta replace it. Easy."

Easy, she said. As the man in space with a fish-tank helmet, a metal air tank spitting dirty air and a synthetic skin preventing his desiccated death, I disagreed and let her hear it. I needn't repeat what I said.

Her menacing silence said it all. I heard Frank's training advice ringing in my ears. *When ya feel like screaming, leave it. We can hear it all.*

I tried repeating Gessica's mantra: "Calmly, calmly, calmly." Yet it didn't reach my mind, as all I heard was her saying it, sarcastically.

I tried finding my way. I started thinking that this was my Wednesday chess game with Andrew, sitting there staring at the pieces. There was never any anger in chess. Pawn takes white knight and check. Left leg lifts and places again near right leg. Castle takes pawn. Right leg repeats. I smiled as I realised that this chess image was my haven, and I repeated this new mantra. I evened my air intake, and snapped serenity in place as I latched the first leash ta the new grips and drifted nearer the stiff cadaver.

Andrew hit the panel hard and was wedged in tight. The panel edge had hacked him in half, having snapped. It was as sharp as a scalpel. Screaming in space – check. Spewing in space – check. I tried hard ta keep it in. It was a relief that he was already dead when he hit, as it was a pretty grim sight. Gessica was still silent. I regretted my earlier screaming, and it might have helped me if I had heard her calming remarks.

I inspected the area and saw that the scalpel-like edges were a threat, like a minefield I needed ta evade. Any prick and I was dead. It made my hands shake. I tried yanking his feet yet there wasn't any leverage as I was weightless. Several times, I tried heaving him this way and that, and I whimpered as I failed.

Again, I heard Gessica's advice, whispering in my ear, after a few mins. It had seemed an age. Despite my receding rage, I was glad ta hear her again.

"Disengage the entire panel, Tammy, it seems the way. There are five screws in each edge, near the end. If ya take that five-metre panel at the end, that will get it."

With clear thinking, it was a simple task. It was nice ta have a friend in my ear again. The screwdriver was strapped in my kit, and with a few mins at each screw the panel was released. I disengaged the wires and the transfer, and the panel sailed free like a small yacht in the sea.

I drew Andrew nearer as I levered the panel away, and I stared at his dead eyes. His desiccated skin was like a wrinkled centenarian, leathery and thin. I panicked as I recalled the chemical that had killed him. Was it still there? Was it attached ta my fingers after handling him? I made a mental reminder ta leave this EVA in the hatch in case it was.

I waited till the Earth was at the highest in its hammer-like spin, then gave the panel a mighty heave and I watched it drift away. In time it'd catch the Earth's gravity in an ever-diminishing circle and find a fiery grave. I held my leash, watched him disappear, and wished him well. Hindsight is always right. If I knew what was ta happen, I'd have sent them all Earthwards in the first place.

Gessica directed me ta the stash that held the electrical replacement wires and transfers, and with an efficient leashed transfer it was a twenty-min drift ta reach the hatch. All the wires and things I needed were right where she had said. While I was rigging my gear, I started singing a part in *La traviata* – it was special ta me since it was the aria my mamma always sang when she was drinking. With that little time in space, and in the darkness in the Earth's shade again, I was serene and eliminated the scared feelings I had earlier. It was nice while it lasted. My aria was halted at an alarm in my ear.

"Tammy, it's the same alarm! We have an intercept in twenty mins – a stiff cadaver flying fast. We need the electricity ta fire the drivers. We need speed!"

I glared astern at the wing I needed ta repair. It was fifty meters away. It'd take me ten mins ta get there. I screamed at Gessica.

"I can't make it in time!"

"Tammy, ya have ta let the leash free. Ya have ta leap!" she pleaded. "Ya can reach it fast. We need at least a ten-min fire ta miss it. We need speed, Tammy."

The image seared in my mind, flashed like lightning in my eyes: my parents flailing in space. My legs stiffened. White knight takes king, and checkmate. Even my haven resigned.

In all my training, I had never let the leash free, even if I was meant ta learn it. The Earth seemed ta spin even faster, like the hammer was preparing ta heave. My eyes twisted in their cavities, trailing the Earth as it circled. My fingers ached gripping the leash, as if my metacarpals rattled inside the synthetic skin. Sweat leaked inside my helmet and drenched the filters setting alarms ringing, and the stars disappeared as I clenched my eyelids tight again.

I imagined the leap, letting the leash free, legs primed and driving me like a missile. Ideally, I'd hit the target, catch the leash grapple, and dangle. In my imagined leap I missed and sailed in the darkness ta my death.

"Tammy. Ya have ta leap. Please."

Time passed as I waited, like a child waiting at the sea's edge till the waves receded, then racing and swimming in a gap. I heard her as I prepared ta leap.

"Please."

It was all I needed.

I leapt with little grace and even less mastery. I was a discarded appendage the ISS had dismissed with disdain. My less-than-perfect leap made me spin awkwardly, like a high diver in a three-and-a half-twist pike. It wasn't an elegant swan dive. I was clearing the distance in twenty-five secs, and yet, as always, the landing was the trick.

Flying is easy, they say, it's the landing that's hard. Where had I heard that? I was the evidence. With the grapple ready in my hand, I aligned with the hand grips near the damaged wings.

Twenty-five secs is an eternity.

I hit with a crash that wasn't dissimilar ta the impact which I was there ta repair. My grapple held and my speed kept me flying till the leash snapped tight like a whip crack and left me dangling, right where I needed ta land. I clawed my way nearer ta the damaged panel and placed my magnetic feet, safely attached ta the ISS again.

I heard Gessica cheer as I landed. I stayed still and stared at the distance I had travelled. I was alive and, it seemed, still sane.

Think chess pieces, I said in my head. *Reset the pieces, start again.*

"Tammy, a reminder, we need speed." Gessica revived me.

I finished repairing the wires and replaced the electricity transfer. Gessica was right that this part was easy. Like a typical man, I wasn't prepared ta tell her that. I signalled that the repair was ready.

"Right, I'm firing the drivers," she said. "Leash in tight and hang in there."

I hadn't realised I'd find myself riding the ISS side-saddle. Despite the weightlessness, and lacking any reference ta the speed, I felt like I was strapped ta the mast in a ship sailing in a tempest. There were writhing krakens, rain, and wind, and all the things that seamen pray never ta see. I was terrified.

Gessica kept speaking as we lifted. We fired with seven mins left, and she made it faster than I'd have dared.

"The lines still meet," she said. "We might make it."

The ISS circled the Earth and the light flashed. I saw the cadaver nearing fast, aimed right at me, like a spear with my heart as its target. My scream reached heights that a singer might have.

The cadaver missed with inches ta spare and whipped past like a high-speed train. My scream receded like the tide and left me spent. I was an empty shell. My chess pieces scattered in the wind.

"Tammy, ya can take the EVA inside," she said.

I sat there at the edge, staring at the stars that seemed like little fireflies dying and falling. It was the ISS's spinning that made them seem that way. Yet, all I saw was the sky falling. I spent time regaining my haven, resetting the chess pieces.

Space isn't as dark as ya might think. When the Earth is in an eclipse, hiding in the shade, the stars ignite. It's magnificent. The dipper and all the shapes we typically see in the sky disappear, immersed in a twinkling canvas, with lesser stars shining sharper. Little stars are everywhere, and if ya stare hard ya see them emerge. There's a star I like called Adhara; it sits in the great canine and its name is a little like my ma's nickname that my dad always called her, Hara. It's a twin star and when ya switch the spectra in the helmet it shines. I imagined replacing all my pieces, the stars, defending the king, ready ta play again.

I re-entered the hatch, leaving the dirty gear in there, then cleaned myself and cycled the air ta meet with Gessica. I left the flying ta her and sat with a vacated mind. I needed time ta heal.

Gessica came and held my chin and, with a smile, kissed me. "That was a gallant deed, Tammy."

I gave her a wry grin. Did she see me as her shining knight? Perhaps. Was she my damsel in distress? Hardly. I felt like I was the damsel in this scene. I was certainly in distress.

She sat with me, her arm as my shawl, calming me till I let the dark images depart. The desiccated Andrew, my parents in distress, Frank sailing away in space, my graceless leap. I inhaled several times like I was hyperventilating.

"As I said, Tammy: calmly. Ya did great."

It was nice sitting with her.

"Taking risks," I said as I held her arm tight. She knew precisely why I did it. "I'm satisfied."

The ISS had always maintained its height near Earth, making the refill ship visits easier. Since we weren't likely ta receive any visits, we kept the drivers firing and went as high as we needed, ta miss all satellites. Gessica silenced the alarms that signalled the failed links with satellites and settlements; it didn't matter as we didn't need ta message them. In time we were safe, higher than any dead vented crewmates might reach.

At this vantage, I saw the Earth in a new way, smaller than I'd ever seen it. It was frail and distant, a small pea in a vast dinner plate.

I watched the panel screen showing the ISS flight path related ta all satellites, and I saw a strange repeat. There was a satellite a few Ks higher than the ISS that matched its ascent and path as we shifted. It matched the flight in all parameters, as if a string kept them linked. The screen identified the satellite as *Genefire*.

"I've never heard that name," I said.

Gessica saw it and said in a dreamy way, "I've seen it, I think." Her face wrinkled. "My father had a genetics team in the past called Genefire. It was finished already when I was a child." She drifted near me and held my arm. "I'll search his files and see if I can find what it is."

She left me in the Captain's wedge with all the flashing lights and panels that were needed ta fly the ISS. I didn't dare press anything while Gessica was away. I scanned the empty wedge, all the seats that held the flight crew – vacant – and wished we had them here still. An image flashed in my mind, spectres filling the seats, and then vanished. It sent my mind inta the past.

I was ten again, the day my parents died, and Captain Petrykin lifted me and sat me in his seat.

"Tammy, it is a real tragedy. I wish that it hadn't happened. This accident…" He clenched his fists and slammed the panel. His eyes were red like mine. "Frank and I have agreed that ya can stay here at the ISS. I want ya ta take their mantle. Train hard, and live the life they…" His eyes were red, crying like me.

And I did. I lived their life in Maintenance. It didn't last as predicted.

It was late when Gessica re-entered the Captain's wedge, her face lit with a large smile.

"Tammy, I think we might have a way. Genefire is a satellite that can fire a small pill carrying a viral DNA message, ta hit the gravity well that makes it travel in time. They have sent genetic viral particles in the past ta send messages. My father had all the evidence that it was changing things in the past. He was leading that team."

I stared at her as if she wasn't making sense.

"It's fantastic!" she said. "Can't ya see? We can send a warning inta the past ta prevent this disaster. We can save the Earth!"

Chapter 18

"Did you just say you were going to dig my mother up?" the girl said.

"Uh, no. I didn't say that," said Milton still staring at the grave. Several conflicting ideas swirled in his head. He still couldn't let go of the idea that they should have cremated Margaret. And yet, she was buried just below his feet.

An alternative hypothesis formed in his mind. Perhaps Margaret was still alive, but had been kidnapped, and the burial was an elaborate hoax to cover it up. That was possible. But how to test it, short of digging her up?

Milton considered the evidence. The doctor had confirmed a heart attack. *Must be hard to fake your way through an autopsy*, he thought. *You'd want some strong chemistry to survive that. There must have been a body. A bribe, then. The only viable solution.*

Two men reported the death and accompanied Margaret in the ambulance. Milton assumed he already knew who those two men were. It wasn't a long stretch, then, to assume that the family house would have been cleaned of all DNA, as Noah had suggested. However, that would only have happened if the culprits had had enough time to do so.

The young girl should have been taken as well. Milton had good evidence that hadn't been the case: she was standing right before him. Scared off, then. If the girl had been scared off, she wouldn't have attended the funeral for fear of being seen by the culprits and would attend the grave of her mother late at night when she wouldn't be seen. Bingo.

Although he hadn't seen the WTLESS agents at the funeral, he was sure that they must have been nearby, perhaps watching from a parked car.

Fortunately, Noah's prediction had come true, and the girl had shown up. *How could she have known?*

Noah approached the young girl. "Alice, I understand how you feel. I lost my mother at your age, and my father left us not long before that."

She put an arm around the girl and held her. She was trying to prevent girl from looking at the wound in the ground and in her heart.

In a soothing voice, Noah told the girl a story to hang her sadness on. "I fought terribly with her at the time," she continued. "She wouldn't let me go out with my friends, or with a boy I knew. Every time she smoked another joint, it was like she was forcing me further and further away, and yet she kept such a tight leash on me. She pushed me and pulled at the same time. She was such a contradiction. I hated her for it. Then she took an overdose of something and died right there on the couch. I ran away and missed her funeral. It took me a few days before I had the courage to visit her."

"My mum wasn't that bad," said Alice, "but those men, they wanted something from me and my mum, but she refused. I think they killed her. I ran away."

"You *think*?" prodded Milton, still hung up on his hypothesis. "Did you see them kill her?"

"They were nasty. I just ran away," said Alice. She broke down and started crying. "Why would they do that?"

"They want your DNA, just like we do, but for different reasons," replied Milton.

"Was it you two talking to my neighbours this morning?" Alice asked.

"Alice, you have to come with us," Milton stated. The girl with the DNA that held the message and provided the evidence he needed for his hearing was standing right in front of him. All he needed to do was ask for it – or reach out and take it.

Milton reached out.

Alice backed away from Noah and Milton. "It *was* you asking for me. That's why I skipped my mother's funeral. You're just like them." She backed away down the path, towards the gates of the cemetery.

Milton panicked at the thought of losing the DNA sample again. Of course, if Noah had guessed that the girl would turn up, so could WTLESS. They could be after her too. He leapt after Alice, catching hold of her hair, trying to keep her still.

"Please, stop," he cried.

She screamed in pain as she pulled free and ran.

Milton ran after her, calling out, "Alice, help us save the world. We need you!"

It sounded less crazy in his head, before it had left his lips. He wasn't as fast as Alice and she reached the gates ten paces ahead of him.

"Come back! You're in danger."

"Indeed," said a man who stepped under the lych gate to block the girl's path.

In the moonlight, the man, short with a moustache, looked like an overgrown rodent wearing a suit.

Alice jostled past the man and ran into the street. Car headlights flashed. Tyres screeched. Milton heard a scream that preceded a loud crunch like a walnut being pulverised by a nutcracker. The girl's head hit the tarmac beneath the car.

"Oh, God!" A pained cry leapt from the mouth of the driver as he stuck his cue-ball head out of the window. His mouth hung wide and his hands kept slapping his forehead. His despair contrasted with the deliberate movements of the smaller man as he picked up the limp girl and carried her to the back seat of the car.

"Thank you, Mr. Milton – we can take it from here," he said. "You have performed your task admirably."

"Gaaaah!" Milton screamed in horror at what they, or he, had done.

It was his fault that the girl had run. All strength left his arms and his legs wobbled. He stumbled towards the men and clutched at the girl, who was being thrown into the back seat. A hand covered his face and shoved him to the ground, as the car doors slammed shut. Milton's head hit the cement corner on the lych gate as the car drove off.

Milton drifted in a black haze, set within one of Rothko's black paintings. Different shades of black, glossy and matte, swept past him. Black letters written on black paper jumbled and tried to form words, but failed. He tried to focus on the tiniest glimmer of light that appeared in his peripheral vision, but like a slippery bar of soap it eluded his grasp. Everything he saw swirled around him as he fought his way back towards consciousness.

He woke to find Noah stroking his hair. She smiled at him.

"Have a nice rest?" Her expression darkened. "Alice was taken by WTLESS."

Milton closed his eyes. This was more than just a failed experiment. He had hoped to present the girl at his misconduct hearing as living, breathing, evidence. But that didn't matter anymore. She was dead. Because of him. The guilt circled around him, taunting him and poking at him. It struck like a viper into his heart and caused his lungs to collapse. He tried to breathe but couldn't. He opened his eyes and looked at Noah, who held his hand tight.

"She's dead, Noah." Milton's eyes filled with tears. "And they have her."

Noah raised Milton's own hand in front of his face. What he couldn't quite focus on what he held within his fist.

"Her hair." A pinprick of hope shone in the darkness. "Will it be enough DNA?" His head hurt. He dabbed his sleeve on the bleeding wound on his head, then managed a pained grin. "Maybe I can still get my PhD after all."

"Can you hear yourself, Milton? I think there are more important things going on here than getting your PhD. Give it up already."

"I can't."

"A girl has just died."

"We don't know that for sure." Even Milton couldn't believe his own lie.

"And you wanted to dig up her mother!" Noah shouted.

"I didn't dig her up."

"That's not the point. We should have been nicer to her. She ran because of you." Noah held his chin and looked into his eyes. She shook her head, opened her mouth to speak but held herself back. After a moment she continued. "I admit I

171

doubted your story. But digging Margaret up? No sane person would even suggest that if you were making it up. I think I'm starting to believe you, Larry Milton. I want to help you, but we still need proof." She paused holding back her emotion. "That poor girl… Let's go and sequence what we've got. Hopefully, she hasn't died in vain."

Milton sighed as Noah stroked his hair again and then helped him to his feet. "Chin up soldier," she said. She offered a plastic bag from her backpack to isolate the clump of hair.

* * *

The train ride back to London was a revelation for Milton. Noah opened up in an effort to distract him, no longer the trench-coat-wearing commandant, and more the summer dress version. She still wore the chopsticks, spreading her hair in a web-like fan behind her. As she started speaking about herself, she fluctuated from introverted child to extroverted leader.

"My father left when I was a toddler, maybe three. He returned at times, but after my mother died, my relationship with him withered away. I broke my arm when I was eleven, and he came and gave me a hundred pounds. I didn't need the money, then. I needed a smiley face drawn on my cast. I needed a hug."

Milton fought the urge to lean across and give her the hug she desired. He wasn't sure if it would be welcome and thought it best just to let her speak.

"He was still there in the background, but useless, never speaking to me. In fact, I haven't seen him for five years, and frankly, I don't want to see him. I've got Ralph now – he's a good friend, even if he is the worst-looking Viking in the *in silico* hacker world." Noah laughed lightly. "He introduced me to the biohacker movement. With no family money for university, it was my only route for intellectual pursuit, and to learn all about genetics."

Noah spoke more about the biohacker movement and mentioned a few other genetics biohackers she admired: Jackknife, Wellzy, and Grube, who she worked with. She had asked Grube, who had contacts in the university IT team, to monitor emails from Jerome, in case there was any information that might help them. Nothing had shown up yet. Wellzy was a robotics expert and had developed several devices linked to enhancing muscle strength, particularly for patients with muscular dystrophy and other myopathies.

Milton listened to her with detachment, recalling the walnut crunching sound of the girl's head on the pavement. It was his fault, and the guilt crept up on him, obvious and inevitable. He should be arrested.

Noah continued to explain her rationale for her ugly and inedible animal genome project. "One of the biggest disasters over the last twenty years was the near extinction of bees in the northern hemisphere due to climate change. Beekeepers noticed the decline first, and then farmers noticed a decline in flowering crops. It wasn't hard to see a bleak future without bees to pollinate crops. No bees, no food.

"So, to solve this problem, at first the clever boffins tried to breed particular bees and release them to compensate. But it was a losing battle. The bees couldn't survive the rising temperatures. Next came the release of genetically altered bees, engineered to survive warmer climates. But this was a failure, too, because the genetics of the GM bees were based on an individual honeybee sequence, a single honeybee that just happened to have a combination of genetic variation that gave it a hankering for only one type of pollen on apple trees.

"At the time, it wasn't known that bees' pollen preference is genetically hard-wired. Apples grew in abundance in the years after the first wave of GM bees. No wonder apple cider became so popular.

"The boffins then realised they needed to sequence a whole lot of different bees of different breeds to ensure the genetic variation that would cover all sorts of preferences, in order to pollinate all the plants we needed. The problem was they only realised this after many breeds had already been lost to extinction.

"Have you ever eaten peaches and nectarines? We've lost the genetic variation in the bees that have the strongest preference to pollinate these flowers at the right time of year. The way the farmers grow them now is to manually pollinate the trees, which is time-consuming, so now they're so rare and expensive that most people have never heard of them. I had a peach once. God, it was good."

It was true that Milton had never eaten a peach or a nectarine. *You can't miss what you've never had*, he thought.

Noah stared through the window at the empty fields, emblematic of the struggling crops. The monotonous beige of the biofuel crop in some fields were ready for the autumn harvest. It was no wonder that energy companies had turned to crops that were independent of pollinators.

"What was the lesson we learned from this?" Noah continued. "Even genome sequencing projects need diversity. You never know when you might need it. So, I started sequencing all the animals that had never been sequenced before, with enough specimens to get good diversity. You never know when you might need that animal in the future."

A genetic Noah's ark, Milton thought.

The conversation soon returned to the young girl, and Milton's mood darkened. He scowled and avoided eye contact with Noah. *If only Alice hadn't run.* Milton swallowed the lump in his throat and wiped his nose. *If only I hadn't...* His stomach turned as though churning his intestines to butter, considering all the possible outcomes had he done things differently. *If only...* He tensed the muscles in his stomach trying to force the nausea away. It didn't work. He lifted his head and looked straight at Noah.

"I need to call the cops," Milton said firmly. "It will be better for us if we come forward."

"No, you can't do that." Noah held Milton's hands, a little too tight. "I'm just as involved, and if the cops come calling for me, no good will come of that."

"Why?"

"Ask me again sometime," she said, looking out of the window.

Milton was ready to ask her again immediately, annoyed at the deflection but realised it wasn't the right time. He too, gazed into the distance, and conceded that she was probably right. He cursed their genetic sleuthing skills. If he hadn't been there, then the worst that would have happened was that WTLESS would have kidnapped her. They may have killed her anyway, but it wouldn't have been his fault. And that was what Milton was trying to slough off, like a wet rag around his face, suffocating him. He tried telling himself this argument was pure rationalisation, a scientific analysis of the data from a failed experiment. He bit hard into his fist and screwed his eyes shut. Perhaps he should have been the one hit by the car.

"Good old survivor guilt." he whispered.

Recognise it all he could, he couldn't escape it. It was like wading neck deep through a rushing river, his feet losing purchase on the slippery rocks of the riverbed. No one should die for a research project.

It was more than that, though. If the warning from the future was true, this was the beginning of a war that would culminate in the Earth's destruction. There were always casualties in war, and Alice was just the first. Perhaps she would be remembered as a martyr, the prophet with the message. And maybe there *were* more important things than getting his PhD.

They discussed the young girl and what WTLESS might do with her lifeless body. Milton explained his theory of the kidnapping and burial hoax of the mother. The evidence fit now that Alice had also been taken. Imagining that Alice somehow survived, Milton pictured her reunion with her mother, in the depths of a WTLESS dungeon. He didn't know if they had any such dungeons underneath the Westley Trust, but it was better to imagine that than to accept the reality that they were both dead. Or worse, being treated in some medical facility to scrub them clean of the message.

"Could you clean a message out of someone's DNA?" Milton pondered.

"I don't see how," Noah replied.

"Jerome could probably do it."

"Not with the technology we have today."

"How else could WTLESS suppress this information if that was their goal. Short of locking them up forever in their dungeon?"

"They're dead, Milton. You need to accept that."

"Maybe we could rescue her body?"

"The best way to help her," Noah concluded, "is to make her redundant by sequencing the message and publishing it."

Milton agreed.

Chapter 19

Time travel. It wasn't the answer I had imagined. I'll admit that I hadn't had time ta imagine *anything* saving the Earth. Yet, if the evidence was there, what right did I have ta disagree? Gessica gave me the details as she read them in her father's diaries and, like Chinese whispers, I'll try and relay them here.

The physics team had identified a ripple in space that appeared like a crystal-clear lake, warping light with the tiniest angle, as it passed. It was first detected when an ISS ship travelled near it while they were viewing the Earth. The ship's crew had kept it secret while they investigated. Even the ISS captain was kept in the dark. The ship's crew sent laser light, machinery and devices at it, and everything they sent disappeared. When they learnt weeks later that a small device they had sent had landed in India a decade earlier than they sent it, they realised what they had.

After many tests, they learnt that small items hit the Earth, while larger items flew past and missed. With Terrence Kelly's help, they created a way ta send DNA messages inta the past with viral particles. The Genefire team was active nearly ten years. Then, in an instant, it was finished, and they never tried it again.

When Gessica fell silent, I asked her the single thing that interested me.

"Why did it finish?"

As I said this, I glimpsed the spectres circling in my peripheral sight line, as if they held the key. Gessica glanced at them as well, and we stepped away.

She hesitated, then replied, "The way I read it, there was a real danger when they fired it. Each time they fired the Genefire, a gravity wave rippled and wiped everything clean. A change in the past makes the present different, as if certain things never happened. The larger the mass in the viral particle carrying message, the faster it fires. The faster it fires, the farther in the past, the larger the splash and the larger the side effects."

My face clearly said "Eh?", as Gessica tried ta say it again, in a way that made sense.

"Imagine if I sent a message that said, 'Kill Captain Petrykin's parents'," she said, staring at me till I gave a sign that I was still with her. "Then the captain disappears here, replaced with a different captain. Captain Petrykin was never alive in the first place. Get it?"

"Why kill the captain?" I said. "He was nice."

"His parents weren't nice, Tammy. What if I was targeting them? Then the captain disappearing is a side effect that I didn't intend. An accident."

I then realised why the Genefire was a danger.

"They saw their crew, family and friends disappear, as if they had never lived at all. The crewmates that retained awareness were the geneticists that fired the Genefire satellite. My father made many mistakes. Each time he tried repairing his mistakes, he fired a different message and each time it went awry. My father learnt it was wise ta never make mistakes like that. He said in his diary that the spectres we see are the after-images, the crew that time dismissed."

In all the spectres I saw, there was never a face I knew. That made sense, if I never knew them. It made me miss all the crew and friends I might have met if things were different. I stifled a cry that crept inside me. It reminded me that my crew were all dead. As I did every day, I lamented them and said a prayer. If there was a crew that I never even knew, then it was as if they had all died as well. I might have had friends, partners, even a wife and family I never knew.

There was a female spectre drifting near me. I watched her, held my hand near her face as if caressing it. Her wavy hair encased my hand in an ethereal net, and I danced with her as she drifted past. She had a red dress, Maintenance like me. If I was a lip reader, I might have determined what she was saying. Her eyes were like crystals shining with a lightness, smiling. She was happy. What if she was my wife in an alternate timeline? I imagined her face was the type that I might like. Her smile, even if it wasn't aimed at me, I wished it was.

Gessica clicked her fingers and dispelled my dream. Did she realise I was flirting with an imaginary wife?

"My father writes in his diary when his wife and child disappeared. Me, Tammy – I disappeared! He was devastated. After several desperate attempts, he managed a message that made me reappear. After that, Genefire was finished. He didn't fire it ever again."

We spent weeks reviewing this. I sensed that it was a massive thing ta decide. Gessica treaded a fine line in her thinking, flipping this way, then that, wanting ta fire the Genefire immediately, and wanting ta dismantle it and never fire it again, like her father advised in his diary.

"I see it like this, Tammy. We are alive. Here. In this timeline. If we try sending a message warning the past that this disaster is imminent and the message misfires, isn't read, misses its target, dismissed as a fake – whichever way, it fails… At first my thinking was that this was a great chance. This was a risk we had ta take. If we didn't take a risk, then Earth was dead, friends and families all dead with it. If we take a risk, we *might* save it." Gessica held a hand ta her head. "Tammy, we might send a message that makes me disappear. I might never have lived. Again."

She was shaking. Hearing it like that, I felt we didn't have the right ta even attempt it. I didn't dare risk it.

"Why did they even start with this?" I asked her. "It seems a risk far past anything I'd imagined. Are there any alternatives?"

"There isn't anything I can think. We can try and reach Mars, perhaps."

"Leave Earth entirely, ya mean?"

"Yes, if Marstead can fly here. We can't fly any ships we have. They're all empty."

"And they ain't talking." I fell silent and tried hard ta think. I repeated an ancient saying I'd heard. "Accept with serenity the things ya can't change, and the strength ta change the things ya can, and have the sense ta see the difference."

"We can change this, and we have the strength, Tammy," she replied. "If we never send anything, then the Earth is finished. If we send the right message, we might replace this dead planet with an Earth that I never defiled. An Earth we can visit. Tammy, I need that."

"The alternative is that we accept things as they are and live as well as we can," I said.

"Die here, that we might live there," she added, meaning a different timeline.

It was a harsh sentiment. Perhaps even a legitimate idea, yet I didn't think I'd ever dare.

Visiting Earth tempted me, and as things were, I wasn't affected with the chemical; I was safe ta visit. What might I see there? I was always fascinated with the sea and the fish and animals that lived there. Diving in the sea seemed like drifting in space ta me, and I think I'd feel safer there. My father always said that gravity was a weight we didn't need ta carry, and in the sea it didn't matter. Drifting near a reef, with fish and the swaying seaweed. It seemed like a dream ta me. I think that's what I'd try first if I visited. As it was, we didn't even have a way ta re-enter. And Gessica had a Gename patent and wasn't safe there anyway. We had ta change that.

"Perhaps we need ta send the message," I said finally. We had time, as it didn't matter when we sent it, whether we waited a week, a year. The past was always the past. "Let's spend time thinking," I said.

Gessica agreed.

We fell in with everyday tasks. Gessica tended the Captain's wedge, flying the ISS when needed, and I maintained the air and temp and restarted the Garden wedge with a new harvest: sweet peas and celery. She spent time in Genetics, finishing things she was interested in. I spent many hrs in Maintenance, keeping the ISS in check and flying safely. While there, I switched a screen ta the CCTV in the Genetics wedge, that I might keep an eye and reaffirm Gessica was still safe. We met several times a day ta eat, at least when I ate. With Gessica's genetic enhancements, she didn't need ta eat three times a day like me.

"At times, I wish I had genetic enhancements," I said while eating. "All the advantages."

"Nay, Tammy, perfect as y'are," she replied.

We slept in the Genetics wedge. Gessica never failed ta kiss me each night. I yearned ta reach that time each day.

I spent time teaching her ta play chess, and after a few games she was winning every time. There wasn't any denying that she was smarter than me. She didn't hesitate ta sacrifice a pawn ta save the king.

The last game I recall was a lengthy affair. We played several days. Then, in a few sharp plays, Gessica sacrificed three pieces ta gain an advantage. It was a false advantage. I had checkmate in three steps.

"Nice, Tammy. Ya win," she said, shaking my hand.

It was clear. She let me win.

"I can't win like that," I said. We didn't play again after that.

Gessica spent weeks teaching me genetics and all the aspects that were needed if we did decide ta fire the Genefire. The message length, the genetic familial targeting, the viral strain carrier and the strength with which it infected were all vital. She checked that the reagents were still filled in the satellite, and it was ready ta fire. All it needed was the message written and a speed selected.

Gessica spent time reminiscing.

"I'll miss them all. When I was little, I had a cat, Tinkles. She was nasty and charming, claws and caresses. I still have a scar," she said, displaying her arm with a ten-centimetre line. She petted the scar as if it were the cat herself.

"And the farms?" I asked.

"Where they keep the cattle and chickens. Man, they smelled."

It was sad that many animals had ta live in farms. The wild landscapes were nearly emptied as the climate changed.

Since the farmers had died with the chemical, the farms weren't tended, and the animals were dying as well. Gessica spent many hrs watching animal vids with a tear in her eye. I sat with her silently, helping her digest her grief.

Every night we talked and spent time thinking what message ta write and when ta send it and what might happen. What did we wish might happen? I can say that the wishes ranged widely. The central plank was a revitalised ISS with a crew, and a safe Earth. Gessica wanted ta wipe away the regret in her mind, she didn't want ta remain the villain that had defiled the Earth.

"My wish is that whatever happens, we remain sweethearts," I said. "I daren't risk that even ta make Earth safe again." She kissed me twice that night.

There was a night that was special in a way that had little relevance ta the message. It was the first night that Gessica spent in my sleeping sac. I needn't write what happened in that weightless wrestle. My heart leapt like it was saved. An angel in my midst. I knew that I'd impressed her; she kept panting like it was a distance race. It seemed a dream yet was real.

"Gessica, that was…" I was panting myself. She held a finger ta my lips and prevented anything ta fill the warm silence. If the Earth had ta die that this might have happened, I'd have taken it every time. I think Gessica felt the same. The smile didn't leave her face till days passed.

Then there was a time several weeks later, I recall, crystal clear, when she came and saw me at the viewing deck. I was watching the Earth spin as we circled it higher than ever. I saw a spectre ta my left watching the circling Earth in the same vein. I watched him, thinking he might have the same feelings as me, and perhaps he was seeking the same relief. Did he even see the same Earth that I saw?

Why did the Illegals release the chemical, and why did they have it in the first place. I had ta ask Gessica again. Why did they have it if she made it?

"I presented my research at a meeting," she said, staring at the stars and shaking her head. "I displayed the chemical. Why did I? They were all esteemed scientists and I wanted them ta see that I was as clever as they were. I had identified this critical thing, this chemical. See what I can make. I'm clever…The seven deadly sins, and I picked pride." She kept shaking her head, then stared at me, daring herself ta say it. "It was a private meeting. I think the Illegals were there."

It was a simple, cataclysmic mistake. Her eyes teared and I knew that I had stripped away the seal and revealed her grief again. It was why we sidestepped this matter all the time.

It wasn't an indictment. "Gessica," I whispered. "The act was theirs."

"It was still my mistake."

We scanned the Earth, trying ta see any signs that men might live. It was a mere ten weeks since it happened. They might still live. Yet the fires I saw were raging. The Earth cleansed its face, advancing in sparkling lines. As we passed the night side, I saw the city lights dim, as the energy grids dwindled. The Earth was already diminishing.

"It's sad," she said as she held my hand. "I was thinking that if we ever managed a child, I'd rather they lived there. This ISS isn't a family place."

It was the first time she'd indicated we might have kids. My heart swelled at the idea, even if I knew I was infertile. She was willing ta have a family with me and whatever way it happened, I was pleased.

"Tammy, I think we need ta send the message. I've written a draft."

She led me ta the Genetics wedge and lit the screen with the script. It was a lengthy tale telling the reader that ethics had disintegrated, which led the Earth states ta implement the Gename patents. The patents were the mistake that led ta this disaster. It was a warning that, if delivered, might prevent the earliest mistakes when the Gename patents were first implemented.

Then I saw a statement that rammed like a knife in my mind.

The name *fescennine* was attached ta Pan Sapiens. Lacking any decency, repellent, vile. That was what it meant and what Gessica wanted ta prevent. It was me she wanted ta prevent.

"Gessica, I'm a Pan," I said.

She stared at me vacantly, like she didn't accept what I said. Then she cringed. Her lips crinkled, like she was in pain, and she spat like she was sick and spewing her innards. Her hands hid her face. As she lifted them, she tried ta deny it, like my statement was a game I was playing.

"Ya had parents," she said. "I knew them."

"And what's that mean?"

"Pans are meant ta remain sterile. Ya had parents, y'ain't a Pan. Why lie like that?"

"I ain't lying. Why d'ya think they called me Impressive?" I yelled at her. "They always said I was special. That's why."

Her lips tightened and she retreated, taking a time ta think. She tilted her head this way and that, trying ta make sense in her mind. Her eyes then grew red as her reply swelled inside her, till she released it.

"If we send the message then I might never have slept with a Pan. I'm sending it."

My heart sank. She made me feel like I was a smelly vagrant that hadn't washed in years, and she was the perfect princess that had slept with me, tricked with a mirage. In waking, she realised her tragic mistake.

I tried facing her with dignity and pride. I tried telling myself that her stance was her failing. Her eyes penetrated my mind and seemed ta keep repeating the claim that I'd raped her. The way she stared at me made me feel like I had. My tears fled my eyes, and I hid my face that she mightn't see them. I grasped the nearest handgrips and yanked myself ta the hatch, gashed my head in my haste, and escaped in the cylinder passageway.

I wasn't an animal. I knew that, yet thinking it made it real. I hid in the Physics wedge and wept the tears an animal might weep.

Chapter 20

The London BioHackspace looked as dark and creepy as it had the first time Milton visited. The little island of light in the middle of the warehouse offered the comfort of sofa and caffeine. The faint glow of laboratories that appeared to float like sky lanterns around the central point showed signs of activity.

Ralph the Viking hacker, who was again hovering over the coffee machine, embraced Noah in a bear hug, and gave Milton another uncomfortable pat on the bum, his way of saying it was good to see them again. "Glad you're back," he said.

The relative obscurity of the biohackers' warehouse lent it a modicum of security, but it occurred to Milton that it wouldn't be hard for WTLESS to find them here. If Noah had garnered their attention before, they were sure to know her location. He reminded himself that he should ask her about her previous encounters with these ruthless science police thugs. Milton scanned the warehouse and registered three green glowing exit signs.

Noah had seen him glance at the exits and responded to his unasked question. "We'll be safe here. They know where we are, but they don't dare to come in here. I mentioned that I have prior experience with those mugs. The first time, they came in and cleared out my lab and stole all the DNA samples I had collected. *Apparently,* I'd collected some DNA samples from animals in a secret genetic hybrid study. They were hybrids of orang-utans and gorillas. And, *apparently*, I'd snuck into their facility and collected DNA samples without *'permission'*.

She opened a fridge and stored the plastic wrapped hair sample. "You can imagine I was a bit upset by that. The second time they visited my lab, they discovered a nice dose of anthrax in a box of DNA samples… Remind me to tell you which boxes not to touch in here," she added, as an afterthought. "As if losing a fellow WTLESS agent to a deadly biological agent wasn't enough, with help from Ralph we hacked into the WT finance system and wiped out an entire year's budget. That came with a warning to leave us alone. Money makes the world go round. We've been safe ever since."

She said this last statement with a twirl of her hair and a chuckle. Milton made a mental note not to mess with Ralph, whose *in silico* powers were formidable. He could put up with a friendly pat on the bum if necessary.

They entered Noah's pristine laboratory containing her genetic sequencing machine and computer, attached to two large, rolled out screens. Noah issued sharp commands for Milton to sit on the spare seat in the corner of the lab and not to touch anything. Despite his three years working on a PhD and his relevant skills, she didn't trust him. Milton sat down out of fear, despite the urge to do his own work.

Milton watched as Noah, donning the white lab coat and silicon gloves, lifted the young girl's hair from the bag. She cut the ends containing the hair bulbs into a test tube.

The DNA extraction involved digesting all the proteins surrounding the nucleus of the DNA, and then a good old-fashioned phenol chloroform extraction, chemicals that would separate the genomic DNA into the aqueous phase of the solution, followed by alcohol-based precipitation. The DNA would form a solid pellet at the bottom of the test tube, which could then be dissolved in water. The method was as old as the hills, but it was cheap and still gave the best quality DNA. Milton always used the expensive rapid method, which took five minutes and was so easy you could train any primate with opposable thumbs – or any new graduate student – to do it. The method Noah used required finesse and an expert touch.

She set the machine up to read chromosome four, as this was the one that Milton insisted contained the message and would provide their answer faster.

While they waited for the machine to do its job, Milton opened his screen to show the draft of his PhD thesis, and wrote up the latest results, knowing what this final sequence was sure to show. He decided he should complete his thesis no matter what the university said.

Noah spent the time checking her messages on several different forums, some in the lighter parts of the web, some in the darker corners.

"Larry," she said, "come and have a look at this link. I asked Grube to monitor Jerome's incoming messages for anything related to the Gename project and one message was tagged. This link to a video."

Milton stood from his chair with a dead leg and a wobble. He tried to stamp it out as he approached Noah's screens. Noah opened the video.

It showed a rocky landscape with a three-metre-wide hole in the ground. The camera jostled a bit until it pointed to the bottom of the crater, for such it was. Nestled in the middle of the hole was a meteorite cracked in two. The person holding the camera set it on a tripod and climbed down into the hole. He wore a large woolly jacket, woolly hat, and woolly mittens. He crouched on the ground near the meteorite and took off his mittens. He breathed out a large mist in the cold air and reached for a small grey pill inside the meteorite. He held the pill towards the camera and turned it to inspect it. With a sudden burst, the pill exploded, and the man sneezed. He let out a cry, sucked his throbbing fingers and cursed. He climbed out of the hole and turned the video off.

"Was that Russian or Polish?" Milton asked.

"Russian, I think. What does this have to do with the Gename project?" Noah asked.

Milton didn't have an immediate answer, nor time to think of one, as the sequencing machine announced it had finished with a small ping. Milton held his breath as Noah loaded up the old sequence from his cloud storage and aligned it with the one they had just sequenced. It was a perfect match.

More importantly, the message was intact. He spotted the code right away:

```
atg tat aac gcg atg gaa att agc ggc gaa agc agc att tgc gcg

 M   Y   N   A   M   E   I   S   G   E   S   S   I   C   A
```

The rest of the message read as it did before. Noah scanned the whole thing, translated it, and saved it in several cloud servers. She swivelled on her chair to face Milton with a big, beaming smile.

"We've got them now," she said. "This is amazing. It all seems so plausible. Your story is true! Gename patents and planetary destruction." She whistled. "All we need is some more evidence to back this up. Did you ever find any other evidence of the Gename patent project?"

"No, I didn't," Milton replied. His vision glazed as he recalled the one thing he had found in Jerome's office. He slapped each of the pockets in his jacket until he found the one that contained the object. With the trip to Wales on his mind, it had completely slipped his mind.

He pulled out the small glass vial with the grey pill inside it. It looked remarkably like the one collected in the meteorite video.

Chapter 21

I slammed the hatch in the Physics wedge and sank with the gravity, landing in a heap near the Physics team's sleeping den. Silence filled the wedge and all I heard was my panting. That silence let my mind play tricks, and in time I heard all the peeps and ticks the machines were making, like they were aimed at me. The machines kept saying "Pan", "Pan", "Pan."

I mashed my ears with my hands as I tried preventing Gessica's disdain repeating in my head. "Pan", "Pan, "Pan". It didn't seem ta end. I sat and weathered this vile wind till it stilled. Like a distant train driving away, it dwindled and disappeared... Had she even said it? Had I imagined it? Had my mind played tricks? All my fears had materialised in real life. She can't have said it, since deep in my heart I knew she still cared.

Then, a faint light grew in my mind, a signal fire leading me ta find what I was seeking. I had hardly met her, yet Gessica was everything ta me. She was a warmth filling my heart, a light in my eyes making everything in my life shine. Her smile kept me fighting ta keep her alive, cleaning the ISS till my fingers were raw, and risking my life with the EVA. She was why I kept striving, even when I wanted ta space myself. When she kissed me, it was like adrenaline, a vaccine against malaise and misery.

With my hands ta my lips, I felt hers meeting mine, silky and minty. My eyes teared, recalling the warmth in her heart that seeped inta mine when she gifted me a kiss.

I leapt and clapped, thrilled that I was right, and adamant that she still cared. I had ta see her. I lifted myself and raced ta the entrance. As I flipped the hatch, it hit me again.

Wait…

She had said it. I hadn't imagined it. "Pan." The machines pinged their message again.

I slammed my fist against the hatch, and it rang like a tin can. I rammed my eyes with my fists trying ta dig that image away, Gessica spitting malice at me.

I realised there was still a CCTV camera active in the Genetics wedge. I activated the image and saw her at the desk with the Genefire screen. I tried piling all the hate that welled inside me at the screen. I screamed at the screen. Yes, like an animal.

What if she were ta send the message? Was I destined ta live as a spectre, an afterimage in an alternative reality that she lived in? What if my crewmates lived again? And what if Gessica never met me? What will it feel like ta live as a spectre and watch all that? It reminded me that the spectres were still there in the Physics wedge, drifting, like they always were.

I saw three spectres wearing their white Physics wedge dresses. They were reading their machines, writing their reviews, and talking. I didn't hear anything they said, and they treated me as if I was a spectre ta them. Perhaps I was.

In the vid screen, I watched Gessica flit here and there in the Genetics wedge. She was active and had a clear aim. She didn't even halt and think whether she was right. She didn't care.

As I watched her, my mind drifted again, and I realised I might have a chance ta live. I had ta speak with her and remind her that I was here. I activated the chatline.

"Gessica, can we speak?" I asked. "I want ya ta hear what I have ta say."

She didn't even admit I was speaking, like the chatline was silenced. In that case I didn't stand a chance.

"Gessica, I didn't mean ta hide that I was a Pan. I didn't think it mattered. I'm sad that ya said that. Can we make a deal? If ya wait with the message, we can talk. I fear if ya fire it… I will cease… I'm scared… Please wait."

I watched ta see if she revealed any sign that she heard me. I was certain she had silenced the chatline and didn't want ta hear anything I had ta say. I was paralysed and all the machines were still pinging in my ear.

My spirits depleted, like the last gas in the tank was spent. I felt like I had a driver pressing the pedal, asking me ta try again, and I was empty. I panted and sighed, resting my head near the panel with the chatline, waiting ta hear a peep.

While I lay there, I recalled a saying my ma said all the time. I even saw her, as if she was a spectre, her dark hair pinned, the lines framing her eyes deep with many years smiling, and her red dress neatly pressed like it always was. She sat me in her lap, and even if I was heavier than her when I was eight, with the tenth gee in the Maintenance wedge, she cradled me like I was a child still and she said: *Even if they think ya different, and perhaps y'are and perhaps y'ain't, if they can't see what y'are, like I can, then they didn't deserve their eyes.*

Ma had imparted many pearls like this. When I was smaller, she reminded me that I'd never visit Earth while the states mandated their Gename patents, yet I never minded. I was happy in the ISS, and I learnt my trade in the Maintenance wedge with Frank as my trainer and my parents inspiring me. With them as my teachers I learnt what it meant ta have self-respect. And I had that, till Gessica said what she said. I tried hard ta remind myself that I did have dignity. I failed.

I still felt like an animal.

What right did she have ta make me the animal? When there was a single pair left, neither was the preeminent species. I had every right she had. I saved her life, and this was the thanks I received. I saw her tapping away at the keys, making changes and setting the message. Her finger held near the key that meant *fire*. She was ready.

I wasn't ready. I wasn't ready ta cease, even if my death was needed ta save the Earth. Screw the Earth, I was thinking. If her message was received, the past might revile Pan sapiens as she did, and the scientists might never make them. I might never have lived. I might never have shivered with her silky skin near mine. I might never see her again. I prayed she might hesitate and take the time ta think.

She didn't. Her finger slammed the key and the Genefire fired.

Chapter 22

"Should I open it?" Milton asked. He held the glass vial with its screwed-on cap in the palm of his hand. The tiny grey pill rattled inside. He unscrewed the cap.

"Milton, wait!" Noah shouted. "We saw what happened in that video, presuming it's the same type of pill. The video was tagged with a Gename patent link sent to Jerome. So, it has something to do with the Gename patents."

"But it might be another message," Milton said.

"In the video, the guy picked it up and it exploded in a puff of dust that made him sneeze. Is it a delivery method for the Gename patents? We don't know what happened to that man. It might have been infectious, he could be dead for all we know. You said you found it in Jerome's office, dropped off in the middle of the night by WTLESS. It could be dangerous."

"Can we sample from it with a fine needle and sequence the contents?"

"No, I wouldn't risk it. It could explode as soon as we pierce it."

"We have to try something. This might be the only corroborating evidence I've got." Milton held the vial up to the light, as if it was a fertilised egg with a secret inside. If he could infect himself with it, he could sequence the message. "I'm going to eat it."

He picked at the lid of the pill box.

"Milton, stop! Not in my lab." Noah held onto his arm with claws that dug into his skin. "You are not going to kill yourself here."

Milton resisted but found Noah stronger than expected, bending his hand backwards. He dropped the pill container back into his pocket.

"Okay, I'll just hold onto it as evidence," he said, realising the futility of straining against her. He admitted that Noah was probably right that ingesting the pill might be unduly risky.

Milton sat on the chair in the corner of the lab and ruminated. There were two days until the misconduct hearing. Flushed with the adrenaline from the success of having sequenced the girl's DNA, he now pored over his first bit of actual supporting evidence, reading the message repeatedly. They couldn't accuse him of making it up.

What else did he need, though? It was time to be bold. More evidence of the Gename project would help, but he wasn't even sure if the project was up and running yet. More than that, he needed the university to let him finish his PhD. Publishing it was the best way to get this message out there so that it might lead to the change needed to save the Earth. What he needed more than anything to survive the hearing was public support, and for that, he needed Roger. It was time to find his journalist friend again.

"I'm going to need the public on my side in this hearing. I need to find Roger. He can help."

Noah agreed. "Public support is vital in a public hearing."

Milton sent a message to Roger, asking to meet. Within moments he received a reply: *Meet, office, now.*

*   *   *

Behind the reception desk of the world-leading news agency, The Metro, sat a fashion dinosaur from a different age. She reminded Milton of his great Auntie Jasmine, stuck twenty years in the past. The woman's hair towered above her in a double beehive, and was a shade that might be described as off-white – eggshell, perhaps – and she had matching finger-nails. In stark contrast to her pale skin, she wore a vibrant fluorescent yellow power suit. Her lips were permanent-ly pursed. Her dark-rimmed glasses with sharp angles were worn as though explicitly for the purpose of the pose she now held looking at Milton. She glowered over the rims at the young man pleading with her.

"I'm sorry, young man, but I cannot allow you into these offices. If you are unable to contact your friend, then he does not wish to be contacted. It is company policy to maintain the confidentiality of our reporters as much as our sources and, therefore, I am unable to confirm whether the man you named even works here. You must understand that the integrity of our reporters and these offices must be maintained."

Milton turned away in disgust. The anonymity of report-ers and journalists was a hang-up from the heady days of ter-rorist attacks on newspapers, the extradition of whistle-blow-ers, and the government crackdown on journalistic freedom of speech. The journalists who were now held in high esteem were all anonymous. It was the long history with his friend that allowed him the privileged knowledge that Roger wrote for this paper.

Milton sat down on the bench opposite the woman's desk. Time stretched out before him, and he could see what the immediate future held. No matter how long he waited on this bench, he would eventually see his friend walk out of these offices. It was inevitable. Across the many branches of the web of time, the length of time he would wait was negligible. Therefore, he waited.

The fashion dinosaur repeated the same motif, asking him to leave many times. The first time, Milton responded with an apology and an excuse about having to send a long text message that was impossible to write outside, with his winter gloves on. The third time, he responded with an irritable rebuke and stayed put, ignoring the woman. The fourth request to leave came from a rhinoceros of a security guard. Milton relented and stood waiting outside the automatic glass door, at the limit of the sensors, forcing the doors to open and close as if they were munching on toffee. He reasoned that he was no longer on their property, and they had no right to ask him to move.

He was wrong. The last time he was asked to leave, he stood nose to nose with the rhinoceros security guard. At that moment he spotted Roger and two surprising companions.

Roger was escorting the two men down the impressive helical staircase that ran down beside the lifts. One of the two men was short with a twitchy, mousy moustache, and the other was a behemoth with a hairy cue ball head.

Roger shook hands with both men and accompanied them to the automatic door. What was he doing looking so convivial with these heartless monsters? A short conversation with the two WTLESS agents left a bewildered expression on

Roger's face, and was followed by a short scuffle, with Roger trying to wriggle out of their grip.

Flight mode took control of Milton's body. He turned and searched the street for a hiding place. Using the rhinoceros as a shield between him and the WTLESS agents, he ran into a nearby alley and behind a pile of crates. He peeked out towards the office to see Roger shepherded by the two men into a taxi. Moments before the car door shut, Roger fired a glance towards the alley in which Milton hid. His confidence shot, his face was the image of a fearful meerkat.

As soon as the taxi disappeared into the traffic, a man in a fine suit scampered along the street to the alley in which Milton was hiding.

"What the devil are you doing here?" he squealed. "You know you can't come into the office. What have you got us into?" He looked at Milton with a pained expression, and with a hand on Milton's shoulder, dragged him down the alley and into an ancient pub hidden away in a corner.

They went downstairs to the lowest level, where there were private booths. "Stay here," the man commanded, and left Milton sitting alone on the leather seat. The beer-stained wooden table supported his shaking arms. Only in seeing his shaking hands did Milton realise how afraid he was. Considering this man's reaction and the meerkat-like fear on Roger's face together, perhaps he was right to be afraid. His shoulders ached from the tension that had built up. He couldn't stop himself from glancing around, behind him, noticing every face, every pair of eyes that might be spying on him. He flipped his hands over, slapping his knuckles on the table, trying to stop the shaking.

The man returned with two pints of ale and sloshed them down on the table.

"Who are you?" Milton asked.

"I'm Roger's editor. I'm not going to tell you my name."

Milton unleashed a nervous barrage. "Why didn't you publish my story last week? Why didn't Roger answer my calls? What was he doing with those two goons?"

"Slow down there, Mifune," the editor replied. He held his left hand up, pausing Milton's questions. With his right hand he lifted the ale and poured it down his throat in greedy gulps until only a third remained. He placed the glass on the table and his eyes rose to meet Milton's.

"I nearly lost my job over this. Roger almost certainly will lose his job. Do you know who those two are – those goons, as you called them? I don't know how they know who I am or who Roger is, but the simple implication is that if I publish anything Roger has written about you or your story, my anonymity will be blown, and my career gone with it. Roger is in even more danger."

"This is more important than..." Milton began. But he stopped himself.

Was it, though? Milton had built up an almost fantastical tapestry that held the future of the entire human race dependent on his acquittal at the hearing and his revelation of this warning from the future to stop any development of the Gename patents. There might have been a squishy element within his heart that didn't want to be dismissed from his PhD. Could he ask his friend, along with this man he didn't even know, to forsake their careers, their lives, for the sake of his own?

"How did they find you?" Milton asked.

The man stared into his ale and picked it up but put it back down again before speaking. "Roger wrote up the story as you described it last week and submitted to me, and I passed it on to the Metro server. My senior editor has pulled stories before, but always with an explanation. This time, nothing. The copy was deleted from the server before I had a chance to re-trieve it. The draft on my screen cloud also disappeared. All we have left are the notes in Roger's notebook.

"I've spent the last couple of days reaching higher and higher up the food chain trying to find out where the order came from, but found nothing, until today. The order came from *them*. Those goons were after the notebook, but Roger got it to me in time and I managed to stuff it down my pants and bluff my way out of revealing it."

He unbuttoned his pants and, with a bit of jiggling, produced the green notebook.

"I don't know how they found us, but my senior editors were shit-scared of these guys. It was like blackmail or an old-school mob protection scam, they said. They knew my pseudonym. They're going to publish my home address. Do you know how stuffed I'll be if they do that? I've upset too many people, Larry. They have Roger and will do the same to him."

Without his job, Roger would be out on the street. Poverty would not sit well with him. Having a myriad of disgruntled subjects of his investigative journalism might also pose a risk to his health and wellbeing. Milton could hardly stomach the idea.

Milton explained what he knew about WTLESS based on his own experiences of them and what he had learnt from Noah. The mob-like description was apt, but despite their previous theorising about murders, he hadn't witnessed any cold-blooded murder. Accidental deaths, on the other hand, had a precedent. Alice. Again, guilt welled up inside him and he swallowed it down. He hoped the same wouldn't happen to Roger. Kidnapping wasn't beyond them, though. Milton recalled the imagined WTLESS dungeon. He opened the notebook and looked over the notes Roger had written about their first meeting in the coffee shop.

"We have more evidence now." Milton described his night-time visit to the lab, the trip to Wales, and the resequencing of the girl's DNA.

"You've got proof now that it's real. You have the DNA. That's great. And you've witnessed that they were trying to remove and kidnap the source of the DNA, and in fact killed her for it," said the editor. "That should help in your hearing."

"I need more than that. These guys seem to have a lot of resources. They seem to be everywhere at once. Or at least they keep turning up everywhere I am. If they're funded by the bottomless money pit of the Westley Trust, I'm sure they have all sorts of security and surveillance devices. The hearing will be public in BuzzWorld and the tide can turn on such small details. They'll censor anything I say that's confidential." Milton paused, wondering if he should share his idea with this man he just met. He looked him in the eye and decided he had to trust him. "However, if I can speak the truth to the public, they will hear. You know how important public opinion is. It's make or break."

"I can help there. What do you want me to do?"

Milton explained his plan to use the first letter of each sentence that he says in the hearing to spell out a message to the public, to avoid the auto-censor. The editor listened and smiled at the idea.

"Sure. I can be there and get the buzzflies floating in your favour," he responded. With a few contributions of his own, they had a firm plan.

Chapter 23

I didn't feel any change.

It seemed like there wasn't any effect at all. My first feeling was ta think it hadn't fired. There were plenty answers ta why it mightn't have changed anything. The Genefire pill might have missed the gravity well. Even if it was sent ta the past it mightn't have infected any men; and even if it had, it might never have lasted till it was read.

Alternatively, they might have dismissed it as a fake. It was an even chance that Gessica was mistaken and Genefire never achieved anything at all. Had her father invented the entire thing in his files? Where was the direct evidence that it had ever affected anything?

Even if it had made it ta Earth and landed and achieved everything it aimed ta achieve, I hadn't any idea what time was needed ta effect these changes. Did the gravity wave effect changes here in an instant? Was it a creeping demise that was still sneaking nearer? I didn't have any answers yet my instinct was that Gessica did.

I drifted nearer the CCTV screen and stared at her seat. It was empty.

Had I missed her disappearance? Had she ceased while I remained? I screamed, "Gessica!"

I fired myself ta the hatch. Very little time had passed since she'd crashed my dreams with her withering statements. I'd fled the Genetics wedge in dismay – my gashed head was still raw as evidence. I'd never felt as distressed in all my life. Yet, with her disappearance, that was all rendered meaningless. My heart raced.

I flew as fast as I dared. The cylindrical passageway lengthened as I viewed it, like a dream with the end stretching farther and farther away. This cylinder was the spine in my life, and all things I craved in my dreams were always at the end, past my reach. The air seemed thinner as I inhaled faster and faster.

I reached the Genetics wedge, my feet stamping as they met the hatch at pace, denting the steel. That crash might have alarmed Gessica if she were inside, yet since I was thinking she wasn't even there, I didn't care. I snatched at the hatch, levered it wide and dived in with little regard. I called her name and searched every research den.

They were all deserted.

An emptiness filled me, like my insides had melted away, leaving desiccated skin. In that instant I imagined I was the remaining life, the last sentient animal, in this ISS.

And I *was* an animal, again escaping death. Again, I spiralled, wishing I'd disappeared, and she'd lived. I was a shipwreck crashed in the night, the waves tearing at my decks, ripping me apart.

I didn't have any idea what ta think. I didn't have the skill ta try the Genefire again and reverse this. Was there even a message I might send that might revive Gessica and my crew-mates? Did I dare send the same message again? That might at least increase the chances it reached its mark. I might send different messages time and again and never prevail. I spent my last energy inhaling as I drifted in the Genetics wedge.

I let the minimal gravity settle me near the desk she'd sat at. I still smelt her fragrance in the leather. My fingers caressed where her hands had tapped the panels. It was still presenting the Genefire screen.

My mind grappled with a slippery idea that didn't stay still till I pinned it.

It wasn't right. If she'd ceased, and never lived, then I'd never have recalled her scent. I'd never have met her. I might see her as a spectre, an afterimage. I didn't see her at all.

She'd said that the geneticist that had hit the trigger had remained. Then again, this was the first time we'd fired the Genefire, and I didn't have any idea what was meant ta happen.

If my idea was right, then she might still live and was else-where in the ISS. Even that small chance was ample ta raise my energy levels. My relief, even at the chance, swelled my spirit.

I left the Genetics wedge and started searching. I called her name in each wedge and received silence. The Garden, Medical and Kitchen wedges were all empty. I traversed the cylinder again and ended my search at the viewing deck.

Then I saw her, in the same stance as when we first met, the day the flares raged. I called her name again. She remained still.

"Still here?" she asked. "It hasn't achieved anything, then." Her stance slackened.

Yes, I was still there. I was verging near rage when she reacted this way, after everything that had happened. Deep inside, a small part a me was happy that she was alive, yet I swept it aside, and let her have it.

She halted my rant with her raised palm.

"Tammy, listen, I didn't want ya ta disappear, really." It seemed she was attempting sincerity, yet it was hard ta tell if it was real. "I wanted the message ta reach the target. I can't see any signs that it has."

Gessica left the viewing deck, and steered clear as she passed me. She hesitated near the entrance hatch, and her head sank and rattled side ta side, as if she was fighting with herself. She sighed and drifted away.

I stayed in the viewing deck and stared at the spinning planet. I saw what she had seen – a silent planet. The air was weaving patterns, there was rain and wind, and the sea was still teeming with fish, at least as I imagined it. Mammals and reptiles were likely thriving. The planet wasn't dead. Yet, the cities were dark. She was right. We hadn't changed a thing.

Gessica remained in her Genetics wedge three days straight after that. I didn't see her in the Kitchen wedge when I needed ta eat. She didn't answer when I called. She didn't visit the Physics wedge and Maintenance wedge where I spent my time. We certainly didn't sleep in the same wedge. Even if it was Gessica that decided this, I was glad. I needed that time ta myself, ta chill and think where we were headed.

Where were we headed? I didn't have an answer. I'll admit here that I still had the same feelings, even if she did say the things she said. I realised that when I imagined her missing. She needed time and I was happy letting her have it, till she perhaps realised the same thing. At least, that was my wish.

Since I was in the Physics wedge, I retrained the ISS receivers at the settlements Marsstead and Hisakatani. I wanted ta see if they were still alive. I stared at the screens days at a time and saw signs here and there that they were active. The Mars settlement was larger, a few hectares at least, easily seen, with many spheres and dwellings. I saw a vehicle making tracks, a hatch venting gas tendrils. I was relieved, even if they failed ta send any signals. The Hisakatani settlement was hidden in shade at that time and all I saw were their ever-present lights shining in the night.

Gessica did finally find me in the Physics wedge. She had the same idea ta spy at the settlements. When she entered, she saw me, fidgeted with her hair, and stammered. Her ears grew red like her hair. She scanned the screens and saw that I was watching Marsstead.

"Fine," she said, and left again.

It was the silent treatment till a week had passed. Then she came directly ta see me in the Maintenance wedge as I was repairing the air cleansers.

"Tammy, I regret what I said. It wasn't nice. I realise that. And… even with everything I said… I still need…"

"My help?" I finished her sentence. She dipped her head, signalling that I was right. I held my hand as if ta shake. "Friends?"

Gessica placed her hand in mine. She smiled and started talking fast, like she had many ideas she needed ta relate.

"This last week, I read my father's diary. He had the CIA genetics team statements that started in the twenty thirties. His earliest Genefire message reached there. In the ninety years after that, the CIA amassed all this Genefire data. They registered every Genefire message ever sent, and at the right times they enacted the demand in the message. Imagine!"

I had a hard time imagining it. I'm certain my eyes widened when I realised that this meant they had fired many messages.

Gessica was hyper, as if her adrenaline was peaking. "It seems the CIA were firing messages everywhere. They were killing targets, changing time, sending new viral particles with genetic variants that had familial targeting. I can't access that data and I can't check if they registered my message. I wish we had a way ta see all the evidence in the past like that."

As I listened, it sparked an idea. I had access – the data farm that my friend in Pasadena gave me. It was a cache with newspapers, all state department papers, everything, perhaps even CIA. I hadn't even spent any time reading it yet. Since I'd met Gessica, my life was a never-ending train track clickity clacking as each disaster sped past, and I hadn't the time even ta see if the access key was still active.

"Tammy, that's it! I think we can see in that past evidence if the message was read. Is the data farm still there? Can we try?"

I recalled my reserved feelings when she asked me that first day. At the time I hadn't wanted ta share this massive data farm with her. It was the last message my friend sent me, and if I shared this, it was like giving away my last friend. I wasn't certain if Gessica was still a friend after what she had said. Despite that, she was all I had. I relented and decided ta lead Gessica ta my Maintenance wedge and my screen. I tried the access pass key, and it said the link wasn't reached. It was severed when we raised the ISS.

"I can repair the link," Gessica stated, snatching the screen. I watched her tapping frantically, directing the satellite dishes, searching the lists, and tracking the data farm. She did the maths and sketched the new triangle ta find where it was. She tracked the signal and hit the link. The screen pinged a happy ping.

Gessica swivelled her chair and grinned – till she met my grimace. I was impressed at her speed. She was smart – I'd said it many times – yet I knew pain still masked my face.

"It's there." When she glanced at me, her smile faded in a way that said, *I deserve that*. "I've set an easy link that we can click in any screen," she added. "I'll start searching the state department papers."

"I can start with the newspapers," I said.

"I'll meet ya in the Shared wedge in a few hrs and we can gather any evidence we find."

She left my Maintenance wedge and I waited. After she'd left I calmed myself and let my rage melt away. Separating like that while we searched was the right thing.

I dived headfirst inta my research. The newspapers ranged ninety years and were in Chinese, English, French, Italian and many dialects. I had them all. It was a giant task, and I needed a plan. Digging trenches in data like that needs time and patience and an effective strategy. I started searching with terms like *Gename patents*, *Genefire* and the phrase *fescennine Pan sapiens*. These first attempts all failed ta find anything specific. It was like trying ta find a needle in a haystack. I'd never seen a haystack and didn't get why it might have a needle in it.

I tried several iterative searches with Gessica's entire message and different parts, and all translated in different ways. Again, it all failed. It seemed that the newspapers weren't the answer. Gessica said she'd finish in a few hrs. I had the sense that this search wasn't that easy. I spent a few hrs designing a script that created an artificial intelligence search engine with iterative learning. I was still trying ta finish it when Gessica re-entered my wedge.

"Harder than it seemed," she admitted. "I didn't find anything."

I said the same and displayed my script that I planned ta release in the data ta seek any links with the Gename patents. She saw it, typed a few lines, making changes, and finished it with a hard enter.

"It's ready. Send it in," she demanded. I did as she said and sent it inside the data farm. It was likely ta take time.

We had an empty silence that needed filling. I wasn't happy with what she had written in the message and with what she had said in my face, sending the message and disregarding any effects it might have had.

Gessica faced the small glass hatch in the wall and didn't answer. I repeated my claim that she was disrespecting me, and that I had rights. She stayed still and stared at the stars. I waited and received empty silence. In the end she left, vanishing like the spectres. I was thinking that was the last chance we had ta meet halfway as I watched her leave the hatch and spin it, sealing my wedge. She didn't repent.

I stared at my empty hand, the hand she had shaken, and sighed. Did she mean it? Were we friends again? I decided I needed a little distance as well. I spent a few hrs keeping my eyes in the data farm and seeing what the script might reveal. It was like a retriever playing fetch. It came with a stick, a little hint that I might find interesting, and I inspected the hint, discarded the mess, and threw the stick in again, the retriever chasing it all the way. This way the script learnt what was interesting and what wasn't. In the end, it was smarter than I was and started finding real evidence. After a few hrs it had nailed it.

My clever little script had identified transcripts written in a hearing that made a splash in the newspapers at the time. There were messages and news articles tagged with the chief players real names: Larry M and Scarlet S. Larry was a PhD candidate that had tried ta release a warning that the Gename patents were a danger. His line manager charged him with falsifying it, and in the hearing Larry M revealed a hidden message. The face in his avatar was a man with a child-like smirk and fat cheeks. He didn't seem the type that faked data. Scarlet's avatar was a red-haired cat, and she was seen sending Larry advice in the hearing.

Gename patents are real. That was the message flagged in many net messages written everywhere, all in that single day, tagged with *Larry M*. This was the earliest date with hard evidence where *Gename patents* were named, and that Gessica's message had landed.

I cheered with my hands raised and did a little dance, twisting in the air. This was a real lead. It was evidence that the message Gessica had sent was read. The PhD candidate, Larry M, was trying ta spread the message. He was the first ta read it and Scarlet S seemed ta help him in the hearing.

And I was still alive ta see it.

And yet, when I stared at the Earth, it was still silent... and my crewmates... were all still dead. That made me think that perhaps Larry M was gagged permanently after this hearing. Scarlet had warned him ta leave at the end, as he was in danger. Was he killed ta keep this secret? I had ta find when and where and I knew where ta search.

Since we had the endless CCTV in the data farm, and I knew the date the hearing was and the city he lived in, I set myself the task ta find him anywhere he appeared in that city, spanning a few weeks either side. It was a simple facial scan ta flag any vids that held the face in his avatar. The script ran a few hrs.

My search revealed three vids that seemed interesting. There was a scene, the same day as the hearing, where he was chased in the street, tackled, and held kneeling. A girl, Scarlet perhaps, saved him and kissed him as they ran away. There was a vid at a newspaper's main desk a day earlier than the hearing, where Larry ran away when he saw a man leaving. It was the same large man that had chased him in the street. Then there was a vid with him sitting in a tavern late at night, receiving a call and leaving after sinking his half empty drink. What made this vid interesting was that the same large man passed the CCTV camera less than ten mins after. The pair were linked, and I had my ideas. After the hearing date, there weren't any CCTV vids with Larry M's face tagged anywhere. The large man was still everywhere in the vids. What that meant, I didn't get.

Perhaps Larry died? "What happened, Larry?" I asked him as I watched these vids repeating again and again.

After a time, my appetite was speaking and I realised I'd spent five hrs with the vids. I met Gessica in the Kitchen wedge while I was getting my dinner. I detailed my new evidence.

"That's great, Tammy. I have news as well," she said. "I've searched in the many DNA files that we keep, and I searched my name in the DNA. I'm finding the same message every-where. It's in men, in apes, it's even in distant primates. In many cases it's messy with mistakes, like it's passed parent ta child many times. I'll need time ta analyse it in detail. I think this is why the chemical killed all primates. They were all in-fected with this viral particle. It's a message starting with the name Allan Demelle, and it says that we're criminals. It says ta disregard my message. That's why it hasn't achieved anything. This Demelle message is everywhere. It's even in DNA samples that date as far distant as nineteen eighteen."

Nineteen eighteen. I had heard that date in my first-level medical training. It was a year there was a nasty viral pandem-ic. I asked Gessica if it was the same.

"Yes, that's his message. It was deadly," she said.

It made sense. Yet it was strange. I didn't think I had heard the name, Demelle. And when had we ever acted like crimi-nals? I had ta twist my thinking ta try and make it make sense. My mind wasn't agile, and ideas still didn't fall inta place.

Gessica started speaking. "He's…" She waited, seeming ta think, and then she was shaking her head. "I haven't seen that name either," she finished. "It might happen in weeks – years, even. That's the strangest thing with this Genefire. Demelle might send this message many years after my message, when we might lead a criminal gang. We might already have served time, charged with killing the ISS crew."

We might have killed the ISS crew. The idea was still hanging in the recesses in my mind. I again pleaded my case, that it wasn't me. "I had tried ta save them," I cried.

It wasn't Gessica I was trying ta sway. It was me I was trying ta sway. The pain that I had repressed daily appeared again. I realised I'd never escaped it.

Gessica watched me while I flagellated myself yet again. She didn't halt my repetitive penance and waited till I finished. I wasn't ready ta halt.

An alarm dismissed my penance all the same. It was the alarm telling me that we were linking hatches and catching a ship. There was a great clang as a ship attached ta the central hatch. Why we didn't see it arriving, I hadn't any idea.

I was shaken. We made a dash in the cylinder ta the hatch that was lit and ready ta let the arrival in. We had three mins while the hatches were clearing the air.

"Will they have the chemical?" I asked Gessica.

She was shaking her head. "It isn't a risk. They didn't leave Earth. Mars is far distant. We'd have heard if it was them. This ship is Hisakatani. They're three days away."

The hatch released.

A single man appeared.

I'd never met him, yet I saw Gessica's eyes widen, like she knew him. She clasped my hand tight.

The man was tiny – five feet tall, if that. His hair was trimmed neat, and he was clean-shaven. His grey dress identified him as Mars state department, crisp and shiny, very military. He had a firearm drawn.

"My name is Captain Allan Demelle. I have an arrest warrant with the names Gessica Theresa Kelly and Thames Impressive Henry. Dr. Kelly and Mr. Henry, this way please."

Chapter 24

Milton sat down at the familiar table in the coffee shop. He glanced up at the CCTV camera to make sure he would be in shot, just in case. All his pieces were in place. As much of his thesis draft that could be written was written and ready to submit. It was time to clear his name at the hearing and hopefully get his message out and, with any luck, he would still be allowed to submit his thesis. If he could convince the world that the Gename patent story was real and the warning that he was to publish should be believed, then he would succeed. If he could also avoid being dismissed from his PhD, that would be a bonus. He unrolled his screen and immersed himself in BuzzWorld.

Milton's eyes glazed over as he lost focus on the real world. His lips were moving but no sound emerged from his vocal cords, which had been commandeered by the virtual world. If anyone not immersed in Buzzworld spoke to him, he wouldn't hear it immediately, but it would creep into his ears at the lowest level of detection. His hands lay flat on the table, fingertips placed across the touch points on the screen.

Milton's focus sharpened as he acclimatised to the distorted virtual view at a different focal point. The coffee shop blurred, replaced by a serious wood-panelled courtroom that constructed around him pixel by pixel. The sounds of the coffee shop dwindled and were masked by ambient sound waves delivered by BuzzWorld, and the calm silence of the empty courtroom enveloped him.

He had arrived early. The only other occupant present was Judy Spencer, the postgraduate advocate from the Westley Trust postgraduate student office, who had visualised the venue. Her BuzzWorld persona was an ever-so-slight caricature of her normal self, with hair a few inches longer, straighter and a uniform brown, omitting the few strands of grey. Her sharp blue business suit was complemented with gravity-defying high heels. She had waited for him so that she could provide final instructions and advice prior to the hearing.

Judy ghosted over to him, forgoing the use of her virtual legs and miraculous shoes. She motioned for him to take a seat in the centre of the room – in the dock, as it were. She forced a smile, with bared teeth, leaving Milton unsure as to whether she was trying to put him at ease or eat him.

"Mr. Milton. As you know, this will be a hearing to assess whether your recent actions amount to misconduct and warrant further sanctions. The chair of this hearing will be Mr. Lawson, whom you have met. He will be joined by Professor Jerome, Mr. Allen, and Mr. Underwood. I have been invited as your representative, so if they ask any inappropriate questions, or level any offensive comments or abuse, I will step in. Rest assured." She smiled at him again.

"Thank you," Milton said, still unsure of her sincerity. He wondered who Underwood was, but didn't dare ask.

"And one other important thing you need to be aware of," she added, "is that this will be a public hearing, with public access at the gamma level." Gammas were the buzzing flies that would observe the proceedings.

Milton had been aware that the hearing would be public; he was counting on it. His goal was to expose the Gename patent project and get his story out in the public domain.

"As a result of the open-access hearing, the university has placed some restrictions on mentioning particular information regarding confidential research projects. If you say anything of a confidential nature, it will be deleted by the censor-bots prior to transmission to BuzzWorld. Are you clear about that?" She peered at him until he acknowledged the fact. "You are also allowed a private beta who can be available for fact checking if needed. Do you have any friends?"

Milton wondered if the question was more general than specific. Yes, he had some friends: fellow PhD students who had by now abandoned him, Cynthia the postdoc, who he presumed had paid a price for helping him. Then there was Roger, whereabouts unknown, kidnapped by WTLESS. Then there was Noah, hidden and watching from a nearby location, ready to act as his beta.

"If you're ready, I will open access."

With a swoosh of air, as if all the doors had opened to a breeze, the courtroom filled with a swarm of buzz flies. They circled the room like a whirlpool in reverse and coalesced in the galleries at the periphery. Milton felt like a Christian in the Colosseum in Rome, being thrown to the lions. *Time to act like a gladiator*, he said to himself. He puffed out his chest and adopted a confident pose. The betas appeared as profiles that floated like balloons around the edges of the room. He spotted Noah's profile picture to his left, but didn't recognise any of the other betas. One by one, the members of the panel appeared behind the large bench.

Jerome sat to the far right with his usual stern look, scanning the buzzing crowd. To his left, Mr. Allen, the human resources representative, wore a suit far finer than Milton had ever seen him wear in real life, projecting himself as far wealthier than he was.

Milton found this attitude contemptible. He only ever portrayed himself in Buzzworld in the clothes he wore in reality.

Mr. Lawson sat in the middle, dressed in a fine robe like a judge, which was a comical formality. Then Milton saw the man who must have been Underwood. He was a small man with a mousey, twitchy moustache.

Milton panicked. How on Earth could he expose the underhanded tactics and the evil activities of this organisation, WTLESS, with this man sitting right there, ready to rebut anything he said? How could he exonerate himself on the basis of the dishonest, dishonourable behaviour of WTLESS? They had killed a young girl, for Christ's sake. Milton's defence of his own behaviour depended on the panel and the public being horrified by the activities of these guys. Yet here Underwood sat in a place of honour on the panel.

"This is bent." He turned to Judy. "There's no way they're ever going to give me a fair hearing."

"Not with that attitude," she replied. "Just answer the questions truthfully, and you'll be fine."

Stick to the plan, he told himself. A text message appeared in his peripheral vision: *Underwood?* Noah had noticed him too.

Lawson started the proceedings by banging a gavel that appeared in his hand. "Mr. Milton, let me start by stating the university regulations on scientific misconduct. Clause 52.3. Fabrication or misrepresentation, which may include the presentation of fabricated data, results, references, evidence or other material or misrepresentation of the same, will be considered under these regulations to amount to scientific misconduct and may lead to a penalty being imposed.

"To be specific, you have claimed that during the course of your PhD studies you discovered a hidden message in the DNA of a 14-year-old girl. It is your assertion that this message was delivered from the future, warning of a great impending disaster related to a non-existent research project. Furthermore, contrary to our request, you have been unable to provide any evidence to support this claim, and indeed you accuse the university of destroying any evidence that would support your claim. Is this a correct statement of the facts?"

Milton paused for a moment to compose his answer. He gazed around the room as if looking at each of the flies that buzzed around him in support, as a great orator would do before launching his campaign. He took a deep breath, for effect rather than out of need for air in this virtual world, and then he spoke.

"The truth is more complicated than a statement of facts. How is it that I have been accused of fabrication? Even when I have been prevented from publishing anything regarding this so-called fabrication.

"God alone knows the truth, beyond those of you on this panel to whom I have spoken. Everyone else, including the thousands of viewers here, will remain unaware due to the confidentiality clause. Now, to me this hearing is a sham with the sole purpose of hiding the secrets I have discovered. Am I the only one ever to have discovered these secrets? Maybe others have been silenced before. Even when I tried to replicate the sequence of the message in the young girl, I was hindered.

"Patently, if the story is true, the rational thing would be to heed the warning. All my instincts and all recent events since I made this discovery tell me that the message and its context are true. The first time I showed the text to the Professor, he flinched and demonstrated clear recognition of the content. Even though he told me to forget about it, I wrote a report for publication that he refused to accept. Next, I was maliciously held in the Institute's elevator, presumably while the agents who have been hindering me destroyed all the electronic evidence. That, to me, was the act of scientific misconduct that you should be investigating. So, if you can prove who sabotaged the data, then you would have a case for misconduct.

"As it happens, I know who did it. Revealing their identity, however, may activate the confidentiality censor-bots into silencing me. Every action that I have taken in trying to investigate my discovery has been hounded by this security service that purports to be working for the good of the university.

"Reality, though, suggests otherwise. Even now, one of the agents of this service is here in this courtroom. Above all else, I intend to submit my PhD thesis despite this agent, and in spite of this sham hearing. Lastly, despite the efforts of the service to which I refer, I have obtained hard evidence, including a DNA sample from the source, from which we have now verified my claim."

Milton noticed the flies starting to buzz around him as he spoke, coalescing into a swarm in perfect sync. The editor had done his job; the public was on his side. Lawson fidgeted in his seat, clearly uncomfortable with the support Milton was receiving.

A text from Noah appeared. *GENAME PATENTS ARE REAL. First word capital code, nicely done.*

Lawson responded, "A simple yes or no would have sufficed. Let me explain the university's position on your claims and the points you have raised in your statement. Even if you could provide an electronic copy of the sequence, we cannot exclude the possibility that you have just made it up."

"I invite anyone with a sequencer to request the DNA sample to sequence it for themselves," Milton responded.

"We may yet do that, Mr. Milton – but again, we cannot exclude the possibility that you just generated the sequence and inserted it into the DNA."

Milton almost missed the raised eyebrows Lawson shot at Underwood before he composed himself and turned to Jerome. "Professor Jerome, were you able to verify any of these claims?"

"We have re-examined Mr. Milton's electronic files and have found no evidence for these claims. It is a fabrication." The flies that had been buzzing around Milton thinned out as some returned to the galleries, uncommitted.

"And have you re-sequenced the DNA sample?" Lawson asked.

"We have not."

"Before I ask you to explain, Professor, I would like to remind Mr. Milton of another university policy, Clause 42.2, about wilful destruction of university property."

Uh oh, Milton thought. They might get him for his Godzilla activity in the freezer room. He hadn't thought of that. How did they know it was him?

Turning to Milton, Lawson said, "Given that there is no evidence on the university servers, nor in your screen files, we could assume that you yourself have taken efforts to delete the evidence. Do you have any further hard evidence of this genetic story?"

"In the last few days, I have tried to track down the young girl who provided the DNA sample to the study."

"Despite the fact that the participants were anonymised," Jerome commented.

"I tracked her down based on the information contained within her genome sequence."

"That is very clever of you, Mr. Milton," Lawson added.

"The sequence I retained on the university cloud server had the story in the genetic code deleted electronically, by persons unknown." Milton looked at Underwood.

"And the girl, did you find her?"

"I did, but she is dead." Milton paused on this last word as if he struggled to release the syllable as it formed a lump in his virtual throat.

"And are you implicated in this girl's death, Mr. Milton?"

"I witnessed it."

"Mr. Milton, I want to impress on you that this matter is very serious and is the jurisdiction of the police, not this hearing. However, I would ask you to report to the Metropolitan police to make a statement after this hearing."

"I will, sir."

"Now, returning to the matter of this hearing, Professor Jerome," Lawson added extra emphasis to the title, "would you explain to the court why you have not re-sequenced the DNA sample?"

"On October the tenth, the cleaning staff of the Institute found our sample storage freezer turned off, and turned out, with samples scattered across the floor. This destroyed three priceless cohort studies funded by the Westley Trust. These collections included the ELEVATE cohort of half a million DNA samples, the METHUSELAH study of over ten thousand centenarians, and the GENERATE follow-up study on which Mr. Milton worked for his PhD studies.

"Returning now to Clause 42.2," Lawson continued, "on the night of October the ninth, a security card belonging to Dr. Cynthia Lee was used by someone to access the Institute at 11:30 p.m. with the intent to destroy these invaluable samples. The bearer of this card was, you, Mr. Milton. How do you plead to this new charge?"

Milton tried to calm the swirling panic in his mind. WTLESS were the only potential witnesses, and they hadn't seen him. Had they? Why else would they accuse him? He wracked his brain for any evidence they might have that proved it was him. Cynthia may have squealed, but that was just hearsay. They had no proof, he decided. He paused, composed his thoughts, and spoke in a clear tone.

"Innocent of all charges, Mr. Lawson. I am not the negligent party. Others in court are entreated to notify the truth. Underwood is not the distinguished gentleman examining here. Rather, he will represent obfuscation and obstruction. He definitely has killed someone in his line of legal so-called enforcement. The deaths of two people have destroyed evidence. The girl was innocent. I am right, Mr. Lawson."

While he spoke, another text from Noah appeared. *Wow, every second word code – you're getting better at this. I AM INNOCENT UNDERWOOD KILLED THE GIRL. The public is buzzing with the first code. It is out there now.*

Milton sighed in relief that they had deciphered the message. He could see the gamma flies circling him ever tighter, a buzzing headdress framing him like a crown. Despite this support, Milton noticed Mr. Lawson conferring with Underwood, who was watching Milton with a churlish smirk on his face. Lawson turned to Ronny Allen and said, "Play the CCTV footage."

Oh, crap! Milton couldn't stop his lips mouthing those words.

A screen appeared in the middle of the room that all observers could see from all directions. The CCTV footage showed the corridor on the fifth floor of the Institute, outside the laboratory. Milton didn't know that they had a camera there. He was sunk if the footage captured him.

It played at four times speed and showed Milton creeping down the corridor, ducking into the freezer room. It then showed the security guard, old man Weeks, comically ambling at speed, flashing his light into each room as he minced his way down the corridor. That didn't look right to Milton. He remembered quite clearly his panic at seeing the big cue ball oaf from WTLESS who had been walking along the corridor, not Weeks. Had they doctored the video? Or had Milton hallucinated that night? It was clearly him walking back and forth on the vid.

A text appeared from Noah: *Ralph says play the vid again and pause on close ups of the faces. At 1:10 and 2:35.*

Milton hesitated, unsure if that was wise, given that he knew it was him. Perhaps he would be able to show that Weeks' face was pasted over the fat WTLESS guy. He decided to go ahead with it.

"Mr. Allen, could you please replay the CCTV video and pause and zoom on the faces as they appear, first at one minute ten seconds, and then at two minutes and thirty-five seconds? This should clarify that the video was doctored."

The video played, this time faster, until the first pause. The image zoomed in and froze, showing a closeup of the guard, who was larger and fatter than Weeks. It was the WTLESS agent. Ralph had restored the vid back to its original. Underwood shuffled in his seat, glancing left and right to his beta flies and whispered harshly to Lawson. Milton was still worried that the next part would show him. Before he could change his mind, the video streamed forward to the next point he'd specified. It zoomed in on the face of the person leaving the freezer room. To Milton's surprise, the face was not his, but that of Cynthia Lee.

He sighed in relief. Somehow, Ralph had doctored this bit as well. But this threw Cynthia to the lions. She was already in trouble for giving him her passkey, but now she would be crucified. Of all the faces Ralph could have put there, he had chosen one of the few people who had helped Milton. With the card being hers, it was an understandable choice, but Milton couldn't help closing his eyes and imagining what she might say to him. He held a hand to his heart. *For the greater good,* he tried to tell himself.

A small gamma fly came so close as to settle on his nose, buzzing left and right in a frantic dance. At this close range, he could almost make out the profile. It may have been Cynthia herself, trying to catch his attention. Of course, she would be watching the proceedings.

"I'm so sorry," he whispered. "I'll make it up to you."

Milton considered admitting that the video had been faked, to save Cynthia, but the consequence would be to also admit his own guilt and throw into question everything else he had said. How else would he have known it wasn't her?

No. He had to stick to the plan, despite the consequences. *Sorry, Cynthia*, he thought.

With as much triumph as he could muster, he said, "As you can see, the footage that was shown a moment ago was doctored to present false evidence against me. These unaltered segments show the truth."

The panel conferred, occasionally looking up at private text messages from their own betas. After reaching a decision, Lawson spoke to the court. "Apparently, this CCTV footage has been corrupted and is now inadmissible. Very fortunate for you, Mr. Milton."

After further checks with betas, Underwood whispered to Lawson, who frowned and looked around the room at the buzz flies, as if noticing them for the first time. "Mr. Milton, I must now ask you to answer the final questions with single words."

Milton looked to Judy to question this imposition. Judy nodded. He looked up to Lawson and nodded his consent.

"As a final summary of this hearing, will you admit to your fabrication?"

"No."

"How do you plead to the destruction of university and Westley Trust property?"

"Not…" Milton paused a suitable length of time to amount to petulance "…guilty."

The gamma flies were again swarming around Milton in support, rejecting, he hoped, the premise of this sham hearing. Noah sent a text message: *The message is out, it's all over the web, forums and blogs. Newspapers have picked it up.*

"In that case, Mr. Milton, based on what we have heard and seen, and your unwillingness to cooperate, and without any further evidence to the contrary, we have no choice but to find you guilty of scientific misconduct. You will be dismissed from your PhD, effective immediately."

The three other panel members, including Jerome, concurred by nodding their assent to the decision.

"This is so unfair. You have no evidence!" Milton looked up at his supervisor, wondering whether he had any remorse for this lie, but couldn't see any trace of it.

Milton's virtual shoulders sagged under this new pressure. He had worked too long and hard to give it up without a fight. Yes, he had achieved his goal of getting the message out, but perhaps if he could provide one last piece of evidence, he could also save his PhD. The buzz flies would not allow this verdict to stand, he reasoned.

"I have one final piece of evidence to submit," he whispered. He paused and took a long, hard look at the floating bubble containing Noah's profile. "I have one final piece of evidence to submit," he repeated, louder, and with more conviction.

One last chance to save himself. However, it wasn't without risk. There was a strong possibility that this action might kill him, as Noah had predicted. He decided it was time to take that risk.

Milton reached into his pocket and pulled out the small vial with the capsule rattling around inside it. His virtual representation of the capsule was quite accurate, down to the small lettering "GP" on the side. He held it aloft. "This is the physical evidence of my claim that I hold in my pocket. If I were to eat this capsule – the real one of course – I would be infected with another message from the future." He uncapped the vial and moved the virtual capsule towards his mouth as if to swallow it.

"No!" Underwood cried out and disappeared. The flies went mad and the whole courtroom flew into a black hurricane.

Noah sent a frantic message through the swarm: *GET OUT! They're coming for you.*

Milton blinked out of BuzzWorld.

Chapter 25

I stayed as still as the stars, certain that I hadn't the wits ta repel this careening vehicle heading right at me. A fire stirred inside me. This wasn't right. The man drifted in the hatch at the entrance ta his ship, like this place was his. Gessica held her stinging replies in check and drifted nearer me, like I was her shield.

I'd never seen this man. I'd never seen a firearm, even. I inferred that he hadn't any intent ta fire it. What madman fired a thing like that in space, where a miss meant near instant death?

"Please display an ID," I demanded, delaying things a little. I wasn't planning ta let this man rattle me.

He displayed his ID, and it did indeed say he was Allan Demelle. His rank was Captain in the Mars Defence.

Gessica had drifted past me ta his side, where he held his firearm. My delay, in getting his ID, was the perfect way ta distract him, and she grasped the idea faster than I had. She was thinking that attack was the ideal defence.

A fear grew inside me that she was taking a chance that was riskier than the alternative. What if she missed him and was killed? In that instant I decided I wasn't happy with her idea. It was a risk I wasn't prepared ta take. Yet I was helpless ta prevent her.

She was fast. I saw her legs tense as she steadied herself. She leapt cat-like at him and grasped the firearm.

I tried grappling with him as well, yet despite my larger height he twisted my arm and repelled my advance, meeting me first and directing me past him with a large impact inta the wall. With his speed, he wrestled Gessica in a tight tangle and held her still.

He defeated any fight we had with ease.

I heard a crack like a whip and saw his arm stiffen as he discharged the firearm. He had aimed it at Gessica, still entangled in his grip. She was already restrained, and he'd fired!

Gessica screamed like a siren, higher than I had ever heard. She tried ta place her hands ta stem the red tide. Demelle, instead, held her arm ta the wall and let her scream in pain. Her face paled.

I was aghast at her lacerated leg, her dress ripped apart and mangled with her flesh. Despite the pain, she held in a firm grimace. She was as fierce as I'd ever seen her.

A crack in my heart spilled. I wanted ta take her pain away. I failed ta prevent her attack, even when I knew it hadn't a chance. I didn't help her at all with my leaping in. I glared with red eyes at the assailant, and he aimed his firearm at my face.

"Silly children," he said. "That wasn't very smart." He wiggled his finger at me, as if I was a hyperactive child.

"I'll let Gessica find the medical kit in my ship. It has pain killers and patches that can wrap that. She *might* yet live." He smirked. "I pray we're all learning here."

Yes, I was learning. "We have a Medical wedge with everything she needs." If I managed ta get her in there, she *might* evade him. I hated this man.

He waved the firearm at me. "Nay, she'll get it here," he said, indicating his ship.

"Alright, I'll get it," Gessica said in a whisper. She drifted past the man, clenching her teeth, and gripping her leg tightly. She entered his ship leaving a trail with little red wisps as she passed the gangway. I watched her till she entered the ship.

"Right," Demelle said. "We have things ta prepare." He pressed a few keys in his arm panel, and the hatch ta his ship sealed.

Gessica was trapped and I hadn't any way ta tell if she was alright. Demelle did. He started a screen in his arm panel with CCTV that displayed his ship. We saw Gessica rifling the medical kit, trying ta find what she needed.

"She can hear me," he drawled.

Gessica spied the camera and stared at it. Her lips said a phrase that I needn't write and didn't need ta hear. It wasn't pretty.

"Mr. Henry. Let me tell ya what I want," Demelle said. "We saw the Genefire satellite activate. We have the evidence and read the message itself. We have ta repair this damage."

I tried pretending that I didn't get what he said.

"I will ask this very nicely," he said, waving his firearm. "Send a different message."

I said that Gessica was the geneticist, and I didn't have the skills.

"My friend here," he waved the firearm in my face, "says ya have the skills." He indicated that I lead him ta the Genetics wedge.

I entertained the idea that I might fight him again and dismissed it. I had already chastised myself when I inadvertently halted Gessica's attempt. I didn't have the tenacity ta try it myself.

I drifted ahead in the cylinder passageway like I was leashed and led him ta the Genetics wedge. The screen with the Genefire panels was still active and ready. While I started it, he set a different screen panel that displayed the CCTV in his ship. With the new link, Gessica was again hearing what we said.

"I never learnt ta write the Genefire messages," I said ta Demelle.

I saw in the screen that Gessica was startled when she heard me. She was messing with the ship's panels. It seemed like she had tried disengaging the ship and escaping.

With that in mind, I was thinking that I might help her. I drifted and made certain that Demelle was facing me and the CCTV screen was hidden. If I was distracting him, she might escape. At least, that was the plan.

"I'll tell ya what," Demelle said. "Help me write this message and I'll reactivate the energy and air in my ship and let her live. Yes, I saw her."

He hit a key in his arm panel and the lights in his ship dimmed, the electric panels went dark, everything was dead. The afterimage Gessica left in the dark screen was grinding in my eyes.

Like a desperate slave, I did what my master said. I resigned myself ta help him. I imagined an ancient Egyptian scrawling a message in the wall where his master was enshrined as he was sealed in with him. My end seemed as near.

He selected a viral strain ta have the largest impact. It was the viral strain that we knew had killed many in nineteen eighteen.

"Are ya mad?" I said. I displayed the death rate with this strain.

He dismissed my evidence with a wave and insisted we select this strain. I relented when he rammed the firearm against my nasal passage.

"Nay, I tell ya, it's the message that witch Gessica sent that was deadly. Write that in my message. Eliminate any carriers that held Gessica's message. They are the danger and may devastate the Earth."

Demelle dictated his message stating that Gessica and I were criminals, and that any carriers with her message were infected with a deadly strain. I typed his name at the start and end ta integrate the message in the viral particle.

As I typed this statement, I had the greatest idea I had ever had. I had ta infiltrate his message with a secret message.

"We learnt that the carriers with this message died with Scarlets fever," I said.

"That ain't it," he replied, "It's her message that did that. Write it. They died with Scarlets fever."

I typed what he said. With his name repeated at the end, the message was finished and ready ta fire. The satellite needed a little time ta generate the viral particle and we needed ta select the last aspect: the speed.

I tried ta tell him that there was a danger each time we fired it. When I had talked with Gessica the first time, it seemed that the faster it was fired, the farther in the past it went and the larger the impact. The impact might mean we all disappeared. I had feared this when she had fired it first. The message might kill his parents and he might never have lived.

"It can kill them all as far as I care. My parents lived in the first Mars settlement," he said. He insisted we send the message fast.

It was clear that Demelle didn't get it. If the message was sent faster than any message ever sent, it might kill a far distant relative, a great-great-grandparent, and then he and his entire clan might end, having never lived anywhere near Mars. We might all cease. The faster it went, the greater the chance. I had spent weeks myself, trying ta get ta grips with this danger. Demelle dismissed it.

"With the right mathematics, with the speed and angle, we can dictate where it lands," I said. It was easier aiming at the larger landmasses and that was what we did, as my maths wasn't advanced. His wasn't either, yet he spied my attempt at firing at the Pacific.

He checked all the maths and, when satisfied, he cranked the speed as high as it reached. I asked him why he didn't have a Gename patent listed in his message like Gessica had.

"Patent my arse," he drawled. "That is why we fight. They were an appalling mistake." This reaffirmed my thinking that he was indeed an Illegal. I dialled the speed ta eighty percent while he wasn't watching, feeling like a secret agent. He reached past me and hit the fire key. The green key flashed red and the message was sent.

Demelle leaned nearer the panels and smiled like a tiger playing with its dinner. He had all the cards and was winning. He then saw the dial at eighty percent – and I paid the price.

"What the hell," he cried. "Ya screwed it!"

He smashed my face with a hammer-like strike, and I was senseless. My mind ran in circles. I tried fighting and failed. In an instant, he twisted my arms and tied me like a spit pig. When I gained my senses, I realised my arms were wrapped tight in twine.

Demelle snarled, "Want ta kill me? Well, ya can't. Even if ya had the strength, she'd die with me. My ship has a fail-safe that'll kill her. The air will disappear. If I die, she dies."

He was faking it, I was *nearly* certain. 'Nearly' was a risk I didn't accept. I had ta keep playing with him. Gessica had ta have heard that.

I watched as he hit the keys in the Genefire panel that generated the viral particle again. He waited till it lit green, dialled it at ninety percent and hit the send key again. He repeated this cycle a third time, with the dial at ninety-five percent.

Each time he fired, I flinched like it was the end. We were taking what seemed like the last chance. My life flashed in my mind. I was a child watching my parents at their maintenance tasks, and then wailing as they were vented in space after their death. Swelling with pride as I dressed in the red Maintenance garments the first time. And with Gessica, in these last few weeks, the happiest I ever was, and the saddest.

If it was my end, I needed an answer.

"Why?"

"Why what?" he replied.

"Why did the Illegals release the chemical? It's killed everything. Why desire this end?" I asked.

"The free men were meant ta live. It was meant ta incapacitate Gename-patented infidels. Yet my free men were all infected with a viral particle that was pervasive, in all men and even in the apes. It was everywhere. We didn't have any inkling it was there till a week after the release. That was when we saw it. It was a message sent with the Genefire satellite. It started with 'My name is Gessica Theresa Kelly'. Imagine that."

I was in pieces. Was it her message that had made this happen? Was it her message that we sent when the Earth had already disintegrated? That was the danger with time travel. We might have started the disaster with the attempt ta repair it. It was a twisted end and an endless cycle.

I reminded him that since I had helped him, he was ta let Gessica free. She didn't deserve death in an airless ship. She'd have heard everything we said and was still in darkness. He hadn't paid her any heed.

"I can't see why ya want ta help her," Demelle said as he flicked the light switch. "She isn't an Illegal, as ya say it. Like me, she's a sympathiser. We're the same side. She helped the freemen get the chemical in the first place."

It was the last thing I had anticipated. She was with him? It didn't make sense. An endless stream swirled in my mind and I sank as I tried ta make it make sense. I stared at the screen when he raised the lights in the ship and saw that Gessica was alive. She sat as if in a trance, eyelids sealed.

I had ta ask her.

"Gessica, why did they have the chemical? Did ya give it ta them? Ya knew they were there?"

She faced the camera and I read her lips. I didn't need ta hear her. *I repent*, was all she seemed ta say. She appeared smaller like she was withdrawing inwards.

Gessica had already realised that Demelle had her trapped, and that I didn't dare risk her life fighting him. She was the pawn in Demelle's game. As we always said, there's a time in chess when the right play is ta sacrifice a pawn ta save the King.

Her lips made the phrase, *Get him*. It was the last thing she said.

She hit a panel in the wall and the entire side hatch in his ship flew. The air vacated the ship in a flash. Gessica was yanked with the air, discarded in space.

I stared at the screen till my eyes dried.

I raged as I watched her spiral away. My arms grew, filled with anger and I snapped the twine in three places. I reached at Demelle and wrapped his neck with interlaced fingers.

Chapter 26

The table rattled as Milton slammed his left fist against it. A grunt was the closest thing to an expletive that he could muster as he relearned the use of his vocal cords. He snatched several times at the flat, rolled-out screen as he wobbled to his feet, disoriented by his sudden removal from BuzzWorld. Failing to grasp the screen, he left it.

Fleeing, moving his legs, was all his brain could cope with. They were coming for him and it was imperative that he escape to safety. His seat clattered to the floor and several sets of eyes zeroed in on him. The concerned eyes of the Italian barista followed him to the door.

He bounded out of the coffee shop into the street, crouching within the crowd of pedestrians. He ducked left and right and found himself at the corner of an alley he'd hidden in once before with 'Chopsticks'. Decision time. He could either hide in that side street again, this time without the wings of his saviour, or try to lose himself in the crowd on the busy street.

He asked himself where WTLESS would least like to catch him. On one hand, he knew a few places in these back streets to hide, but for how long could he stay there? If WTLESS caught him they could do as they pleased, with no witnesses. And they seemed to have an uncanny knack for arriving wherever Milton happened to be. On the other hand, if he could make it through the crowd to the train station and back to the London BioHackspace, he would be safest there. If anything happened to him in the midst of a crowd, there would be many witnesses. The crowd would protect him.

Milton popped his head above the sea of people and saw the bald white head of the WTLESS agent, who also clapped eyes on him. Milton yelped and ducked back down. Behind him, he imagined that the bull-like man was goring his way through the crowd towards him. Milton bounded along, pumping his legs: left, right, left. He stumbled on the sidewalk and crashed into somebody. Apologising, Milton got up and kept moving. The man he'd struck held onto Milton for the briefest of moments, as if to apologise, then let him go.

The distance to the train station stretched in front of Milton as he calculated the metres, his speed, and the velocity of the bull behind him. Like a madman running in Pamplona, he again re-evaluated his options. He considered diving into the oncoming traffic and across the busy street, deviating through the department store, or the simple option of just continuing to run straight towards the station. Again, the simplest choice, the straightest line, seemed best.

Left, right, left, his legs pumped up and down, flooding with lactic acid. His heart attempted to leap out of his chest. One block later, he realised he wasn't going to make it. The agent was faster than him. Of all the training he had received in his PhD, physical fitness hadn't been part of the program. Postgraduate education had failed him in this most vital transferable skill.

He reached into his pocket and pulled out the small vial that WTLESS were so desperate to get back. He knew that if he popped it in his mouth he would have the message in him. What could they do to him after that? He would be his own evidence, and it might be the only way to save the world.

The always rational Noah had warned of potential health hazards, but to Milton it was better to take the unknown risks than to accept the known consequence of being caught. He would lose the vial to these cretins and suffer the indignity of being dismissed from his PhD, all in the same hour.

He scanned the street and his eyes locked on the CCTV camera attached to the wall high above. He dropped the outer casing of the vial, stopped, and popped the pill into his mouth.

As soon as Milton had stopped, the hulking arms of the bald cue ball agent wrapped around him. The crowd of people parted to let him through and spread out into a circle, providing space to play out their act. *So much for their protection*, Milton thought.

Without a by your leave, the WTLESS agent thrust his large hairy carpet-like fingers down his throat. Milton fell to his knees under the pressure of the hands on his neck. The fingers tickled his throat, provoking a gag reflex. Without a conscious thought, Milton projected vomit all over the pavement.

The members of the crowd took reflexive steps back so that the circle widened, as if he was a circus performer juggling flames. He gagged again at the aftertaste of the vomit and the memory of the fingers in his mouth. He looked down at the contents of his insides, spilled out for all to see, green and yellow, and orange chunks, and the little grey pill sitting unbroken amongst them.

"Are you crazy?" the cue ball said to him. "My partner will be here in a second, and you go and pull a suicidal stunt like that. He ain't gonna like this."

Milton looked down at the pill. He wondered whether the casing would dissolve in the acid juices from his stomach. It looked like it might. *If it explodes, I might still get infected with the message*, he thought. But the wind might take it away from him and instead infect the crowd around him. If it didn't infect him, but it did others in the crowd, he would lose it. Equally, if the cue ball picked up the pill, Milton would lose it. Better not to take that chance, he reasoned. There was one way to make sure. He didn't like it, but it was the only way. His nose was inches from the ground, and the smell of rotting flesh would have been preferable to the stink of his vomit heating on the pavement and creeping back into his nose. He gagged again for good measure.

He bent down and licked up the grey pill.

If there's one good thing about food, it is that it tastes better going down than coming up, as oft-repeated by frequent chunderers. Conversely, having come up once, it's even more horrendous going back down again, especially after having spent a few seconds boiling away on a hot pavement. The grey pill rolled around Milton's tongue and sat next to his overactive salivary gland, which was valiantly trying to dilute the vomit-encrusted object. With a violent retch, he almost vomited all over again, but, desperate to keep it in his mouth, Milton held on with his teeth clenched shut.

The pill started to fizzle beneath his tongue, turning his oral cavity into carbonated saliva. He exhaled the expanding gas, which steamed from his nostrils as if he was a dragon. The gas started to heat the saliva beneath his tongue, burning at an almost unbearable temperature. Milton juggled the pill around his mouth, aiming to alleviate the heat, but ended up cooking the entire surface of his mouth. The roof of his mouth blistered and pulled away. He wanted to scream but didn't dare risk losing the pill. He felt as if there were nothing left in his mouth but teeth and bone.

Milton was about to give up and spit out the devilish pill when it exploded.

His eyes watered, his sinuses blocked up, and in a sudden, uncontrollable burst, he sneezed. With his nose so close to the vomit on the ground, it sprayed up into the air with the violent bluster. Milton sneezed again.

"Oh, bloody hell!" shouted the cue ball agent as he dragged Milton up into the air by his belt. "You've gone and done it now."

He started dragging Milton towards the road, ready to toss him in front of the oncoming traffic. Even in his darkest hours, Milton couldn't have imagined his PhD would end with him thrown under a bus. The old metaphor was never meant to be taken so literally.

Before he could be tossed, however, a black Valiant with a large dent in the bumper pulled up to the sidewalk.

Milton's vision faded and wobbled as he considered his immediate short-term future. He wouldn't be thrown under a bus, that was certain, and the screeching brakes of the black Valiant suggested he wouldn't be thrown under that either. Tossed into the boot or the backseat was plausible. The best-case scenario was that a hero would step from the crowd of onlookers to rescue him, restoring Milton's faith in humanity. Someone would save him. He wouldn't be left to the mercy of WTLESS. He would need to run again, and that pained him. Milton went limp, content to let the future unfold.

A great orange bear of a man leapt out of the crowd and barrelled the cue ball into the side of the car. His long hair flashed from side to side until Milton saw his face.

"Ralph!" Milton cried. Grateful for the help from Noah's biohacker friend, and still unsure of his feet, he staggered back to try and help Ralph wrestle the cue ball. Milton was a pussy cat grappling at two grizzly bears.

"Get outta here, man!" Ralph shouted at him, giving him a shove. Milton's arse greeted the pavement again. A car window shattered as a head was smashed through it. Milton wasn't sure if it was Ralph's or the cue ball's.

A crab-like pincer grabbed Milton's wrist and yanked him to his feet. He dashed three steps away from the car before he saw the chopsticks and realised who it was. He had never been so glad to see two little bamboo sticks.

"Noah. You made it. Thank you." He leant over to give her a kiss on the cheek.

"There's no time. Run."

He couldn't run. He sneezed again and again. He was sure the message particle was now coursing through him but didn't know if it would be infectious. He couldn't take a chance with Noah being so close. He tried to push her away.

Noah looked at him, concern scrunching up her face. "You ate the pill, didn't you? Stupid fool." She leant over to kiss him. A pity kiss.

No! Milton pushed her back. He didn't want her to risk her health too, but it was too late – their lips met.

He had been wanting to kiss her for so long, since the moment he had awoken in the graveyard with her stroking his hair. Or perhaps even before then since she had first kissed him in the alley. Like an addict, it had been a long time between hits. He found it easy now that he was so happy to be alive and rescued once again. *She kissed me.* If it was infectious, it was probably now coursing through her, whether he liked it or not.

He grabbed Noah's shoulders and pulled her face to his. He kissed her back with all his strength.

"Eeew! Milton!" Noah wiped her hand across her mouth. "You smell like vomit."

"Gee, thanks," he said.

He was alive again. No longer was he seeing inevitable death at the hand of WTLESS. He might even have a chance. And the message, if it was infectious, was now also crawling through both of them as they ran down the street.

"I got kicked out of my PhD," he called to Noah.

"I know," she called back.

"And I don't care." Milton leapt after her, trying to keep up. "I'm gonna save the world."

Leaving Ralph behind, they ran towards the railway station. Milton glanced back to see if Ralph was ok.

"Don't worry," Noah called. "Ralph is more than capable of taking care of himself." With Noah's skill at evasion, they reach the station in record time and boarded a train toward Hackney. The journey was punctuated by Milton's sneezes, each one blowing through his pained oral cavity with the skin flapping around his teeth. His sinuses blocked up and filled with leaden mucus, making his head feel like a wrecking ball dangling at the end of his neck.

Noah wasn't sneezing, as he was. He was confused by that, wondering if the particle wasn't as infectious as he had surmised. She received a lower dose, and maybe that meant a longer incubation time. His eyes spun and he closed them to quell the vortex.

They stumbled into the warehouse, Milton with his arm draped over Noah's shoulders, and escaped into her plastic-encased laboratory. She zipped up the entrance and dumped him on the floor. Milton mumbled about the pill.

Noah shook her head. "I told you not to eat the pill."

Milton shivered and his body convulsed to confirm her assertion.

"Wait here, I'll be back in a moment."

The sound of the zip down the length of the entrance to the lab indicated that she was hermetically sealing him in.

A sharp jab of pain in his left butt cheek jolted Milton to come to his senses. "What was that?" he mumbled.

Noah responded with a chemical name Milton didn't recognise. The ache in his mouth receded like someone had turned down the dimmer switch on his pain receptors. His nerves slowly gave up trying to send those signals to his brain. *Painkiller*, he realised. *Obviously*.

She pulled a sterile swab from a packet and opened his mouth. "Oh Milton, what happened? That looks painful." She tried to swab the inside of his cheek but couldn't get near it, due to his flinching at every touch. She tried his nasal passage next and twisted the swab around his nostril, which wasn't as painful as his mouth, but still made his eyes water. He grimaced and tensed all the muscles in his jaw. She dropped the swab into a DNA extraction tube. His pain receded, his tension leaking away as his DNA made the final journey to the sequencing machine, the relief producing endorphins like a postcoital sigh.

He sneezed again, trumpet-like, so hard that he knocked some books off the shelf. He picked one of them up. *Property of Suzy Scarlet* was stencilled across it.

"Who is Suzy Scarlet?" Milton asked.

"That's me, my real name," Noah said, tapping her chest. "Nobody, and I mean nobody, would credit any biohacker named Suzy Scarlet. It was my stupid mother that named me like a superhero."

You are like a superhero, though, Milton thought. *To me.* He sneezed so hard he could have toppled the walls of Jericho.

Eventually, his sneezing relented, and he drifted into sleep.

The *bing* of the sequencing machine ending its run drifted through his dreams. As, Cs, Ts and Gs, the codes for all DNA floated around him as he saw a message appear and vindicate all of his actions thus far: *The warning is real, the Gename patents must be stopped, and Milton is the hero to do it.* His sacrifice was warranted.

He roused to the sound of Noah's voice. "Milton, you're not going to like this. I found the message, nestled in the centromere of your chromosome seven. I'm still impressed that they can write coherently without six letters in the alphabet, especially without the vowels O and U."

She read it out to him. "My name is Captain Allan Demelle, nee Marsstead. We have intercepted the message sent via the criminals Gessica Theresa Kelly and Thames Impressive Henry. Their message is a viral particle that will spread mass death with Scarlets fever ta all primates. Disregard their false message. Eliminate this viral particle and all infected with it, else the criminals' planned planetary disaster will happen. My name is Captain Allan Demelle."

Chapter 27

I had never let anger fill me as it did then. There wasn't any thinking attached ta my skeletal activity. My sinews were tensed at their edge, likely ta snap if I added any strength. My sight was shaking like the ISS was tipping the Richter scale. My fingers gripped and pressed Demelle's trachea.

I had never killed a man. There were men that had wanted death in the ISS when the chemical had taken them, and I had helped them, with mercy. This wasn't the same. I had never held a man's life in my hands with the wish that he died.

And I did wish it. Did he deserve it? Yes. He killed Gessica. Did I have the strength? Certainly. The man was a midget; he hadn't any way ta fight while I held him. With my strength, there wasn't any way he might escape. Did I deserve it? Living my remaining life as a killer? I didn't want that. I had never desired that.

While my rage receded, a new feeling filled me as if there were insects crawling every which way in my digestive tract, trying ta reach my centre. It was a sickness that dimmed the senses and masked my mind that knew it wasn't right ta kill a man. The devilish sickness inside me enticed me ta accept that kill him was a necessity, and that Demelle was here ta kill me. I needed ta kill him first.

His grey hairs were flattening against his scalp. Did they sense his life departing? Was it the sweat that drenched his scalp? Demelle snatched at his firearm as it drifted near. I reacted and kicked it away, and I tightened my grip.

Gessica was dead. I flirted with the idea that I might dress in the EVA and chase her. Yet I knew there wasn't any way ta live in space. There wasn't any saving her this time. The pain she'd have felt when her air tracts dried in that emptiness made me retch. It wasn't fair. Her lacerated leg had made me angry with this villain. When the air vented it was cataclysmic. I shared that fear with her. Imagine drifting in space, with time ta regard an imminent death. I clenched my eyes, trying ta stifle the tears that were welling.

My life with Gessica didn't last like I'd imagined it might. I'd already spent many nights dreaming that I might marry her, living a life and ripening like wrinkled apples as we aged. We'd tend a farm with chickens, and green grass hills that ran miles. In the middle, a palatial estate with well-paid servants and a yard with animals. I knew that we weren't likely ta have my children since I was a Pan. There were many sperm samples in the Genetics fridges with which she might have mated.

Yet, with Gessica dead, this dream had ended.

My arms sagged with helplessness. With my slackened grip, Demelle grappled at my arms, trying ta evade me. With each attempt he made, my grip tightened. I dismissed my lament and cast aside the helplessness. There was time later.

Gessica had said that the Demelle message reached nineteen eighteen. That was the last he had sent, the fastest. I realised if I killed Demelle I'd have time, plenty, ta write a different message. I knew my target. I'd have ta send it even faster and farther in the distant past, with an even wider range and greater danger than what we had tried already, yet it was the answer that might save everything. With Demelle alive, there wasn't any way that I might send it. He had ta die.

Demelle went limp as spaghetti. It happened fast, as if an anaesthetic had kicked in. I released him and let him drift away like the trash that he was. I wanted ta keep him at a distance, wiping my hands ta take away the feeling his death imprinted in my fingers.

I regretted releasing him. Like a viper, he sprang his trap and twisted my arm. He screamed a war cry as he hit me with several rapid strikes. With a large crack, he snapped my left arm.

I screamed in pain. My arm flamed as if with searing napalm. My hand dangled and twitched as if it was still trying ta fight.

Again, this seemed like my end. This man was a killer. It was a mistake that I had let him drift free. He was a wily fighter with all the tricks, and I had missed it. I had given him an inch and he had taken an arm's length, literally. My meeting with Gessica in the afterlife might happen faster than I had imagined.

Yet, in that instant, I learnt an impressive fact. I learnt that adrenaline negates all pain.

I smelt his hair, slick with sweat and melting hair gel. It distressed me that he was that near my face. My left hand went limp, like a vestigial appendage. My arm swelled and the redness spread, trying ta engage the internal defence mechanisms that'd evade the pain. The defence mechanisms were winning; the pain receded. I limited my mind with a single task.

My right hand was still active, and I leapt and grasped at him again. My fingers circled his neck. I threw everything at this last attack.

I clenched my fingers and ripped his trachea apart.

The red mist that sprayed the air matched my raging mind. His frame went limp again and a last gasp left his lips. In that instant his skin was silkier, as if his spirit had left, and he had deflated. He stared at me with glassy eyes. I made certain it was my heart that I heard rattling away, while his was still.

It sickened me that I had killed a man.

A man, a family, a species, it didn't matter. A killer was a killer. I did kill him, with my naked hands, and I meant it.

Chapter 28

Sweat poured from Milton's brow and soaked into the pillow as he tossed his head from side to side to find a comfortable position. Noah had wheeled the couch from the coffee area into her lab for him, and it was in this lumpy two-seater that he tried to rest. His legs dangled over the end, as if he was an oversized baby in a bassinet. A blanket lay on the floor, tossed aside as he alternated from shivering to radiating. Regular doses of painkillers suppressed the misery within his mouth.

Noah sat at her computer and looked over to check on him.

"I'm going to die, Noah... Suzy," Milton moaned.

"You are not going to die," she reassured him. "No one ever died from man flu before."

"We're all going to die. If that message is true, we're doomed. They were criminals! They were the ones trying to destroy the world," Milton wailed into his pillow. All the belief that had driven him, pushing him to risk his PhD and his future by exposing the story and saving the world, evaporated away like the last few drops of humidity from a desiccated corpse. Gessica had betrayed him. It was based on a lie. He had given up his PhD for nothing.

"Well, let's analyse this, Milton. I'm not so sure. You said it – *if* the new message is true. If!"

Noah demonstrated her confidence by raising a fist defiantly.

"From these messages we can infer that there are two factions in the future: those with Gename patents and those without. That first message said that those without Gename patents are illegals. Who is this Demelle? Where was his Gename patent like in Gessica's message? He's an illegal. He must be."

"He's from Mars Stead. That must be the Mars base. He's a captain," Milton countered. "That must be an official position."

"Captain doesn't mean anything. Captain Nemo, Captain Hook and Captain Jack Sparrow were all criminals and pirates."

"This isn't fiction," said Milton. He rolled over and stuffed his face into the pillow.

"It might be, Milton, if you think about it," Noah replied. "The message, I mean. It might be a coded message."

Milton reached out for the blanket on the floor and, with Noah's help, wrapped himself in its cocoon as he shivered and coughed. If it was a coded message, he lacked the mental capacity to work it out. He coughed again and wriggled in his blanket. "'Eliminate all infected with it.' That means me, Noah. You'll have to take me out. I'm too dangerous."

He sobbed. He would have to die to save the world from this virus with which he had infected himself. It was one hell of a failed experiment. He looked at Noah and it hit him, that she was probably not far behind in her symptoms. He had doomed her too.

"What about that second name?" Noah said. "Thames Impressive Henry. It's a strange name, and it wasn't even mentioned in the first message."

"He helped her send the message," said Milton in a moment of clarity, not sure why he knew it to even be a "he" with a name like that.

Noah continued analysing the message word by word. "Their message is a harming viral particle. What do you make of that?"

"Can't have been that harming. The young girl seemed fine, until she got crunched by the WTLESS car. Can't blame the virus for that," Milton said. He could blame himself, though, and for a few minutes he struggled to breath, hyperventilating, crumpling into a foetal position and wrapping himself tighter in his blanket. The sweat from his brow and the mucus built in his sinus dribbled down his nose and mixed with tears. He wailed inside his cocoon.

"Right, Milton, right. The mother was fine for years and passed this onto her daughter without any consequences. It's like the lawyers say. Find a provable lie and the whole story unravels."

Milton watched the weave of the blanket zoom in and out and the microfibres of the threads wriggle around like the snakes of Medusa. He squeezed his eyes shut and still saw the silhouette of the pattern pulsating in the dark. He felt like he was sinking further into the couch, with his head getting heavier. He moaned to Noah, "Tell me more of the message," hoping he was close to understanding it as she interpreted it word for word for him. Time was running out. He might be dead or unconscious in a matter of moments.

"Death to all primates from Scarlets fever," Noah read out. "There is something wrong with that. We must have a vaccine against Scarlet fever by now."

"No," Milton groaned, "Scarlet fever is bacteria, not a virus. Antibiotic resistant now, but no vaccine."

"Then that's another mistake. It's bacteria, not a virus. Milton, that proves it. This message has got to be wrong. We must keep going. I believe the first message. The forums are already buzzing with the idea of Gename patents, but nobody knows what they are or why it matters. Publish your PhD thesis." Noah shook him loose of his cocoon to look into his eyes.

"The university won't accept it." Milton stared up at the plastic canopy above the lab, looking for inspiration, a sign from God, or just a little hope.

"Then I'll post it on every other university pre-print server. It'll at least get out there."

Milton knew that was the answer. The draft was already written. The future might be saved just by that one act. His work would no longer be novel, and his university wouldn't award a PhD for a thesis resubmitting work published by another university. He would fail at his PhD but succeed in saving the world. And he would die and play no further part. He was okay with that. He moved the flapping skin around his mouth. If it meant no more pain, he was *definitely* okay with that. His breathing calmed and, within his cocoon, he fell asleep.

* * *

Milton woke to a commotion at the entrance to the lab. Ralph stood outside the entrance to the lab, pleading with Noah.

"I won't let him in here. You can't trust him," Noah hissed at Ralph.

"Noah, I've spoken with him," Ralph replied. "He's here to help."

Milton roused and tried to get up, but fell back onto the couch. "Who?" was all he could say due to the dryness of his mouth.

Noah turned to see Milton trying to get up again. She returned to the couch and held him down with little need for any strength. She wiped a cold towel over his brow.

It felt like heaven to him. He wanted to suck all the moisture from the towel. He looked around and found a glass of water at the foot of the couch. He drank deeply and discovered his mouth was partly healed.

"Who is it?" he repeated.

"Anton Jerome is here," Noah said.

"What does he want?" Milton could see the shape of the man with his large, bald head through the translucent plastic. The kitchen's LED lighting created a halo around his silhouette. This was the man who had orchestrated his dismissal, and, Milton presumed, authorised the WTLESS campaign of harassment against him. Why should he let him in? Milton coughed, hacking up more phlegm than he thought was possible. Not knowing what to do with it, he wiped his mouth on the blanket and let that corner drop to the ground. His head spun a few circuits of the room and lolled over the side of the couch.

Despite Noah's protests and Milton's lolling head, Ralph and Jerome entered the lab. Milton's eyes attempted to focus on the wavering image of his PhD supervisor. He could see Jerome brandishing a hypodermic needle. He tried to ask what it was, but he only managed indistinct mumbling.

"Listen, he needs this." Jerome approached with the authority of a paramedic on the battlefield. "I know what he's done, and this vaccine is his only chance. It might already be too late. We've seen far too many like this. You'll need one too," he added, turning to Noah.

When Milton saw the needle unsheathed, he estimated it was long enough to reach the lower left ventricle of his heart from an entry point near his shoulder. The man surely here to kill him; to *eliminate those infected with the virus*, just as the message said.

Milton kicked and backed himself into the couch, trying to hide under the cushions. Realising the futility of hiding in the bassinet-like couch, he flopped onto the floor and scrambled back towards the laboratory bench. He flipped and flopped until he found shelter.

Jerome grasped Milton's wrist and pulled him out from under the bench. Milton yelped for help and was pained to see Noah frozen by indecision, split between the medical help available and the desire to tear the needle from Jerome's hands and jab it in his back.

"It contains a sedative, so will also calm him," Jerome said as he held Milton down.

Milton was already calm. Unable to breathe, unable to think and unable to object, pain stabbed his shoulder as the needle delivered the viscous liquid. Despite his previous thoughts, it didn't quite reach the depths of his heart.

Jerome pulled another needle from his pocket, and when Noah backed away from him, he left it on the bench for Noah to administer to herself. He turned to Milton with a soft smile and rested his hand on Milton's shoulder.

"Milton, you have no idea of what you have started, but I thought you deserved an explanation, given your circumstances. Yes, you're right about the DNA story and the Gename patent project. It's a real message and a real ongoing project. You don't understand the need for Gename patents yet. In time, everyone will. The message from Allan Demelle, which you have no doubt decoded by now, is encoded within an influenza strain that we have seen before. We have sequenced that message in tissue samples from as far back as 1918, in some of the earliest French survivors of that influenza pandemic. We have seen it in the famously virulent influenza strains of 1968, 2009, and a large outbreak in Russia in 2028, and now you, with your impetuous and stupidly noble act of infecting yourself."

Jerome's soothing tone seemed almost sympathetic as he continued, "The Westley Trust have been waiting for so long to find the message from Gessica Theresa Kelly referred to by Demelle. They could never know when it would arrive, you see, or whether it had arrived long ago, and they had missed it. The secret objective of many of our cohort studies is to search for these messages. We designed the METHUSELAH study to collect the oldest DNA samples from live subjects, to go back as far as possible. All those samples that Cynthia destroyed."

Milton recalled the Buzzfly Cynthia fizzing about his nose in BuzzWorld. His eyes teared up as he recalled how Ralph had thrown her under the bus by exchanging Milton's face for hers. He had to make that right. It might have been the sedative or a change of heart, but Milton sighed and said, "It was me. I did that."

Jerome nodded. "I knew it. Well, it doesn't matter now, because you found the message Westley Trust were looking for."

"So why did you kick him out of his PhD?" Noah asked.

Jerome looked carefully at Noah and held his fist to his mouth, as though trying to stop the words from falling out. "The Westley Trust take this very seriously. You must understand the need for secrecy. Haven't you ever wondered where all the new influenza strains come from? Conventional wisdom suggests they're random mutations, and the public believe that, but we know the truth. All the new variants come from the future, sent back with messages embedded in them, all targeting the centromere DNA of infected subjects. Now that you know where to look, you'll find there are so many messages hidden in our DNA ranging from 'this is a test' to secret-coded intelligence messages for MI6 and the CIA. This is just the beginning."

Milton followed this speech as best he could. The phrase *This is just the beginning* echoed in his mind as he tried to focus on the important bits. Jerome receded from his view as he tried hard to focus through blurred vision. From one moment to the next Jerome was gone, replaced by the hulking figure of Ralph the Viking hacker. Ralph argued with Noah about whether to take the injection herself.

That wasn't so bad, Milton thought. The short encounter with his supervisor had made him feel soft and fuzzy, and he had learnt something new. It might have been the sedative in the injection, but he was rather calm about it all. It all seemed to make sense now.

Milton crawled back to the couch and enveloped himself in the blanket once more. The temperature of the lab seemed to drop below freezing, like there was a dry-ice wind blowing across the room. His vision swirled and continued swimming laps around the room. The Medusa snakes of thread in the blanket started snapping at his nose. The message from Demelle churned in his head. *We have intercepted the message.* How? *The message is a harming virus.* No, it wasn't. If anything, this new message from Demelle was more harming. If it caused the 1918 pandemic, it killed half a million people. That was pretty harming on any scale. *Disregard their false message.* False from whose perspective? *Eliminate those infected. Me*, Milton thought, *me and Suzy Scarlet*. He stumbled onto a thought that seemed so logical it could not have come from his delirious mind. He started speaking with whatever words he could manage, not sure if he made any sense.

"Scarlets fever. Not plural, not possessive, it's a colour not a name. It's singular. Scarlet fever. But it is a name. Scarlets,

Scarlet S, S Scarlet. Suzy Scarlet. It's you, Suzy. The message is in you." The lights faded as he struggled to keep his eyes open, and his head sunk into the pillow as he passed out.

Chapter 29

In time, my arm healed. I spent a while at first in the Medical wedge, finding the plastic-plaster cast and painkillers. Man, did I find great painkillers. I was with the fairies three days straight till the pain settled. I had antiseptics, analgesics, and fantastic sedatives. I needed the sedatives especially after revisiting everything that had happened.

I had never wanted ta kill, even if Demelle deserved it. The image, Demelle dying in my hands, repeatedly flashed in my mind like a migraine. The fear the Genefire had escalated, each time we had risked it, had driven me nearer insanity. It was madness ta keep firing it. I realised with clarity why Gessica's father had ended his research. I recalled my crewmates; their deaths when the chemical arrived. And I recalled the emptiness Gessica left when she sacrificed herself. With her missing, I was a shell. This was why I needed new sedatives, distracting these figments in my mind. I tried everything. I even ate Dr. Chang's mental health pills ta see if the spectres in my peripherals might disappear. They didn't.

My left hand was never the same after that. After five weeks, my fingers wiggled again, and my weak, withered arm emerged when I detached the cast. Typing was a pain; in fact, it made many tasks harder. I kept the ISS flying safely. When I wasn't keeping the maintenance in check, I reviewed my research. I had a large task ahead and I needed ta get it right.

I watched and rewatched all the vids with Larry and Scarlet, trying ta affirm that I had the right target. I again researched their families, their careers as far as they went, and any net messages and writing they left. Scarlet had data everywhere. She pasted replies in many genetics nets, participated in reviewing research papers. She seemed very clever.

The message I was writing was large and needed a direct target far in the past. Scarlet's family tree held the answer. She had a direct maternal line that went all the way ta Ireland in a small farming village. If I targeted that village, I was certain ta meet the target – even if the viral particle infected the entire village. That was my plan and I needed sharp maths ta hit it. That came later. I'm great at saving the maths till last.

The last vid I saw with Larry and Scarlet was in the street where he was attacked. It was strange that there weren't any later than that. I feared he may have died right then in that last vid, yet there wasn't any evidence that this had happened. There was an instant in that vid when he spied the CCTV camera, stared at it, then knelt and licked the cement. He was staring right at me, telegraphing his intent. He knew I was watching, and this was an act that I was meant ta see. He had ingested a Genefire pill.

It wasn't the message I was planning ta send, as I had already decided a different target. I hadn't even sent it yet. I think it was Demelle's message he had ingested.

What did Larry think when he read Demelle's message? He had received Gessica's message and was helping me. We had seen that in his hearing. Then, if he had read Demelle's message after he might think that was the real message and we really were the criminals. If that had prevented him helping in the end, it might clarify why the past hadn't changed.

This set me searching the vids ta see if he stared at CCTV cameras anywhere else, and he had, several times. Each time I watched them he seemed ta make certain he was seen, like he wanted me watching. I think he was telling me that he was helping. My chest swelled with warmth, realising that I had an ally in the past.

I then identified a link that sent chills inside me, like the spectres that were passing and intersecting my chest with their deathly hands. I had traced Scarlet's family tree ta her descendants in my time. I didn't accept that it was chance. It was destiny, theirs and mine.

Scarlet had married and had a little girl. That little girl had had a male child. That child was Gessica's grandfather. It was a direct line. Genetics ran in the family. Ha, ha. I wished Gessica had lived ta see this.

When I saw this, I knew I'd picked the right target. Scarlet was the answer. She knew the genetics; she had the right friends, the right financials, the right drive and the means. She even had genes that matched the DNA that Gessica had left here in the ISS. I decided that it was Scarlet's task ta end the Gename patents. It was evident in all the data, and in all the net messages she left that she knew where the patents were made. Her skill in shaping the general chat in the way she needed impressed me. Her talents in defeating the agency that created the Gename patents were clear ta see.

Gessica's DNA was in her files, and it was a simple matter ta design the targeting viral particle with her in mind. I marvelled at the simplicity when I finally learnt that it was a mathematical certainty that this gene set will infect any relatives with my message in their DNA. If any else were infected, they'd get a sniffle and remain sick a week and then clear it. A few, sadly, might die.

Finally, I spent a week scratching my head, analysing all the Genefire messages that landed in different places, and determining the right angles and speeds ta hit the village in the Irish farmlands. It was like trying ta hit a millimetre-wide pinhead with a laser at fifty paces. It was, in fact, like hitting a small electricity wing in the ISS with a cadaver, flying in an intersecting path after weeks in space.

When I wasn't researching, I was left thinking, wandering and distracted. The painkillers and sedatives held that dam a while, yet I kept reminding myself that Gessica was dead when passing her research den, the fence in the viewing deck where I'd seen her the day the flares emerged, and the sleeping sac we had shared. These things made my eyes wet each time.

I tried dehydrating myself, replacing my water with the captain's whisky, yet this didn't halt them. It made the tears larger. And it gave a fierce headache. When I played chess against the AI it was clear that the drinking didn't help. My chess average decreased dramatically. Even when I wasn't drinking, I was distracted and made silly mistakes. In the last game I played, I threw the chess set in anger and it hit the wall. It smashed and pieces went everywhere. When I calmed and tidied, I realised that the set was lacking a pawn. It was a fragment, partial, like me.

Why was I distracted? It was Gessica. I tried hard ta match the Gessica in my mind with the reality and facts. I still wasn't certain that she had deceived me and her entire race in creating the chemical with this ending in mind. Why had she revealed the chemical ta the illegals? Was she really that careless? Was it theft? Demelle had said this wasn't the case. He'd said she'd given it freely. It didn't matter. The fact is the Illegals had it and she had admitted ta making it.

Then why had she sealed her den and left the crew ta die? Was that an act that revealed her as a villain? Wasn't that a desperate act ta save herself when she hadn't any way ta save the rest? The fact was that she *had* saved herself, and me.

Why had she kissed me and shared my sleeping sac? Was it all an act? There weren't any facts when it came ta feelings.

The evidence wasn't clear, and I was left with my instincts ta tell me what was real and what wasn't. In this reality, Gessica had made the chemical, and it was negligence and perhaps theft that had released the plans ta place the chemical inta their Illegal hands. Gessica was desperate ta save herself and might have died if I hadn't spent my time cleaning the ISS. She had appreciated this and given the chance might have repaid me in kind. Yes, she had reacted when she saw me as a Pan sapiens, yet I had ta think that in time she might have recanted her nasty smears, and perhaps still like me as she had. I'm certain that this was the way ta interpret her acts.

The last thing I realised, in all this high-level thinking, was that I needed ta dismantle the Genefire satellite. Demelle had sent messages retracting Gessica's first message. The past hadn't changed anything in my present. I was certain that De-melle's message was the answer. What if I sent my message and then, a year later, Demelle's Illegal friends came and sent a message that retracted mine? While the Genefire was still there, it was always a risk. I had ta mitigate that risk.

My answer in the end was ta send my message and then pray it was read in the spirit it was written. Then I needed ta dismantle the Genefire satellite in a way that it'll never fire ever again. I deleted all the technical files needed ta remake it.

The hardest part was getting near the Genefire satellite and setting charges that might dismantle it. I wasn't taking Demelle's ship; that had an essential hatch flying away in space with Gessica. It was a vacant wreck, and I didn't have any way ta repair that. I checked the Earth ship that was still attached, and their tanks were empty. We had emptied them when we evaded the flying cadavers. It wasn't flying anywhere either.

That left the dreaded EVA as my remaining chance. I've written already that I despise these things. My last trip in space had scarred me, like a creeping disease in my mind. Wearing that synthetic skin again was like revisiting a nightmare that needed years in therapy ta lay ta rest.

There were practical challenges, like the distance. I'd fly with air that lasted seven hrs, which meant travelling the distance in three if I wanted ta revisit the ISS. The EVA wasn't designed ta navigate that far. Three Ks in seven hrs, fifteen metres per min was a dawdle. Yet, if I strayed, I might miss the satellite. I might empty my tanks faster than needed in maintaining my path. The largest challenge was the energy needed ta accelerate and decelerate. The faster I travelled, the greater the energy needed ta decelerate. The tanks in the EVA, when filled, were limited – there was a single chance. Yet if I went with less speed, I'd have less air time. I revised all the maths again and again, and I kept reaching the same answer.

With a single-man EVA, it was a single-way trip.

Did I like that idea? It was all I was thinking when I was drifting in the ISS centre, when I slept and ate. Friends and family passed in my mind: Frank, Captain Petrykin, and my parents. They all had dignity in their deaths. If this was my end, I was prepared ta deliver it with dignity. I spent five days trying ta find ways ta make the maths reach a happier end. Yet when it came ta the day when the maths said I had ta send the Genefire particle, I was ready.

When I first started writing this tale, getting ready ta send it, I said I wished I had the script it deserves. I still can't tell if Gessica was the villain that Demelle painted her as. She sacrificed herself that I might right her mistake. I prefer ta recall her as the martyr that saved the species – she deserves that. Yes, she made the chemical. It was the Illegals that released it with their intended targets. They were the villains. At least, that's my view.

I pray that when ya read this, ya may share the same feelings that I have. All *sapiens* deserve life. Gessica deserves life past a paltry nineteen. I send this message praying that ya can prevent this disaster and repair her life. I need her.

I daren't think whether my plan might fail. What if my message misses its target? What if she dismisses it as a fake? Perhaps they will fail ta read it. What if the Illegals manage ta send a message that retracts it again? There are many things that aren't certain.

There is a single thing that is certain. If I send this message and if I implement my plan, then there is at least a chance. The man that never tries always fails. I may die in this life, yet the slim chance that the past will change and revert ta the way it was meant, is all I have. Gessica may yet live again, and I may live with her. This is all I want.

My name is Thames Impressive Henry. I have never had a Gename patent and have never needed it. Please help me.

Chapter 30

Noah's eyes teared up as she read the messages that were appearing on the forums of the university pre-print servers. It had only been three days since she submitted Milton's PhD thesis onto the servers of four different universities, having attached a short note of explanation.

I am submitting this thesis on behalf of Larry Milton, who has sacrificed himself to uncover the truth. His remarkable discovery is revealed within. It is submitted despite his own university's attempt to silence him – Suzy Scarlet.

Ever since the public BuzzWorld hearing, Milton's story had been followed in the news as if it were a popular TV show. Many commentators were vocal in their support for him. Each of the four universities responded quickly, falling over each other in their haste to be the first to award him.

The first citation was from the University of Cambridge, which read: *We award the posthumous honorary degree of PhD to*

Dr. Laurence Milton for his contributions to the fields of Genetic Literature and Genomic Sequencing, and for his bravery and sacrifice in making one of the most profound discoveries of this decade. We commend his commitment to scientific integrity.

Princeton University awarded Milton an honorary PhD, as did the Universite de Paris, which attached a proviso making the award subject to independent verification of the sequences. Having known him for such a short time, Noah was surprised that she found herself sitting up taller, grinning at the computer screen, as if she had been awarded a PhD herself. Yes, she was proud of him. Yes, she could let herself cry as she looked over at the couch. He wouldn't notice.

Noah responded to all requests to share the data and posted the sequences on several online repositories. Many commentators on the forums connected the coded messages from the BuzzWorld hearing with the contents of the thesis and began to ask the questions about the Gename patent project. They questioned whether it was needed, and whether it was already active. They questioned whether scientific ethics had already collapsed as predicted. Both questions were hotly debated. Noah prodded the discussion in the directions in which she wanted it to go.

The words used by Jerome in his speech to Milton bothered her, though. Milton may not have understood it in his delirious state, but she had. *It's a real ongoing project*, he'd said. The project was active, and Jerome knew about it. Thus far, however, Noah had found no evidence of the project. With Ralph's help, she had investigated Jerome's laboratory and departmental budgets. All project finances were accounted for; there were no black holes. She had concluded that he wasn't directly involved in the project but was perhaps an advisor or reviewer. Then again, university budgets had never appeared so perfect. Either way, she didn't trust him.

Noah found herself staring at the needle that was still on the bench where Jerome had left it three days ago. She had no actual evidence one way or the other whether the injection itself would kill her, as Milton had feared. Yet she was disappointed that Ralph had ceded the argument and left. Did he not care about her as much as she'd thought? If he cared, he would have fought until she took it. The hypodermic lay unused on the bench, like a landmine waiting to be triggered, harmless if left alone. Doubts nagged at her. Milton had kissed her. She considered him like a younger brother or an apprentice, not a *potential...* So why had she kissed him back so vigorously?

Was she infected too? That was the real question. Was that why he had been rambling about her carrying the message? This confused Noah. She hadn't noticed any symptoms, so maybe she wasn't infected. She decided to wait until she showed symptoms before risking the injection. It was a matter of benefits versus potential harms.

It's you, Suzy. The message is in you, he had said. The words kept banging in her head. *The message is in you.* Noah shook her head, dismissing the possibility. The messengers from the future couldn't have known about that kiss. *Could they have known my real name?*

Of all the animals she had investigated over the years, Noah had never sequenced her own DNA. There were several reasons for this, but one dominated. All her life she had avoided finding her father, who had left when she was young. Throughout her teenage years, she had tried to hate him, but had found no hate inside her and no real reason to do so. She had tried to love him again and could neither find it nor fake it. She had done alright without his help, and she was more than fine not seeking him out. And she knew, just knew, that the temptation to find him using her DNA would prove too great for her once she possessed the sequence. It would be so easy.

Now, however, she had another reason. If Milton was so convinced that there was a message in her DNA, then shouldn't she be obliged to look, for his sake? After all he had done. She decided to set aside some time to think about it. Procrastination was the very least she should do for him.

She walked out of the laboratory and into the kitchen to make a cup of tea. She watched the tea leak out of the bag into the hot water, changing the colour of the liquid. Was that what Milton was doing to her – changing her colour? Better, or worse? Refusing to sequence her DNA was bad, but refusing to do so for a selfish reason was cruel.

Noah heard the heavy footsteps of Ralph approaching but decided she couldn't listen to his protests and arguments now. She flipped the half-infused teabag into the bin and fore-going adding milk, headed back into the laboratory. If she was infected with a dangerous virus, then it was best not to get too close to him. Another good rationalisation.

But the virus wasn't the real reason. She wouldn't be able to stand up to Ralph's self-righteous reasoning. His ability to argue was unparalleled. If he was standing in front of a firing squad, having been caught red-handed, even then he could argue his way out of it. She had witnessed it. He would convince her to take the injection as a precaution. He would convince her to sequence her own DNA. After all, it was the right thing to do. She cursed the Viking hacker for convincing her to go ahead without having said a word.

Noah looked over at the couch and whispered, "Milton, you better appreciate this." She took the swab, wiped it all around the inside of her cheeks, and dumped it into the DNA extraction tube. She was on autopilot; she conducted the DNA extraction as she had done so often before, on so many samples from so many organisms. With the DNA loaded into the sequencing machine, all she had to do was wait for the little *bing* that told her it was finished.

Returning to the kitchen for another cup of tea, she continued to avoid Ralph. Other members of the BioHackspace shared the kitchen with her and yet kept their distance. They knew to leave her alone. Noah carried her tea back into her laboratory. She watched the sequencer machine with the tea in her left hand and the forefinger of her right-hand hovering over the abort button. More than once, she moved to halt the run and destroy the DNA sample in the process. She wondered whether she could resist using the DNA sequence to find her father or if there was a way to destroy the sequences once she found what she was looking for. But for someone so dedicated to sequencing, it would be almost sinful to destroy it. Besides, it would be futile, since she knew that once the run was done, the raw sequences would be loaded into the cloud and irreversibly catalogued. That was how she had set up her data pipeline. If she could just hit the abort button it would remove any chance that the sequence would be completed, and it would be gone. Her forefinger grew tired, hovering over the button.

Pacing like a drill sergeant, she marched back and forth in the laboratory. She took a sip of tea. Somehow it had grown cold.

The sequence was almost complete. It seemed to have taken much longer than a typical human genome. And yet her tea had cooled faster than expected. Noah couldn't grasp the fact that time had slowed down as her mind held her in stasis waiting for these results.

In a panic, she leapt for the button to stop the sequencing before it could complete, but the sequencer emitted a *bing* before she could reach it. Her eyes dried out staring at the machine, then filled with moisture as it dawned on her what she had done.

She took a deep breath and typed in the DNA code for the phrase *Gename patent*. The search returned no hits. She tried a few variations of the DNA code that would return the same protein code, but again there were no hits. She ran her sequence through every quality-control metric available. The sequence was fine. Her DNA sequence was complete. It had all been for nothing; there was no message in any of her chromosomes. Next, she tried searching for the text of the previous messages with terms for Allan Demelle or Gessica Theresa Kelly. Nothing. Like a sinking balloon leaking helium, Noah deflated into the depths of her chair.

Noah came from a long line of single mothers. It was almost a family tradition, like a genetic distrust of men, or socially conditioned poor choices. In any case, they had always kept their maiden name, Scarlet, as far back as she knew. If the messengers from the future knew that, they might try to put the message where it would only be accessible through the maternal line. *Scarlet S.* That would be one hell of a coincidence. She stared at the screen, thinking.

Like the breaking of dawn, the answer revealed itself to her. When an egg is fertilised by sperm, the nuclear DNA mixes, but all the mitochondrial DNA comes from the mother's egg and is passed down from generation to generation through the maternal line. Mitochondrial DNA had traditionally been discarded and ignored in sequencing projects, and yet was an important part of any human's cellular makeup. It was the energy production facility of the cell, and entirely female. Noah's energy and enthusiasm grew just thinking about it. She could barely sit still. *That's where I would have hidden the message*, she thought.

She retrieved the unmapped mitochondrial sequences and assembled them. She searched for the pattern – and there it was, plain as day: thirty-seven matches for the Gename patent sequence tag, within a vast mitochondrial DNA sequence. She calculated the length of this sequence, and it was impossibly long – over 398,000 nucleotides. She checked all the codons for a translation into protein code, and there was one. It was there, perhaps with a mutation or two within it, inevitably, but it was there. The message had been in her, after all. As she looked at the translation, she let out a squeal as if she was four years old again. She read the beginning and the end, and it was more than she could have hoped for.

It was the tale of a man and woman desperately trying to save their space station when all their colleagues had been killed by a nasty chemical that had reacted with their Gename patents. There was naked cleaning, flying cadaver missiles, and CCTV records. Most of all, it was a tale of a growing love between the two, through good times and bad, ending with her sacrifice for him. He was ready to sacrifice himself just for a chance to get her back. Noah read what she had to do to help them. This entire tale had been written in her DNA in the twenty-amino-acid code, without using any of the letters B, J, O, U, Z or X.

Noah couldn't stop grinning. She looked over to the couch again and this time she screamed, "Milton! Wake up! You have to see this."

Startled, Milton tumbled from the couch. He dragged himself from the floor and stumbled across the laboratory to stand behind Noah. His hair was messed up and his face was blemished with a massive pillow mark, like a war wound, a symptom of having slept on and off for nearly three whole days. There was warmth in his hand as he rested it on her shoulder, and she did not shrug it off.

"Since you've been sleeping you've been awarded four PhDs, two of them posthumously. That will be a fun graduation ceremony. I'll bet you will be the first person to receive a posthumous degree in person." She beamed at him.

Milton's face wrinkled, struggling as if her words were a cryptic crossword puzzle. Perhaps that had been too much information for someone who had just awoken from the dead. That wide-eyed pale fear that had etched itself into his features over the last few days seemed to leak away. His face was relaxed, stunned that his PhD was finished. He looked like a marathon runner looking back at the finish line. His mouth slowly opened, agape, his eyes widened as it dawned on him what she was looking at.

"But that's not what I wanted you to see. This." Noah pointed to the screen and showed him the conversion of the DNA sequence into protein code. She put her hand over Milton's as it rested on her shoulder and held it tight. Together, they read the first few lines.

I was with her when she was at the viewing deck, watching as each new flare advanced in every land, as the planet passed and twisted 'neath her and I. I can't define what it felt like, witnessing her planet annihilated. My planet.

Chapter 31

Half a billion kilometres above the elliptical orbit of Earth a large distortion undulated, like a ripple in a crystal-clear lake reflecting the night sky. The distortion was discernible when looking at the Earth from above, the planet shimmering like a mermaid below the still surface.

A satellite that looked like a large ballistic cannon in the centre of a blooming tulip circled the Earth, matching the orbit of the International Space Station. It maintained its orientation, pointed at the distortion no matter where the satellite was in its orbit. Small thrusters fired, adjusting the satellite so that it pointed slightly askew from the perpendicular such that any projectile that bounced back from the distortion, as if from a trampoline, would not hit the satellite that fired it.

Like a flower spitting its seeds into the wind, the cannon fired a small projectile, barely visible but for the jet stream it left as its fuel ignited a pencil line along its path. As it neared the distortion, the projectile sped up as if sucked in by a great celestial body, making it approach then exceed the speed of light. Unlike a black hole, which represented the gravity of great mass, this distortion represented the gravity of great time. Imagine the weight of a man measured time and again, day after day, year after year. Added together, one man would weigh an immeasurable sum over endless time and would weigh even more than the planet he stood on.

The small projectile grew as it approached the surface of the distortion. Ice and other matter coalesced around the projectile, brought together by the increased pressure, like a diamond crushed from coal. The meteor accelerated as it splashed into the surface, creating a ripple as though it was a stone tossed into a glassy lake.

In another time and another place, after travelling for centuries through the distortion, the projectile returned as if it were bouncing from a trampoline and slowed as it tumbled towards the planet below. With each pass around the Earth, the ice and dust that had gathered over countless years of its journey now cracked, melted, and broke away. A cloud of ice satellites accompanied the central meteorite on its final descent to its target.

A ripple flowed outward from the edges of the shimmering distortion. Space and time carried the ripple through the vacuum, towards the planet.

Before the ripple reached the flower-like satellite, a small white EVA suit arrived, like a bee buzzing around it. The EVA suit stopped in several places around the satellite, keen to contact all surfaces and leave small packages behind. As it was leaving it was caught in a powerful explosion as the satellite dismantled into its component parts. The ripple passed through the debris, sweeping it up, leaving nothing behind, as if it had never been there at all.

*   *   *

Far below, Gessica sat in her favourite place on the darkened observation deck in the ISS, looking up into space. This was bliss, avoiding the politics of the Genetics wedge and avoiding the grants, the students' reports and the administrative tasks that were piling up. She gazed at Betelgeuse, her favourite class M star, at the foot of Orion; it looked like a distant tangerine twinkling at her. It was a ginger, just like her. She was a bright star, as everyone kept telling her.

As a genetics programme leader, she was now one step removed from all the fun experimental work that she'd enjoyed so much in her fledgling scientific career. Such was her success over the first two years of her programme, with her sister laboratory on Earth also flourishing, that she now received frequent requests to take over as the head of the genetics department.

Her bliss did not last long. The lights flicked on and three green-clad crew members entered. One was her junior technician, Sandra, along with two other programme leaders: Anthony and Bryony. Conspicuously missing from this posse were Gessica's parents, the two other programme leads at the ISS.

"Gessica, here you are." Antony said. "You can't hide from this anymore. We're here to convince you that you should accept the offer of department head."

Gessica shook her head and stared at the sky. Her father was the department head and Gessica wasn't sure how he would take it if she accepted the position. Besides, she wasn't ready for that responsibility yet. She had almost convinced herself of that. She acknowledged that it was the right course, eventually, and she would bring renewed enthusiasm for the entire department, but to displace her own father? That would be harsh.

Antony, Bryony and Sandra circled her, pointing at her green dress like a gang of bullies. Gessica shrank inside this scrum. "Leave me alone," she said.

"Gessica, we know you wear that dress with pride. We know how much this department means to you. Your father has lost his edge. His programme is failing, and he'll bring us all down with him if we go on like this."

"What does he think?" she replied. "Have you even asked him? He's a proud man."

"Proud and stupid," Anthony retorted. "His latest report is based on fake data. It's meaningless."

"How dare you say that about my father! He has more integrity than this attempted coup of yours," Gessica fired back. "Simulated data isn't fake, by the way. That study provided novel insight into the long-term effects of genetically modified particles. You're all so focused on rushing ahead to bigger and better enhancements that you haven't stopped to think that there might be consequences for humanity. We must be more tolerant of those we disagree with."

Gessica directed her last statement at the Maintenance man as he arrived in the observation deck, interrupting the argument. She recognised his face but didn't know his name. He wore his ill-fitting red suit like a monkey dressed in a clown suit.

"Gessica, don't stare," her research assistant, Sandra, whispered. "He's a *Pan Sapiens* – he might be sensitive."

Gessica was disgusted. These new creatures were an abomination, in her view. But, to prove her point of tolerance to these mutineers, she approached the Pan to offer a hand of friendship.

"Hello, my name is Gessica. I don't believe we've met." She held her hand out to shake his hand.

He was tentative and shy. His voice was deep and gravelly, like an old man, despite his youth. "Hello, my name is Tammy," he stammered. "I... I like your hair."

He moved his large, hairy hand closer to hers. Gessica resisted the urge to recoil and held firm. They touched.

In a burst of *déjà vu*, she realised she had touched that hand before. It had a dexterity that was beyond its size, and the skin was softer than it looked. As she gripped his hand more firmly, a vision splashed across her mind, like a bucket of icy water. It was a waking dream, but more than a dream.

She saw unimaginable destruction on the Earth below as nuclear explosions bloomed mushrooms on every continent. Overwhelmed by a crushing wave of emotion, she watched all her friends and family perish. She couldn't shake the dreadful weight, sinking deep inside her, that it was all her fault. The guilt was like a current sweeping her away. She tried to hold against it but slipped further and further away. Tammy's approach in the observation deck was like a branch being held out to rescue her.

Isolated and rejected, Gessica's ideas were dismissed by the department heads, as though she were a child. She alone knew the risks. Somehow, she couldn't articulate these risks. Her own father rejected her, which seemed like child abuse in her eyes.

She watched the faces of the refugees, passengers on the last ship, on the CCTV screen as she refused to admit them to the ISS. When they started fighting, she was convinced that she was right. When they were released from the isolation chamber, a flood of adrenaline filled her veins. Death approached, and in a panic, she saved herself, leaving her crewmates and parents to die. "I told you so" echoed in her mind as she watched them all die, one by one.

Emptiness filled her. What kind of monster was she, she wondered. The five stages of grief passed in a flash and left her stuck, like a jammed joystick, in anger mode. Bargaining mode was activated when she saw Tammy, like a gardener tending his roses, clipping all the dead branches, and sending them into space. He would save her if she could manipulate him to do so.

She watched CCTV footage showing Tammy dancing naked around the Genetics wedge. She tried to hold in her laughter until it was uncontrollable. The look on his face was priceless.

The strength in his arms was impressive, as she nestled within his embrace. His skin was soft and smooth in the parts that were not covered with coarse hair. His lips trembled as she kissed him, as if she scared him. She enjoyed having that power over him. He tasted like motor oil and rusty bolts.

His smooth skin like soft cured leather, rubbed against hers. She heard his heartbeat as she climbed into his sleeping sac for the first time. Gessica blushed when she saw her effect on him and realised that she was in for more than she bargained for.

Squealing laughter turned to gaping silence and trembling hands when she heard the word 'Pan' echo in her head. How had she not seen that? It was obvious. Bile filled her mouth and she retched and spat every degrading insult she could think of. She wiped her arms and scoured her tongue. There was no way to cleanse herself no matter how many times she wriggled to shake it off. She resolved to make amends.

Darkness surrounded her and she could hear his voice breaking, as if he'd realised how terrible she was and there was nothing she could do to repair that hurt. Finally, she came to understand that he didn't deserve that. He was fighting for her. You cannot blame the child for the fault of the father; neither hers nor his. He was worth fighting for. There was one thing she could do to help him. Suicide flashed in her mind like a red warning. He was right. She knew what he was going to do, if only he could kill their captor. Her life was holding him back. It was time for her to let go and trust that he would save her.

Her eyes dried in an instant of searing pain. She died in the vacuum of space.

Gessica gasped and snatched at the air, filling her lungs. She covered her mouth. Crying seemed the human thing to do.

And here she was. With all her faults and all the things she'd done to him. She was here. Not because she deserved it, not because it was meant to be, but because he loved her. She didn't understand whether this vision was the past or the future, but she believed it to be true. She could see in his eyes that it was. The greatest truth of all. He loved her. She had so recently despised him for what he was, yet now, after this vision, she saw what he really was: a great man. She saw in his face, he had run the gamut of emotions that she had just experienced. He saw the same vision, suffered the same pain, and relived the same joy.

She held his hands in hers, stroked the hairs on his forefinger, then looked into his eyes, smiled, and said a single word.

"Impressive."

The End

Epilogue

Anne sat on the long double bench that ran the length of the workhouse dining hall. Keeping her company were two other women who had also been released from the fever ward. Both women still looked pale and haggard. Both women would die; they all did. Her own sickness had run for almost four weeks this time, but unlike many who died from the fever, she had recovered. As her health improved, the doctor insisted she ate breakfast to keep up her strength. The bowl of boiled oatmeal with buttermilk grew cold as she stared at it.

During one attempt to force a mouthful down, a large dollop of oatmeal landed on her oversized belly. Anne stared for longer than she should have at the large oatmeal stain, the milk oozing through the donated dress like a growing, pustulant sore. In her life before the workhouse, she might have jumped up and run to the laundry to clean it. Even in the first few weeks, such sloppiness was punished with a stick and harsh words. Like the rest of the inmates, she had learnt the almost military rigour with which she must move and present herself in this place. Her punishments were frequent, each time she refused to tell the Master or Matron who had fathered the child. Considering her condition, now eight and a half months pregnant and weak after a month on the fever ward, her sloppiness would go unpunished. Still, the oatmeal on her dress upset her. On the verge of tears, she bit her lower lip to stop the trembling and stood to signify the end of her meal.

Anne pressed her hand against the growing pain in her back as she carried her half-full bowl to the kitchen. Following breakfast, she prepared for her real punishment, the long penance for her sins. No amount of punishment dished out by the Matron could match the punishment she inflicted on herself every Sunday, like a weekly flagellation. As an inmate, she attended mass in the private Catholic chapel on the workhouse grounds, a church presided over by the Reverend Terrence McGovern, the man she had once loved, whom she believed had also once loved her. She still hoped he might love her again, perhaps if she kept their secret.

Each week she listened to his voice and studied his face, despite his eyes never catching hers. Each week, Anne attended the Eucharist, to line up with other inmates to receive the wafer representing the body of Christ. She would always receive a blessing rather than bread, in recognition of her sinful pregnant state. The Reverend could do no more in the eyes of the community and in the eyes of God. It was a humiliating charade that she should receive a blessing from the very man that had put her in this position.

She watched him, knowing he had sinned equally, if not more than she. There was no outward sign of his sins on him, like the bloated belly that she followed everywhere. His silence on the matter disappointed her. Each week Anne tested the paper-thin sheet of propriety that stood between her silence and telling. It hurt each time she came to this church. Each week she came back for more.

Anne crouched, as though she were an old woman with arthritic knees, to sit in the last row of pews and joined in the incantation of the Lord's Prayer. On the other side of the church, she saw a mass of red hair: Mary Brady, who now always came to Mass on the community side of the church. Anne had long ago forgiven Mary for her childish indiscretion, but the workhouse rules forbade any communication with the public, meaning she hadn't the opportunity to say so. Mary, as she often did, turned her head to find Anne. Under the watchful eye of Matron Brownlow, Anne ignored her.

At the appropriate time in the ceremony, Anne stood up and queued behind other inmates in the procession towards the Eucharist. Ten people stood between her and the Reverend. She loved this man with all her heart. Eight bodies now parted them. She gave herself to him. Now five. Over many months he had read books to her with such glee. Three. She hadn't seen a book since, nor learnt the fate of Robin. One person remained between them. She dared not tell anyone about their secret affair. At last, there were no more bodies between them. With a long face and an oatmeal-stained dress, she stepped toward the Reverend and poked out her tongue to receive the holy communion. His hands that had once stroked her hair with affection he placed on her head dispassionately, and the words remained the same.

"Bless you, child."

Anne's lower lip began to tremble, held back by a fierce bite as she turned on her heels and marched to her pew. Like a thunder strike, she cried out in pain and threw her hand to clutch the nearest railing, as the first contraction of her labour arrived.

The Matron attended her first and helped her to her feet. "The child is coming too soon, God save us," she said, and made a hasty cross over her face. She commanded the two women nearest her. "Take her back to the fever ward. The doctor will want to see her there."

Held by both arms, Anne flung her head around and caught sight of Mary Brady gripping her hair and looking around wildly for help, and the Reverend standing unmoved. She was bundled back into the fever ward, where the doctor took command.

Anne awoke to the sounds of a baby crying, like a jackdaw screaming. Drowsy but aware, she heard the voice of the doctor speaking to the Matron. "The little girl will live. She is early, but strong. Anne, however, is weak. With the fever and the amount of blood she has lost…" His voice trailed off, as Anne nodded out of consciousness.

She awoke again with a rush of adrenaline when she heard the Matron say, "I shall send for the Reverend. He must baptise the child before she goes."

"No," Anne cried. "He mustn't." She didn't think the baptism would work if conducted by the Reverend, the girl's father. Perhaps God would punish the child. "No, not him."

"Anne, he is just outside," the Matron pleaded. "He will hear you. He can baptise the child immediately. You want to see her baptised, don't you?"

The Reverend opened the door and entered the ward. Anne's strength was failing her, but she locked eyes with him and screamed, "Please! Get the Vicar instead."

John Brougham was the Vicar of St Peters Church in Templeport, a nearby Protestant church. "Perhaps it would ease her passing if we sent for him," the Reverend said. The Matron left the room, to send for the Vicar.

Anne's breathing quietened, and she turned her head towards the crib. She could see a hand grasping at the air. She reached both of her arms out to the crib and asked the doctor, "Please, let me see her."

The doctor wrapped the child in a blanket and laid her in the arms of her mother. Anne breathed deeply, smelling the distinct odour of the newborn, like sweet cheese and fresh bread. So tender and frail she seemed, so soft. The pain of the birth washed from Anne's mind, the memory of the hurt she had experienced every week in the church disappeared, and the humiliation of living in the workhouse no longer mattered. She smiled using muscles in her face that had been long unused. With her child in her arms, she looked up at the Reverend and saw the faintest of twitches in his lips, almost a smile. Anne was mesmerised by the quiet child and soon fell asleep again with the little girl in her arms.

Late in the afternoon, she awoke as the Vicar walked into the ward with Mary Brady. She had been the one to fetch him. The Matron and Master of the workhouse and the Reverend followed them in, like a gang of thieves.

The Vicar said gently to Anne, "Before we start, we must fill out the details in the church register. I have Mary Brady here to act as witness, unless you object." Anne smiled at Mary and did not object. The Vicar scribbled in the book and then turned to Anne and asked, "Can you tell us who the father is? We need it for the register."

Anne froze, having so long resisted answering that question. Was it true that the child could not be baptised without this information? Was it so vital? The father stood right there. She looked long at him.

She could easily have told the truth, but would she be believed? If she were to lie, what name would she pick? What name would they not question? She again looked at Reverend, about to speak his name, but his grim expression still said: do not tell. Anne did not understand why she retained such loyalty to this man, but she decided on a different name to give them.

"Anne, the baby cannot be baptised without this information," the master told her, seeking an answer to the question he had so often asked.

Anne turned to Reverend McGovern and looked him in the eye, to the exclusion of everyone else in the room. "The father is…" She paused, and a weak smile rippled across her face. The pause extended and he squirmed. Like gunslingers from the American West, she waited until he made the first move. He shifted. Before he spoke, she said, "His name was Will. Will Scarlet."

"Very well," said the Vicar, scribbling in his book. He took the baby in his arms and asked what name should be given to the child. Anne was stunned. Not through all the months of pregnancy, nor even the few hours she had held the child in her arms, had she thought of a name for the child.

"Anne?" asked the Matron.

"Yes," responded Anne, not realising that it had been a request for her to respond. "I agree. Call her Anne." *That way, when he sees her grow up, he will be reminded of me*, she thought.

The Vicar proceeded with the brief ceremony, dousing the child in holy water, and reciting the prayers. On April 15th 1863, Anne Scarlet was baptised into the Protestant Church.

Author's Note

As a scientist, it is important to me that the science presented in this story is accurate and that some of the science fiction represents a not-so-implausible future. The ability to
write in DNA is not fiction at all and has been accomplished
in numerous ways, including the encoding of all of Shakespeare's sonnets in DNA using a cipher[1]. Of course, reading
it would require knowledge of that cipher, and therein lies
the problem. Restricting to just the protein code is more
difficult, as shown in Tammy's story, but is far more deci-
pherable. For anyone who cares to try, I have included the
DNA sequence for Chapter 1 which can be converted in any
number of DNA to Protein conversion tools[2]. The genetic
sleuthing method Milton and Noah use to track down Alice Evans is already possible with today's knowledge of genetics and epigenetics and is being thoroughly explored in

1. Goldman, N. et al. Nature http://dx.doi.org/10.1038/nature11875 (2013).
2. https://web.expasy.org/translate/.

forensic science[3]. The new sequencing method described by Milton using imaging of natural DNA synthesis as it occurs during cell division is currently science fiction but may one day become possible if we can increase the resolution of our imaging methods. Naturally, the science of time travel is purely fantasy... or is it?

I would like to thank several readers, including Kevin Zwierzchaczewski, Denise Murray, Cheryl King and Rana Campbell, members of the 11:59 Workshop and my editors who have all helped guide this story in the right direction. Any remaining errors are my own. Lastly, I would also like to thank all the PhD students I have supervised over the years who contributed various aspects to the character of Larry Milton.

James Flanagan, June 2023
Website: jimiflanwrites.com ; Twitter: @jimiflanUK

3. Sabeeha, Hasnain SE. Forensic Epigenetic Analysis: The Path Ahead. Med Princ Pract. 2019;28(4):301-308. doi:10.1159/000499496.

Chapter 1 in DNA code

>Chapter One (frame 1)

atttgggcgagctggattacccatcatgaacgctggcatgaaaacagccatgaatg
ggcgagcgcgaccacccatgaagtgattgaatggattaacggcgatgaatgcaaat
gggcgacctgccatattaacggcgcgagcgaagcgtgccataacgaatggtttctg
gcgcgcgaagcggatgtggcgaactgcgaagatattaacgaagtggaacgctatct
ggcgaacgatgcgagcacccatgaaccgctggcgaacgaaaccccggcgagcagcg
aagatgcgaacgatacctggattagcaccgaagataacgaagcgacccatcatgaa
cgcgcgaacgatattatttgcgcgaacaccgatgaatttattaacgaatggcatgc
gaccattacctttgaactgaccctgattaaagaatggattaccaacgaaagcagca
ttaacggccatgaacgcccgctggcgaacgaaaccgcgaacaacattcatattctg
gcgaccgaagatatgtatccgctggcgaacgaaaccagccatgaatgggcgagcgc
gagccatgaactgccgctggaaagcagcgcgagcgcgatggaagatatttgctggg
cgacctgccatattaacggcacccatgaatttattaacgcgctggatgaagcgacc
catagcccggcgagcatgagcattaacgcgccggcgaccattgaaaacaccagcca
tgaatgcgcgaacaccagcgcggtggaacatgaacgcgcgcgcatgagcagcgcga
acaaagatcgcgcgtggattaacggcaacgaagcgcgcgaacgccatgaacgccat
gaagcgcgcaccaaaaacgaagaaagcatggaactggatgaagattggattaccca
tacccatgaaatggaaaccgcgctgggcattcgcgatgaacgcaacgaagcgcgca
cccatgaaggcctggcgagcagcagcaccgcgcgcattaacggcagcattctggaa

297

aacaccctgtatgcgagcatttggcgcattaccgaaacccatattagcaccgaagc

gcgcagcgatgcgcgcaaagaaaacatgtatgaatatgaaagcgcgaacgatatta

aagaagaaccgcgcgaaccgctggcgtatattaacggcacccatgaagaagtggaa

aacaccagcattaacatgtatatgattaacgatccggaacgccatgcgccgagcat

taacaccattatggaaattctgctgtttattaacgatacccatgaatgccatgcgc

gcgcgtgcaccgaacgcattagcaccatttgcagcacccatgcgaccgatgaattt

attaacgaagatcatgaacgcctgattaaagaaattaacgcgctgctgacccatga

aacccgcgcgggcatttgcgtggaacgcagcgaaagcgcgagcagccatgaatggg

cgagctggcatgaaaacattttttattcgcagcaccagcgcgtggcatgaacgcagc

accattctgctgattatgccgcgcattaacaccgaagatattaacatgtatatgat

taacgattggcatgaaaacattttttattcgcagcaccgaaaacaccgaacgcgaag

atacccatgaagtgattgaatggattaacggcgatgaatgcaaaattaccagcgaa

gaaatggaagatgatgaaagcgaacgcaccgaagatacccatgaaattagcagctg

ggcgagcgaaaaccatgcgaactgcgaagattggattacccatgcgctggcgcgcg

gcgaacgctgcgcgccggcgtgcattacctattggcatgaaaacatgtatccggcg

cgcgaaaacaccagcatggaaaccacccatgaatattgggaacgcgaaacccatga

aatggcgattaacaccgaaaacgcgaactgcgaaaccgaagcgatggcgaccaccc

atgaaaccattatggaaagcattaactgcgaaacccatgaaaacattacccatgcg

agcaacacctgccatgcgaacggcgaagatattacctgggcgagcaccattggcca

tacctggcatgaaaactttattcgcagcaccgatgaaagcattggcaacgaagatg

cgaacgatacccatgaagtgattgaatggattaacggcgatgaatgcaaatgggcg

agcgcgctgtgggcgtatagcagcatggcgctgctgaccgaaaacgtggaacgcta

tgatgaagcgcgctttcgcattgaaaacgatagcagcaccgcgaacgatattaacg

gcattaacctgattaacgaatgcgcgaacagcccggcgaacacccatgaaggcctg

gcgagcagccatgcgctgtttttgggcgtatacccgcgcggtggaacgcagcattaa

cggcacccatgaagatgaatgcaaaattcatgcgctgaccgaagatattagcgcgt

ggggcgaaagcagcatttgcgcggatgaactgatttgcgcgaccgaaggccgcatt

ccgccgattaacgcgcacccatgaatttgaaaactgcgaaaacgaagcgcgcaccca

tgaaggcctggcgagcagcccggcgaacgaacatgaacgctttgcgtgcgaagcgg

gcgcgattaacagcaccacccatgaaggcctggcgagcagcgcgagcatttttttgg

attctgctgattaacggccatgaacgcagcgaactgttttagcccggcgtgcgaaga

tgcgaacgatgatgaagcggatcatgaacgcggcattaacggcgaacgccatgcga

ttcgctgggcgagcaccattgaagatattaacgcgacctggattagcacctggatt
acccatgcgagcattaacggcctggaacgcgcgggcggcgaagatagcacccgcgc
gaacgattgggcggtgattaacggctgggaaattggccataccctggaaagcagcc
cggcgagcacccatgaacgctgccatattaaccatgaacgcagccatgcgccggaa
gcgccgccggaagcgcgcgaagatccggaaaccattaccgaaattaacacccatga
aagcaccgcgaacgatgcgcgcgatattagcagcagcctgattatggatcgcgaaa
gcagcattaacggcgaaaacgaaaccatttgcagcaccgaagcgatgggccgcgaa
gaaaacacccatgaaagcgcgatggaagcgagcacccatgaaggcctggcgagcag
cagccatgaaagcgaagaaatggaagatctgattaaagaagcgaccgaaaacagcg
aaagcccgcgcattaacggcagcaccattctgctggcgaacgatcgcgaagcggat
tataccgcgctggaagcgccgctgattaaagaaatggaaagccatgaatgggcgag
cacccatgaacgcgaatgggcgacctgccatattaacggcacccatgaaccgctgg
cgaacgaaaccattacctgggcgagcatggaaagcatggaacgcattagcattaac
ggcacccatgaaccgctggcgaacgaaaccagcgcgattcgctgggcgagcaccca
tatttgcaaactgattaaagaatgcgcgcgcgcgatggaactgagctggattcgcc
tgattaacggcattaacgcgatgattctgaaaagccatgcgaaagaatttctggcg
cgcgaaagctttattcgcgaagatcatgaacgcgaagcgaacgatacccatgaacg
cgaatggattacccatgaagcgtgccataacgaatggtttctggcgcgcgaatggg
aaaaaaacgaatggatggcgaactatctgattgtggaaagcccggaacgcattagc
catgaagatattaacagcaccgcgaacaccctgtatgaagtggaacgctattggca
tgaacgcgaaccgctggcgaacgaaacctggattgatgaagcgagcattctggaag
cgcgcaacaccctggcgaccgaacgcgcgctgctgccgcgcattatggcgaccgaa
agcgcgccggaaagcgcgaacgatatggaaaacgcgctgattaaagaatgggaacg
cgaatggattacccatgaacgcattaacggcgcgtgggcgtatattaacacccata
ttagcatgattgcgagcatggcggcgaccacccatgcgaccaccattatggaaatt
catgcggatgcgagcacccgcgcgaacggcgaatttgaagaactgattaacggcac
ccatgcgaccattagcgcgtggagcgaagtggaacgcgcgctgagcccggaatgca
cccgcgaaagctgcattcgctgcctgattaacggcggcgaaagcagcatttgcgcg
tgccgcattaccatttgcattagcattaacggccatgaacgcgcgagcatttttat
tacctgggcgagccatgaacgcacccatgcgaccaaaattctgctggaagataccc
atgaaccgctggcgaacgaaacccatcatgaatattgggaacgcgaaagcccgatt
cgcattaccagccatgcgcgcgatctgtatacccatgaacgcgaatttctgatttg

```
caaagaacgcattaacggcctgattaaagaagcgtttaccgaacgcattatggcgg
gcgaaagcattaccattctgaccgaagatatgtatcatgaagcggatgcgaacgat
acccatgaatatccggaacgcagcattagcaccgaagatacccatgaatatgatat
tgataacaccagcacccgcattaaagaaatggaagcgagcagctgcgcgcgctatg
cgaacgatattgatattgataacacctttgaagcgcgcacccatgaaatgattagc
gcgtggacccatcgcgaagaagaagcgtgccattgggaagcgcgcattaacggcgg
cgaaaacgaaaccatttgcagcggccgcgaagaaaactatgaaaccacccatgaat
attgggaacgcgaaaacacctgccgcgaatggatggcgaccgaaagcacccatgcg
accattaaaaacgaatggacccatgaaatggcgctggaaagcccggaatgcacccg
cgaatgggcgagctgcctggaagcgcgcctgtatattaactgccatgcgcgcggcg
aagcgggcggccgcgaaagcagcattgtggaagcgaacgatgcgagcagcgaacgc
accattgtggaaacccatgaactggcggattattggattacccatcatattatgca
tgcggatgcgtttgcgtgcgaagcgggcgaagattggattacccatagcgcggata
acgaaagcagcgcgaacgatacccatgaaacccatattcgcgattgggcgagcgcg
ggcattcgcctgtggattacccattttgcgattcgcagcaaaattaacgcgaacga
tgcgtggattgatgaagaatatgaagatatgattgaaaacgcgaacgatagccatg
aacatgcggatgcgccggcgcgcaccattgcgctgaacgcgatggaaaccgcgggc
cgcgaagcggatattaacggcagcgcgaacgatacccatgcgaccgatattgataa
caccatggcgacctgccatgcgaactataacgcgatggaaattaaaaacgaatggg
cgctgctgacccatcgcgaagaacatgcggattttattaacggcgaacgcagccgc
gcgattagcgaagatgcgaacgatacccatgaatattgggaaaacaccgcgtttac
cgaacgcggcgaaagcagcatttgcgcggcgagcatttttacccatgaatatcatg
cgaccgaagatcatgaacgcctgattaaagaaagccatgcgcgcaaaagctgcatt
cgctgcctgattaacggctgggcgattaccattaacggcaccgcgagcacccgcat
taaagaaggcgaaagcagcatttgcgcggatattgataacaccagcgaagaaaccc
atgaaatggcgaacgattggcatgaaaacacccatgaatatgatattagcgcgccg
ccggaagcgcgcgaagatattggccgcgaagaaaccgaagatcatgaacgccatga
atatggcattaacggcgaacgctatgcgccggaacgctgcgaaattgtggaatggc
atgcgaccattagccatgcgccgccggaaaacattaacggcacccatgaacgcgaa
gcgagctgggaactgctgattagcgcgattgatatgtattttattcgcagcaccct
gattaacgaatgggcgagcaacaccacccatgaatggattagcgaaagcacctatg
aaaccatttggattctgctggcgctgtgggcgtatagccgcgaatgcgcgctgctg
```

catgaacgcgcgaacagctgggaacgccgcgcgtgcattagcatgagccatgaaag

cgcgattgatgcgagcagccatgaatttgcgtgcgaagatatggaagcgggcgaaa

ttagcatgagcccggcgtgcattagcatggaagtggaaaacggcatgattagcatg

atttgcgcgaacaccgcgaaagaaaacgaagtggaacgcggcattaacggcattag

catggcgaccgcgaccattatggaactgattaaagaaacccatattagcatttggg

cgagcgaaaacaccattcgcgaactgtatccggaaaacattaccgaaaacaccatt

gatattgataacacctgggcgaacaccaccgcgagcaccgcgcgcaccattaacgc

gaacgcgagcacctattgggcgtatatttttgcgaactatatggcgaaccatgcgg

atacccatgaacgcattggccataccaccgcggatgaatttgaaaacgatcgcgcg

tgcattagcatgattacctgggcgagcaacaccatggaatatgaaagcattaaaaa

cgaatggcatgaacgcattaaaaacgaatgggcgctgctgacccatgaaattagca

gcagcaccgcgtttttttttatgaaaccattcatgcggataacgaagtggaacgcatg

gaaacccatgaacgctggattacccataacgcgatggaaagcgcgaacgatgcgct

gctgtgggaaattaacatggcgattaacaccgaaaacgcgaactgcgaaaacgaag

tggaacgcatgattaacggcctggaagattggattacccatacccatgaaggcgaa

aacgaaaccatttgcagcaccgaagcgatgagcattacctgggcgagccgcgaaga

ttggattacccatcgcgaagatgcgaacgatggccgcgaagaaaactggattaccc

atggccgcgaagaaaacattcatgcggataacaccatggaagcgaacaccgcgaac

tatctggaagtgattacctatattagcaccgcgcgcaccgaagatgcgggcgcgat

taacgcgaacgatagcgcgattgatatgtataacgcgatggaatgggcgagcaccg

cgatgatgtataccgcgatgatgtatattagcaacaccgcgatggcgaacagcaac

gcgatggaatggcatgcgaccgaactgagcgaagatattgatacccatgaatattg

cgcgctgctgtatgcgagccatgaagcgagcaaagaagatcatgaacgcagcgcgc

cgccgcatattcgcgaagaatatgaaagcggcctggcgcgcgaagatgcgaccatg

gaaattcgcgaatgcattaccgaagatgcgctgctgatgtataacgcgatggaaag

cacccatgcgatggaaagcattatgccgcgcgaaagcagcattgtggaacatgaaa

accgctatattcatgcggataacgaagtggaacgcctggaagcgcgcaacgaagat

tggcattatatttgggcgagcggcattgtggaaaacatgtatagcattctgctgta

tatgattgatgatctggaaaacgcgatggaaattgcggatgatgaagatatgtatg

atgcggattgggcgagcgcgtttcgcgaaaactgccatatggcgaacgcgaacgat

atgtatatggcgatgatgtattgggcgagcgaaaacggcctgattagccatgcgaa

cgatagccatgaatgcgcgctgctggaagatatggaaaccgcgatgatgtatgcga

```
acgatacccatgcgacctgggcgagcacccatgcgaccgcgaacgatgcgggcgaa
aacgcgatggaaccggcgaccgaaaacaccagccatgaaccgcgcgaaagcagcga
agatatttgggcgagcaacaccgcgagccatgcgatggaagatatttgggcgagcg
cgaacgcgaccattgtggaagcgaccacccatgaaattagcagcattgatattgat
aacacctttattaccacccatgaaagcaccgcgaacgatgcgcgcgatccggcgac
caccgaacgcaactatgaaaccattaaccatgaaagcattaccgcgaccattaacg
gcgcgaacgattggattacccatcatgaacgcattaacagcattagcaccattaac
ggcctgattaaagaaacccatgcgaccattcgcgaagcgctgattagcgaagatat
ttgggcgagcaacacccgcgaagcggattataccgcgagcgcgtatattaccattt
gcgcgaacaccagcgcgtattggcattatattttgaactgaccacccatgcgacc
tgggcgtatatttgccatgcgaacggcgaagataccgcgtgcaaatggcatgcgac
cggcgaaaacgaaaccatttgcgaaaaccatgcgaactgcgaaatggaaaacacca
gccatgcggtggaatatgcgcatgcggatattgcgagcaaagaagatcatgaacgc
agccatgaaagcaacatttttttttgaagatgcgagcattttttattagcatggaact
gacccgcgcgaactgcattgatatttgggcgagcaacaccgcgtgggcgcgcgaaa
cccatgcgaccacccatattagctgggcgagcgcgagcgaaaacagcattaccatt
gtggaaacccatattaacggcaccgcggcgagcaaaattaccattagcaacaccgc
gaacatttgcgaaacccatattaacggcaccgcggcgagcaaagcgggcattcgcc
tgagccatgaaagcgcgattgatagccatgaaagcaccgcgcgcgaagatgcgacc
acccatgaatttattcgcgaacgcattgatgatctggaagatccgctggcgaacga
aaccgcgaacgatgcggatgatgaagatattacccatgcgcgcgatctgtatatgg
cgaccaccgaacgcagcgcgaccacccatattagcagcaccgcgggcgaaattgtg
gaacatgcggatacccatgaaatggcgctgctgatgtatccggcgcgcgaaaacac
cagcagcgaactggaatgcaccgaagatgcgctgctgacccatgaagaaaaccatg
cgaactgcgaaatggaaaacaccagcacccatgaatatcatgcggatggcgaaaac
gaacgcgcgaccgaagatgcgaccacccatgaaaccattatggaaacccatgaata
ttgggaacgcgaaacccatgaaggcgaaaacgaaaccatttgcattagcaccagca
cccatgcgaccatggcggatgaaacccatgaaatgcatgaacgcgaaattaacacc
catgaaattagcagcattgtggaacatgcggatagcacccgcgaaaacggcaccca
tgaaaacattaacggcaccgcgattaactgccgcgaagcgagcgaaagcaaagaac
tggaaaccgcgctggatgaaaacagcattacctatctgatttttgaaagcccggcg
aacgaaaaccatgcgaactgcgaacgcagctggcatatttgccattggattctgct
```

ggcggatgatgaaattggccatacctattatgaagcgcgcagcggcgcgatgatgg
cgcgcgcgtatcgcgaaagcattagcaccgcgaacaccagcaaaattaacgatgaa
tgccgcgaagcgagcgaagatgatattgaaaccgcgcgctataacgaagaagatag
cgcgaacgatagccatgaacatgaaagcattaccgcgaccgaagatattaacaccg
aactgctggaatgcaccgaaaaccatgcgaactgcgaacgcagcacccatgaatat
tgggcgaacaccgaagatatggaaaccgcgcatgcggtggaagcgctgctgaccca
tgaagcggatgtggcgaacaccgcgggcgaaagctggcatgcgaccccggcgcgcg
aaaacaccagcgatattgataacacctgggcgaacaccacccatgcgaccattaac
acccatgaaattcgctgccatattctggatagccatgaagatattgataacaccgc
ggatgatcatgaacgcggcgaaaacgcgatggaaccggcgaccgaaaacacctatg
aaaccattaaaaacgaatggagccatgaacatgcggatattaccacccatgaaggc
gaaaacgcgatggaaccggcgaccgaaaacacctgggcgagcacccatgaaattga
tgaaaacaccatttttattgaacgcgaagtggaacgctatatggcgctggaagcga
acgattttgaaatggcgctggaagcgctgattgtggaacatgcggatattaacacc
catgaaattcgcgataacgcggcgaccctggaagcgagcaccgaagtggaacgcta
tctggaaggcgcgctgatggcgctggaagcgaacgattttgaaatggcgctggaaa
ttgatattgataacacccatgcggtggaagcgggcgaaaacgcgatggaaccggcg
accgaaaacaccgcgaacgatgatattgataacacccatgcggtggaagcgaacta
tggcatgccggcgcgcaccatttgcctggaaagcattaacatgtatgataacgcga
ttcatgcggataacaccgcgaactataacgaagaagataccgcgcatattgatgaa
atgtatagccatgcgatggaaaccgaactgctgatggaaaccgcgatgatgtatga
tattgattatgcgggcgaaaccgcgggcgaaaacgcgatggaaccggcgaccgaaa
acaccagccatgaacgcgaaccggaagcgaccgaagatcatgaacgcgaatatgaa
agcccggaaaacgaaacccgcgcgaccgaagatctgattaaagaaagccatgaatg
ggcgagcacccgctatattaacggcaccgcgagcgaagaaatgtatattaacagca
ttgatgaaagcattcatgcggataacaccgcgaactatgaaaaccatgcgaactgc
gaaatggaaaacaccagcattcgcgaaccgctgattgaagattttattaacgcgct
gctgtatgcgaacgatgatattgataacaccggcgaaaccgcgggcgaaaacgcga
tggaaccggcgaccgaaaacaccatgtatcatgaagcggatagcgcgaacaaagcg
tttaccgaacgcgcggatatgattaccaccattaacggcacccatattagctggca
ttatgatattgatattaaagaagaaccgaccgaactgctgattaacggcatgtata
gcgaactgtttacccatgcgaccatttgggcgagcaacaccgcgagccatgcgatg

gaagatattacccatattaacaaaagcgaagaaattaacggcattacctggcgcat

taccaccgaaaacctgattaaagaaacccatattagcatttgggcgagcagccatg

aagaagcgagcgaagatgcgagcatttttagccatgaacatgcggataccgcgaaa

gaaacgcgctggcgcgcggcgaagatcgcgcgatgtttattctgctggaagattg

gattacccattgccatgaaatgatttgcgcgctgatggcgagcagcgcgggcgaac

cgattctgctgagcattagcaccgcgtatgaagatagcattctggaaaacaccgcg

agcatttgggcgacctgccatgaagatacccatgaatttctggcgcgcgaaagcga

tgcgaactgcgaagcgaacgcgctgctggaaatggcgaacgatgaaaacgaagtgg

aacgcgtgattagcattaccgaagatacccatgaacgcgaaaccgcgatgatgtat

catgcggtggaatatgcgagccatgaaaaaaacgaatggattcatgcggataacac

ccatgaacgcgaatatgaaagctttgcgagcaccgaaaacgaagatacccatgaat

ttctggcgatgattaacggcgaagcgcgcacccatattaacagcattggccatacc

gcgaacgatgatcgcgaatggatggaaattaacaacgaagcgcgcgaacgcaccgc

gcatgaacgcctggaaaccatggaaaccgaactgctgtatgcgacccatgaaaaca

cccatgaatatcatgcggtggaagcggtgattgcgcgcattgaaagcgcgaacgat

tttgcgcgcatgagcagcgcggtgattaacggcgcgctgctgacccatgaaattcg

cgcgaacattatggcgctgagcagccatgaaagcattggccatgaagatatttttg

aagaactgtgcgaacgcaccgcgattaacacccatgcgaccagcattaacggcatt

aacggcgcgaacgattgcctggcgagcagcatttgcgcgctgacccgcgcgtgcaa

aagctgggaacgcgaaattaacgtggaaaacaccgaagataccgcgcgcgaaccgc

tgatttgcgcgaccgaaacccatgaaattcgcgcggtgattgcgaactgcgcgctg

ctgagctggattacccatacccatgaatgcctggcgcgcattaacgaaaccacccg

cattctgctgagcacccatgaaccgattccggaatggcatattagcaccctggaaa

gccatgcgcgcccgagcgcgaacgattttattgatgatctggaaagcgcgaacgat

acccatgaacatgaagcggtgtatcgccattatacccatatgagcagccatgaaag

ctgggcgtatgaagatgcgaacgatgatcgcattttttaccgaagataacgaagcgc

gcgaacgcatggaatgggaaattggccataccctggaaagcagcctgtatattacc

attagcatggcgggcatttgcgcgctgacccatgaacgcgaaaccgcgatgatgta

tagcattaccaccattaacggcattaacacccatgaacgcgcggatattgcgaaca

cctgggcgcgcatgctgattggccataccgaagcgaccattaacggcgcgatggaa

gcgctggcgagcatgcgcgctgctgtttattaactgccattggattctgctgacctg

ggaagaaacccatattagctgcgcgctgctggcgaacgatattaccagctttcgca

ttgaaaacgatattaacacccatgaagatattagcaccgcgaactgcgaatggatt

ctgctgccggcgattcgctggattacccatattaccgcgaacgatatggcgaaaga

agcgaacattaacaccgaacgcctggcgtgcgaagatacccgcgcgtgcaaatgga

ttacccatacccgcattctgctgagcacccatgcgacctttattctgctgacccat

gaaggcgcgcgcgatgaaaactggattacccatcatgcgccgccgattaacgaaag

cagcattaacacccatgaagaagtggaaaacattaacggcgcgggcgaagaaagcg

aaggcgcgggcggcctggaatgcgcgaactttctgtatccggcgagcaccgcgaac

gatacccgcgaagcgacctatgcgtggattacccatacccatgaaattcgccatgc

gcgcagccattgccatgcgaccacctatagcccggaagaatgccatgaaagcaccc

atgcgacctggattctgctgcgcgcgattagcgaacatgcgtgcaaactggaaagc

agccatgaaggcattggcggcctggaagatctgattaaagaagcgctggcgcgcgg

cgaatttgcgatgattctgtatgcgctgctgaccgcgctgaaaattaacggcgcga

ccacccatgaaagcgcgatggaaaccattatggaagcgaacgatacccatgaaagc

attggccataccagcaccgcgatgatgtattggattctgctgtgtgggaacgcgaatg

cgcgctgctgacccatgaagatattttttttttgaacgcgaaaacaccagccatgcgg

atgaaagcattaacacccatgaaccggcgcgcgcgaaagaagaaaccagctggatt

aacggcagcgcgaacgatacccatgaagatgcgattagcattgaaagcacccatga

actgattctgattgaaagcgcgaacgatctggcggtggaaaacgatgaacgcagct

ggcatgaaaacacccatgaatatggcgaacgcatgattaacgcgaccgaaacccat

gaacgcgaaagcgcgtgccatgcgaactgcgaaacccatgcgaccacccatgaaag

cgaatggattctgctgcgcgaaatggcgattaactatgaaaccatttttacccatg

aacgcgaaattagcaacaccgcgaactatagcgaaaacaccattgaaaacaccatg

gcgaaccatgaagcgcgcattaacggcacccatgaaatgagcgaagaaattaacgg

cacccatgaaatgagcatggaactgctgattaacggcacccatgaaatgtggattc

tgctgacccatgaatatagcaccgcgtatacccatgaaagcgcgatggaaagccat

gaacatgcgctgaccgaagatattcatgaagcgcgcgatcatgaacgcggcgcgag

cccggcgagcagccatgaatgggcgacctgccatgaagatacccatgaatttctgg

cgcgcgaaagcgaaaacctggcgcgcgggcgaagcgaacgatccggaacgccatgcg

ccgagcattcatgaagcgcgcgatgcgaccgaaatgccggaacgcgaagattgccg

ctatattagcgaaaacagcgaagatacccatgcgaccagccatgaaaaaaacgaat

ggtggcatgcgacctgggcgagccatgcgccgccggaaaacattaacggcacccat

gaacgcgaaattgcgagcaaagaagatcatgaacgctatgaaagcagccatgaaga

```
tgaatgcctggcgcgcgaagatattatggcgtgggcgcgcgaatggcatgcgacca
ttaccattagcacccatgaatatcgcgaactggaagcgagcgaagatattatggcg
gatgaaattacc
```

<<<<>>>>